# Too Hard to Forget

## by

## Amanda Balfour

**Too Hard to Forget**

Cover Art by *Debbie Taylor*

The Wild Rose Press, Inc.
PO Box 708
Adams Basin, NY 14410-0708
Visit us at www.thewildrosepress.com

Publishing History
First Tea Rose Edition, 2016
Print ISBN 978-1-5092-0935-4
Digital ISBN 978-1-5092-0936-1

Published in the United States of America

**"I am yours in name, nothing more."**

She turned away, trying to shrug off his hand. He removed it from her shoulder, and she stood and faced him. She wanted to say more, but the lump in her throat prevented her speaking.

"Very well, madam! Listen to what I have to say. You will not be indiscreet under my roof or with my friends." His voice sounded as sharp as flint.

"Perhaps you have a list, so I will know who your friends are." Nicole glared at him through narrowed eyes.

"No doubt you dislike me, and what I represent. You will agree I have not treated you badly. I have given you my name, and although it may not mean much to you, it means a great deal to me."

"You...you, sir, come into my chamber accusing me of things you know I have not done. You speak of your name as if it were akin to the Holy Grail. If you thought so much of your name, your father would not have put that ridiculous clause in the will, and I would not be here. You offered marriage because you must, not from any tender feeling for me. Never fear, my lord, I will live up to my end of the bargain. When a year is up, hold on to your hat because I'll beat Woodrose's record getting out of your sight." Her eyes flashed as she snapped her fingers in his face.

# Dedication

To Sean, Stefanie, Leah, and Andrew

Chapter One

A poorly sprung mail coach lurched and rattled into the yard of the White Bear Tavern and Inn near Fiddler-on-the-Sea, a tourist destination on the coast northeast of London in 1792. The driver swung to the ground, opened the coach door, and lowered the steps. Lone passenger Miss Nicole Waltham peered out of the darkened coach. The morning's molten sun burnt through the clouds in streaks.

A low-hanging ground fog surrounding the inn did nothing to lighten her mood. She gave her hand to the driver as she stepped to the ground. Her gaze wandered over the surrounding bleak landscape with growing dread.

"Miss, it's been raining, and there's mud puddles everywhere. Be careful. If ye'll wait where ye are, ye can follow me into the inn after I fetch your corded trunk and valise from the boot." The driver disappeared in the fog.

She wrung her hands and waited.

The driver called from the back of the coach, "I'll soon have yer baggage sorted out and take ye into the White Bear. It's respectable. No need to worry. I'll introduce ye to Mrs. Carter, and ye can wait there until yer people come for ye."

He came around the coach carrying her baggage. "There, that's sorted. I'll just leave yer baggage here.

I'll be back quicker than a cat can lick its whiskers." He turned and went behind the coach again.

"Thank you," Nicole called after his disappearing backside.

Still standing next to the carriage, now with baggage at her feet, she stared off into the distance. A short six months ago, she had servants to command and never knew a time when she wanted for anything.

Today told a different story.

Her fiancé had abandoned her. Her father, whether through his bout of melancholia or shame, deserted her on the last stop into London. Aunt Helena had agreed to take them into her home but not before writing to her father in which she lectured him on his sins through a five-page missive. Nicole's pride refused to let her remain in her aunt's house any longer than necessary. Aunt Helena had made it obvious she took her in as a charitable act but did not appreciate having an impoverished relative foisted upon her. Nicole shook her head trying to be rid of her gloomy musings.

She had agreed to be a companion to Lady Annis Scott, a widow in poor health from an apoplexy. Her son Lord Robert Scott had procured the services of Miss Nicole Waltham from the Melrose Agency in London. She expected her employer to send a cart to meet her, and at the sound of someone coming around the bend in the road, she turned and craned her neck in anticipation. To her dismay, a speeding curricle and four were bearing down on her. Stunned, she did not have the presence of mind to move. The curricle continued at its reckless pace, missing her by inches. The vehicle ran through a large mud puddle in front of her sending a shower of dirty water, drenching her from head to toe.

Her mouth opened in surprise. "O-o-o-h, mercy me, of all the…" Words failed her as she held her dripping hands away from her clothes. She stomped her foot and stared after the rapidly disappearing curricle.

"Just look at my clothes! They're ruined. Of all the harebrained creatures… Oh, what am I to do?" she called to no one in particular, looking heavenward.

The driver came from the direction of the inn and glimpsed the young woman. "Upon my soul—just look at ye. Well, I'll be a jiggered. This way, oh, my, miss. Let me take ye into the inn. Mrs. Carter will look after ye. She'll know what to do. Now don't ye fret none. She'll have ye cleaned up in no time. I'll take yer trunk in, and ye can change yer clothes."

The coachman hurried through the hall of the inn to the back parlor with Nicole trailing. She looked over her shoulder and saw a woman come out of the kitchen wiping her hands on her apron. Mrs. Carter hurried after them and called to the coachman as they entered the parlor.

"John, what's the meaning of this? And be quiet. I have people sleeping. Just look at my floors. There's mud all over my clean floors."

Nicole turned toward the woman stepping into the parlor.

The portly innkeeper stopped short when she took in Nicole's condition. "Well, I hope I never. Whatever happened to the young lady?"

"Sorry, Mrs. Carter. I had to take the young lady somewhere."

"Mrs. Carter, can you help me? An idiot whipster flying over the rise in the road splashed mud over me from head to toe, as you can see. Today is my first day as Lady Annis Scott's companion. I can't go to her looking like this." On the verge of tears, Nicole sniffed and took a deep breath.

"Of course, you can't, my dear. Now calm yourself. I'll bring hot water so's you can clean up. You can change your clothes in here. There's a lock on the door. We'll have you neat as nine pence before you know it."

Nicole touched her auburn hair and felt the sticky mess. "My hair, oh my hair. It must have a bucket of mud in it."

"Now, dear, we'll wash it, and you can dry it by the fire. It's so thick that even if Lady Scott's man comes for you before it dries, we can make a bun at the nape of your neck. No one will ever guess what happened. You get out of those muddy clothes, and I'll get the hot water." Mrs. Carter hurried away.

Nicole looked at herself in a tarnished piece of a mirror leaning on the fireplace mantel, and her heart sank. At her wit's end and with nowhere else to go, she could not lose this position. "I'll not go crawling back to my aunt. That is not an option." She crossed her arms and stomped her foot, then brushed a tear away and paced the floor. The drying mud was making her clothes stiff and sticky. If Mrs. Carter did not hurry, she soon would be unable to move.

\*\*\*\*

A short way past the bend in the road, the curricle and four pulled to a stop. The reckless whipster turned his rig and headed back to the inn. A tall, inebriated man stepped lightly from the curricle and entered the inn. Swaying somewhat once inside the door, he glanced around the darkened room. Nothing but the ghost of old ales greeted him.

Dressed in a careless fashion, his once mirror polished hessians were mud splattered. He draped his many caped greatcoat in a slapdash fashion over a chair and threw his gold trimmed hat on the table. A diamond pin held his loosely tied cravat in place. Shaking loose the ribbon that held his dark hair away from his face, he stumbled into the hallway leading to the inn's parlors.

"Innkeeper! Innkeeper! Where the devil is everyone?" the young man called and pounded his whip handle on the table in the hall. Not one to wait long, he sauntered down the hallway in search of Mrs. Carter. Glimpsing her with a brass water can and a towel going through a doorway, he followed down the hall and pounded on the door.

"Mrs. Carter, do you have the young lady I splashed? Is she hurt? Very careless of me. Open this door. Where is everyone?" He continued to rattle the door with his whip handle.

"Get away from the door. How dare you? You cannot come in here. I'm not decent. You have a nerve showing your face after you nearly killed me." The young woman's angry words penetrated the closed door.

Mrs. Carter quieted the young lady. "S-sh, my dear, that's Lord—"

"I don't care who he is. Someone should take a whip to him!"

The coachman stepped out of the shadows and sidled between the door and the young man. He cleared his throat and removed his hat. "Begging yer pardon, my lord, but Mrs. Carter is attending to the young lady you splashed. They're trying to repair her outfit. I'm afraid it looks hopeless. She can't attend ye now." The coachman blocked the way between the young man and the door.

"I want to apologize. Dashed awkward. I didn't notice her until it was too late. Why the deuce was she standing in the middle of the road? On my way to Southend, trying to break Woodrose's record. Is she hurt?" He sighed and all of a sudden slouched on the nearest bench.

The coachman continued to stand with his hat in his hands staring at a point on the floor. "No, sir, just angrier than a swarm of bees. She wasn't in the road but standing beside the coach. Ye missed her by inches."

"Well, what's to complain about? A miss is a miss, after all. A little dirt hurts no one. May I at least speak to the innkeeper?"

"If ye wouldn't mind going back into the tavern, my lord, I'll get her for ye."

The young man watched the coachman depart before he returned to the tavern. He chose a table nearest the bar and sat with his long legs sprawled out and his head resting on his uplifted hand. While he waited for Mrs. Carter, he dozed and then awoke with a jerk when he heard her clear her throat. He looked up from under half-closed eyes.

"Lord Montagu, how may I help you?"

"I wish to apologize to the young woman whose costume I muddied. I must make amends for this unfortunate accident."

"Your lordship, with respect, now is not a good time. She's dreadfully upset. She's trying to make herself presentable. You understand, she's going to your aunt's as her companion, and this is her first day. I recommend waiting until she calms down before approaching her."

"Yes, I understand. If you would be so kind and oblige me, please secure the young lady's soiled clothing on the pretense of having them cleaned. Give them to me, and my man'll take care of the chore."

"Very good, my lord. I'll take care of it." She bowed and hurried back to Nicole.

Lord Montagu received the wrapped bundle from Mrs. Carter a short time later and left the inn.

****

A carriage arrived a short time after the reckless whipster left. It surprised Nicole to find a coach waiting to take her to Lady Scott's home. Usually, an employer sent an ordinary cart to fetch an employee, but Lady Scott sent her old-fashioned traveling coach, a much more comfortable conveyance. She'd made Nicole wait nearly two hours, but this did not annoy Nicole. In this instance, it had given her time to make herself presentable and catch her breath.

Lady Scott's servant led her to the coach and helped her inside. When she sat on the bench, he put a traveling rug made of sheepskin over her knees. This unheard of consideration eased a few of her fears. She pulled the rug closer around her and enjoyed the little luxury. The servant tipped his hat, put up the steps, and closed the door. As the coach moved away from the inn at a neat pace, Nicole leaned back and sighed. She let her mind wander into the past when she would not have considered this a luxury.

The coach brought Nicole to Lady Scott's door a short time later, apparently only a short distance from the inn. She looked out the window of the carriage at a large, square, three-storied home with dormers and a huge bay window. The house was an off white with blue shutters. Ivy curled around an ornately carved oak door at the entrance. Rose bushes in full bloom punctuated the large well-maintained gardens surrounding the front of the house. Nicole gazed at sea gulls soaring overhead in the gentle breeze.

A groom appeared and opened the door of the carriage, then lowered the steps. Nicole stepped out and walked to the door.

The butler answered her knock at once and looked her over. "May I help you?"

"I'm La...er...Miss Waltham to see Lady Scott. Lord Scott sent me. I'm to fill the position of companion."

"I'll tell Lady Scott you're here. Please remain in the foyer," the butler said in clipped tones, then allowed her to step inside and retreated down the hall.

Nicole looked around the foyer with its high cornice ceilings. A dogleg staircase rose to the first floor landing just below a large stained-glass window. Not sure what else to do, she sat on a bench and waited.

She wondered idly if all butlers were related. Lady Scott's butler could have been a relative of her old butler, Biggers. They had the same straight as a poker posture and were full of dignity, giving the impression no one coming to the door was worthy to enter. They always seemed to go bald for some unknown reason, and one never could decide what color their eyes were.

The waiting played on her nerves. Nicole bit her lower lip and looked around the hallway. Everything appeared clean and well appointed, and the smell of the sea breeze coming through the open windows was comforting. She hoped she could get on with Lady Scott. If she lost this position, she had no choice but to return to Aunt Helena's home. Neither of them wanted that. She took a deep breath, let it out to the count of five, and turned when she heard the butler's footsteps approaching.

"Lady Scott will see you now." The butler motioned for her to follow him down a narrow pine paneled hallway darkened by age.

When they entered the sitting room, Lady Scott sat by the French doors gazing out on the garden. She sat awkwardly upright in an invalid's chair with two large wheels in back and one small wheel in front. There were hand cranks attached at the front of the chair, and it had a reclining back and adjustable foot rests. When she turned her chair around, Nicole saw someone she recognized. High cheekbones, piercing eyes, and sharp nose reminded her of Aunt Helena.

The light of recognition dawned in Lady Scott's piercing blue eyes at the same time. She looked to be in her late seventies, and her gray hair was pulled tight in a bun at the nape of her neck. Her skin looked paper-thin, and her gnarled left hand lay in her lap.

Nicole swallowed hard and wondered if she had jumped too soon at this offer of employment. She had been to parties at Lady Scott's in London with her father and aunt when she had her first season.

"That will be all, Corbin." Lady Scott waited for the butler to close the door and motioned with her finger. "Come here, young lady, and let me get a look at you. My eyes are not what they used to be."

She looked Nicole up and down before nodding.

9

Her intense blue eyes found Nicole's face before she crossed her arms over her chest. "Just as I thought. What flummery is this? Are you not Lady Nicole Waltham whose father is the Marquess of Beverley?" Lady Scott's eyes flashed in demand of an answer.

"Yes, ma'am, but there is no flummery. I am here to be your companion. Lord Scott hired me from the Melrose Agency in London."

"Why are you taking a position so beneath you?" Lady Scott observed her with narrowed eyes.

Nicole had no trouble telling from her demeanor that she would be satisfied with nothing but the unvarnished truth. "I'm forced to seek employment out of necessity. I find myself charged with providing for my personal welfare."

"How can that be? Are you in disgrace, or on the outs with your father? A love affair gone wrong, no doubt. Your father is one of the wealthiest men in England."

"*Was* the wealthiest. I'm embarrassed to tell my story. Since I will dwell under your roof, I understand you wanting the whole sad tale of our downfall. You must have heard of my father's misfortune?"

"No, I have not. I live here instead of in London for that very reason. I do not wish to listen to the latest. Come, sit, and tell me why I may boast of my good fortune in engaging a marquess's daughter as my companion."

"I'm sorry. I thought everyone knew. As you may or may not be familiar with my family history…my mother died in childbirth along with the child, a boy, nearly five years ago. After she died, my father did outlandish things. He went through over a year of deep depression. At first, he slept most of the day and night. Then he went the other direction and suffered from insomnia. He refused to leave the estate or even go outside our home. When he rode to the hounds once again, I hoped his depression had lifted. He became more outgoing, appearing to enjoy life again. Aunt Tess agreed to sponsor me in my first season, and my father brought me to town. I still had a few concerns regarding him, but the parties and excitement of my first season carried me away. When I realized he had run amok, it was too late to do anything. Until that time, he had a well-run, prosperous estate. He'd inherited a fortune and made another.

"After I became engaged, everything went from dire to worse. Inexplicably, he gambled in notorious gaming hells and threw money at worthless investments. He never gambled before this time, but in doing so, he forgot about running his estate. And he forgot about me. I imagine he just wanted to forget everything." Nicole shrugged and stared out the window a few moments.

Turning back to Lady Scott, Nicole said, "To make matters worse, he bet recklessly. He lost fantastic sums of money at a single sitting. I, along with his friends, tried talking to him. He refused to listen to anyone. He drank to excess and lost more and more money until he even began sponging off his friends. That is, what friends he had left. He was forced to sell our townhouse in London. To avoid debtor's prison and further embarrassment, he signed over everything to the men holding his gambling chits. The men he owed money to confiscated the houses and land. They sold or auctioned off everything to pay his debts. They even took the jewelry my mother gave me. I narrowly escaped with the clothes on my back, and what few clothes I convinced his creditors to let me keep.

"We didn't have enough money between us to cover our passage on the mail coach or for traveling necessities. I was forced to swallow my pride and borrow twelve pounds from my old governess before we could travel to London. At the last stop into London, my father abandoned the coach and left me to travel to Aunt Helena's home alone. He never said good-bye. He just vanished." Nicole's eyes brimmed with tears. She took a deep breath to control her emotions.

"Aunt Helena didn't appreciate my coming to her. She told me I might stay until I found a position, but she could not afford to take me in for an indefinite time. I accepted the only position offered, and here I am." She shrugged and looked up to find Lady Scott scrutinizing her. "I prefer that no one be told of my title. I plan to go on as Miss Waltham."

"It appears you're unlucky in your choice of relatives. Was there no one else you might turn to in your time of need?"

"I could have gone to my Aunt Tess. A warm welcome would have been mine. She lives in Italy, however, I lacked the money to travel there. My mother's sister lives in York. I could have gone there if I had asked. She has six children under the age of fourteen, and my going there would have posed a hardship. I can't blame my Aunt Helena over much. No one wants the responsibility of a female with no prospects.

"At any rate, I prefer to pay my own way. I don't want to be beholding to anyone, let alone a relative. I have often observed the plight of impoverished relatives. If I must work for my room and board, I prefer to be paid for it."

"I admire your sentiment and spunk. How old are you?"

"Two weeks ago I turned one and twenty."

"I didn't imagine you were that old. You appear much younger. It doesn't signify. I didn't ask for a companion. This is my son's doing. I had no way of knowing you were coming until I received my son's post yesterday with instructions to pick you up today. My son is acting as he always has: without consideration for anyone else." She frowned and shook her head.

"I hope the scandal doesn't turn you off my coming here. I'm truly sorry to be thrown at you without your consent. It never occurred to me."

"On the contrary, it makes you interesting and warms my heart that I can pull one over my son. I will be so annoying to two of my other servants that they will give notice. My son will be called upon to provide me with two more, which will inconvenience him. It pleases me to keep him busy and be one up on him." She looked at Nicole and chuckled.

"Have you seen your father since he left you?"

"No, I tried to find him in London, but no one I asked knew where he was. He must be in London somewhere. One day, I believed I glimpsed him, but the man ran away from me before I could be sure. My time was occupied with obtaining a position, so I had to give up the search. I've been beside myself with worry." Nicole wrinkled her brow and looked at her clasped hands.

"I'm sure he'll turn up. Try not to worry, my dear. These things have a way of working themselves out. If he comes to your Aunt Helena, as he must, she can direct him here." Lady Scott smiled at Nicole. "Did you enjoy a pleasant trip, my dear? I'm assuming you came by mail coach. By the way, do you realize there's dirt or something on your left ear?"

Nicole reached up, and a piece of dried mud came away in her hand. She closed her fist around it and felt her face burn with embarrassment. She looked for a place to dispose of the dirt, and when she could see no options, resigned to hold it cupped in her hand.

"A most uneventful trip until I arrived at the White Bear Inn. A drunken whip splashed muddy water all over me. No one but a bubble headed brute drives his team in that manner. I had to change my clothes before I came. I caught a glimpse of his face, and if I ever run into him again, I hope to give him a piece of my mind." Nicole's anger returned just thinking of the whipster.

"Well, I hope you don't run into him again or the other way around. Tell me what shall we do? I've never had a companion before this."

"I hoped you might guide me for I've never been one." Nicole smiled and sensed a little of her tension leave when Lady Scott returned her smile with a twinkle in her eye.

"My health has affected my eyes, making it difficult for me to read. Do you care to read to me?"

"I'd love to. What shall I read?"

"My dear friend Elizabeth de Grey sent me a novel that's all the rage in her circle. It's *The Old English Baron* by Cara Reeve. If you don't mind reading novels with a romantic and somewhat risqué turn, that is my choice."

"I don't mind at all. Shall we begin?" Nicole walked to the door and threw her dirt into the garden. She came back to the seat beside Lady Scott, sat, made herself comfortable, picked up the book from the table, and opened to the first chapter.

The next time she looked up, Lady Scott was dozing in the early afternoon, and her rug had slipped onto the floor. After adjusting the rug across Lady Scott's lap, she tiptoed from the room. She backed out the sitting room door and turned around to find Corbin lurking in the hall. He showed her to her bedchamber. The apartment was painted a pale yellow and trimmed in white. A bay window at one end filled the room with sunshine. The canopied bed had linens of pale yellow trimmed in antique lace. She was pleasantly surprised at such comfort. After exploring every nook and cranny, she put her clothes away.

Nicole fell into her chair to rest, leaned back, and as soon as she closed her eyes, nodded off into a restful slumber. A maid woke her and said she had less than half an hour to get dressed for dinner. It did not take her long to get ready with only one suitable, plain black dress to change into for dinner. She had been adding a scarf or a piece of costume jewelry to change the appearance each time she wore it. Nicole made haste to pile her hair in plaits on top of her head and hurried to the sitting room. She found Lady Scott waiting.

"I trust you had a pleasant nap and are rested from your journey."

"Yes, my lady. I only meant to rest my eyes for a minute or two, and the next thing I knew a maid was shaking me. I guess I'm more tired than I thought."

"Well, my dear, I believe we did fine for our first day. Shall we go in to dinner?" Lady Scott smiled and took Nicole's hand. Corbin pushed her invalid's chair into the dining room.

After dinner, Nicole and Lady Scott returned to the small drawing room. Lady Scott sat by the fire, and Nicole picked up her needle and thread. "Do you get many visitors?" Nicole asked while bending over her embroidery.

"No, I'm afraid it will not be awfully exciting for you. I prefer to be left alone. The only people I let visit me are my nephew and my doctor. My nephew, Lord Montagu, lives a short distance from here. He should return to the country soon. He's exceedingly entertaining. I'm sure you'll like him."

"Is your nephew Lord Brandon Montagu?" Nicole looked up from her needlework.

"Why yes, that's him. Do you know him?"

"Merely by reputation. I'm afraid we don't travel in the same circles."

"By the look on your face, I think you must be familiar with his reputation. I have to admit he is a bit reckless and head strong. I blame his father for that. He neglected the boy shamefully." Lady Scott shook her head.

"I'm told he's considered a nonpareil horseman. The way he races his curricle, I'm always afraid he'll break his neck. He is forever doing something outrageous if you can trust gossiping opinion. I have always had a soft spot in my heart for the boy. He's more like my son than my real son is. Brandon visits me more often. He always brings me a box of Belgian chocolates, my favorite."

"That's most kind of him. I look forward to meeting Lord Montagu." Nicole bent over her sewing again. She did not want Lady Scott to notice the disapproval in her face. She had indeed heard of his exploits. None of them did a gentleman credit.

****

Nicole had been at Lady Scott's home for a week and enjoyed herself more than she thought she could. Lady Scott treated her as a member of the family, and the tension she felt at first was eased quickly.

At the end of her first week, Nicole met Dr. Peterson during his regular weekly visit to check on his patient. When he understood Nicole was to be Lady Scott's companion, he gave her instructions for helping Lady Scott regain her mobility. "Lady Scott, I see no reason you cannot get out of your invalid's chair and walk with a cane. Miss Waltham is a capable young lady. I've given her instructions for your exercise, and I expect you to be much improved on my next visit."

"Why should I be subjected to this badgering at my age? I'm two and seventy years of age. Not long for the bone yard. Leave me in peace." Lady Scott waved a dismissive hand and turned her head to gaze out of the bay window.

Dr. Peterson ignored her and turned to Nicole. "Nothing but drivel. She'll out live us all from sheer perverseness if nothing else." He turned to Lady Scott and smiled. "I'll not wrap you in cotton balls. Outside of a touch of arthritis, you're in good health for a woman of your age. If you exercised, the stroke's damage would be minimal."

Dr. Peterson winked at Nicole and turned to gather up his bag and coat. "She has refused to exercise since her self-imposed confinement. Her stubbornness to exercise has made her weak and unable to stand for more than a few minutes much less take a step. I'm counting on you to help change her mind and start her exercising." The doctor moved between the lady and the window. "Lady Scott, you can do whatever you set your mind to do."

"Fiddlesticks, you say things like that to aggravate me. I'm a sick old woman. Leave me in peace." Lady Scott chuckled.

"I'll visit you next week. I expect to see you much improved." Dr. Peterson bowed over Lady Scott's hand before turning to leave.

"Nicole, show this charlatan out and tell Corbin not to admit him again," Lady Scott called after Nicole.

"My dear, you look forward to my visits as much as I do. I'll visit you next Wednesday."

"You'll have to find me first."

"It won't be difficult if you don't do your exercises," Dr. Peterson threw back. He laughed and left the room.

Watching their interaction, Nicole realized they both looked forward to these visits and the good-natured verbal sparring. She stepped into the hall and gave the doctor the lead, then walked to the front door behind him. Before he took his leave, he handed Nicole a piece of paper. "My dear, do not worry about Lady Scott or become discouraged. I could tell she likes you. A little gentle urging will go a long way with her. I don't expect too much at first. We must get her walking again. Don't worry that she complains she is too frail. Except for the ravages of the apoplexy, she is strong and should be able to walk a few steps by the time I return.

"I've written directions for her care on the sheet of paper I handed you. Don't let her tire you out." Dr. Peterson gave Nicole a pat on the back and left.

In the days that followed, Nicole cajoled and sweetly bullied Lady Scott until she tried the exercises. At first, Corbin had to help Nicole hold her up, but as the days wore on, she regained more strength. With each day, she improved thanks to Nicole's gentle urging. Her returning good health improved her disposition at the same time.

It had been a month since Nicole arrived at Lady Scott's home. She left her lady enjoying the gardens in brilliant bloom while she brought cut flowers into the house and arranged them in tall crystal vases. She placed a vase of flowers on the round hallway table and was carrying another to the sitting room when the door flew open. A man's silhouette filled the doorway and stepped through the threshold. His unexpected entrance caused Nicole to instinctively raise the vase over her head, ready to throw. The man closed the door, spun toward her, and stopped in mid stride awe struck.

The man she'd been hoping to confront was the last person she expected to see barging in as if he owned the place. By his expression, he did not expect to find Nicole standing in the hallway by the stairs either. They stared at each other unable to speak.

Nicole sputtered, but no words came out.

"Now, miss, let's not do anything rash." He held his hands up.

"It's y-you," she said through clenched teeth.

Chapter Two

Nicole continued holding the vase above her head with both hands. If looks could kill, the man she had been waiting to give a set down would lay at her feet. Nicole's rising anger choked her speechless.

The reckless whipster did not move or speak either. He looked from Nicole to Corbin standing behind his accuser. Nicole turned toward Corbin who shrugged and looked from one to the other. She turned back to the whipster, a handsome man above average in height. He had blue-black hair and striking azure blue eyes. His wide shoulders and well-shaped calves needed no padding as he filled out his clothes to perfection. He tied his longish hair with a ribbon and left it unpowdered. Dressed in buckskins and a russet coat with silver buttons, he looked the perfect country gentleman. His Hessian boots shined to perfection. Nicole took this in, but it did not raise him in her estimation. That he quizzed her with his glass did nothing to calm her rising anger. In her ire she forgot the vase of flowers in her hands.

He backed up a step. "Before you throw that vase at me, let me explain." He held the palm of his hand up and moved sideways. Nicole turned and followed him with narrowed eyes. "My name is Lord Brandon Montagu, Duke of Ancaster. Lady Scott is my aunt. I didn't mean to splash you, I swear. I didn't notice you standing there. You understand I had a wager. I meant to beat Woodrose's record to Southend. You somehow got into the way. Lost my bet, by the way."

He took a deep breath. "Please stay calm. I want to make amends. I-I brought a p-present for you. Please wait where you are." He disappeared through the door into the foyer before she had time to respond, then quickly came through the door again with a wrapped parcel. He held the present out to her with his best smile. A smile Nicole was sure had seduced many a lovely lady.

"Lost your bet is all you have to say! Of all the nerve. You're bringing me a present? I don't want a present. The outfit you ruined just happened to be my favorite. Mrs. Carter said she would have it cleaned for me, if it can be cleaned. Whatever it costs; it is your responsibility to pay." Her nostrils flared, and a tight expression dared him to argue.

As she talked, she swayed the vase and droplets of water splashed on Nicole and the floor, but neither Corbin nor Lord Montagu dared mention it.

"Sad to say, but the outfit could not be cleaned. However, my man found your dressmaker's name sewn in the jacket. He took it to London, and the seamstress remembered it. She ran up another outfit just like the first with the same color and duplicate everything. Here is your costume. Please accept it with my sincere apologies. Please say I'm forgiven." Another dazzling smile brightened his chiseled features.

Nicole observed his eyes glitter as he looked her over. "Why are you looking at me in that calculating manner?"

"Force of habit. I'm an observer. I'm rather good at

guessing people's secrets, age, weight, and so on."

"Is that a fact? You must be in great demand at parties." Nicole smirked.

"It occurs to me you're too young to be on your own. From your sharp tongue, my guess is you're used to giving orders, maybe a merchant's daughter. I guess your age at less than twenty years. Your thick, lustrous, auburn hair and intelligent looking slate gray eyes leave nothing to be desired. You have a petite frame with pleasant, softly molded features and a delicate fine-drawn mouth. Although not a great beauty, you're obviously pretty. I wonder why a young lad hasn't stolen your heart. Is that it? You've taken this position with my aunt until you can mend a broken heart?" He smiled at her and cut his eyes mischievously.

"My looks, or lack of, are no concern of yours. I do not appreciate being looked over as so much chattel. You're wrong on just about every one of your observations as well. If you live much longer, you'll find ladies do not want their age guessed or to be ogled by strangers."

He smiled charmingly and bowed low. "I apologize for my impertinence."

She returned his smile with a frown. If the gossip was to be accepted as true, Nicole could see how his smile had won many hearts. A calculated smile did not cause her heart to melt. To give the devil his due, she had to admit that she had not seen a more charming smile.

The vase grew heavy in Nicole's outstretched hands. Her anger waning, she looked at it as if wondering what it was doing there. She turned to Corbin who took the vase and set it on the hall table, then back to Lord Montagu. With pursed lips and an outstretched hand, she accepted the package. Corbin sighed in relief behind her. She tore into the package and found an exact duplicate of her original outfit. Her jaw dropped in surprise. From under her eyelashes, she peeked at Lord Montagu and smiled for the first time.

"Oh, my! Thank you. I hope you understand this does not excuse your callous behavior. Since this is your aunt's home, and we will meet occasionally, I guess I will forgive you after all. Your aunt is on the terrace. I'll just put this away. Again, thank you." Nicole curtsied and left the room.

\*\*\*\*

Brandon strolled out on the terrace and found his aunt in the shade of a maple tree studying two robins building a nest. His footsteps on the stone pavement caused her to turn in her chair. Her smile at his approach made his day. He walked over to her, kissed her on the cheek, and pulled up a chair next to hers.

"Sweets for my favorite aunt." He handed her a box of Belgian chocolates. "I see you've added to your household. An exquisite creature."

Lady Scott nodded, tearing into her chocolates. "I didn't suppose she would go unnoticed for too long. Delighted to see you, my boy. You're too kind to remember your poor old aunt. I thank you for the chocolates. I hope you're going to be here for a spell." She popped a chocolate in her mouth and chewed.

Brandon watched her smile with pleasure.

She looked Brandon over in an appraising way. "The addition to my household is courtesy of my son. Robert sent me a companion without even telling me until the day before she arrived. He had to know I wouldn't be pleased. He assumes this will annoy me, and I won't require him to visit me for a while. The joke's on him. I like her. We've been getting along like a house o' fire.

"But enough about me. What have you been up to, dear boy? No good I'll wager."

"Now Aunt Annis you shouldn't listen to wagging tongues. I fear your companion is unhappy with me."

"Pray tell, why is that?" She looked him over with an indulgent smile. "Oh, Brandon, what have you done?"

"I had a bet with Lord Haversham that I could beat Woodrose's time to Southend. I splashed her by accident along the way. Head to toe with mud. I stopped and went back to the inn to make sure I hadn't hurt her. She refused to see me. I lost my bet if anyone is interested."

"You must make amends. When she told me what happened, I realized it must be you, you rapscallion. Have you apologized?"

"Yes, I had her dressmaker remake the outfit. I hope I'm forgiven. I didn't mean to splash her."

"That reminds me. Brandon, if you had not come, I planned to send for you. It concerns the answer to the problem of your twenty-fifth birthday. My companion, Nicole Waltham, would be most suitable. She's a marquess's daughter fallen upon hard times. As far as I know, there is not a whisper against her. There is nothing for your executors to object to."

"Did you say Waltham?"

"Yes, the Marquess of Beverly. Are you acquainted with him?"

"By reputation mostly. I've seen no one with such

a disastrous run of luck. In the gambling hells, they were taking bets on how much he might lose in a night. Then all of a sudden he dropped out of sight."

"That's what you do when you lose your mind and your money. Nicole has been trying to find him. He abandoned her on their trip into London, and to make matters worse, her fiancé abandoned her also."

"She *has* had a run of bad luck. Who was her fiancé?"

"A Lord Bedlington, I believe."

"Well, blast and tarnation…"

"Brandon, I take it you are acquainted with this Bedlington."

"You're correct. I've had dealings with him. I should marry her for that reason alone and no other." Brandon laughed and looked at his aunt with downcast eyes.

When he looked up, he found her eyes on him with a puzzled expression. "But in reality, Aunt, this scheme of yours is insane. How might I convince her to marry me on this short of an acquaintance? At this moment, she would sooner shoot me than marry me. We did not meet under ideal circumstances initially. Secondly, my reputation is such that no respectable woman would agree to be tied to me. The tales, whether real or imagined, are legend. I've given up the idea and feel sure I'll be living by my wits in another year. I will not even keep my title."

"Brandon, listen to what I'm saying. All that can change. Don't let your father win this one. He raised as much cane as the next one until he took to religion. Begging your pardon, but by the time he died, he had become insufferably sanctimonious. It's a wonder the good Lord didn't send a chariot to take him to Heaven like Elijah in the Bible.

"Show her you can conduct yourself like a gentleman. Make yourself agreeable, and in another week or two, we'll talk to her. Make love to her. From the hearsay that passes my ears, you don't have a big problem making young ladies fall in love. It will be to both her advantage and yours. A word of warning. I like her, and I will not see her abused or hurt in any way."

"In truth, Aunt, of all the things that are said about me, no one can say I ever hurt a lady deliberately. I've never dallied with any paramour that was not familiar with the rules of the game. I can't imagine why I should do as you ask. Being married has never appealed to me. My life suits me the way it is now."

"Consider what you'll be giving up if you don't do this. Do you want the titles, land, and money going to your cousin—that pompous ass, Lord Dover? Time is running short. Your twenty-fourth birthday is coming up in a month if I'm not very much mistaken. This would be a marriage of convenience, nothing more. After the year's up, you can continue on your own path."

They both looked up at the sound of Nicole's footsteps coming across the sett terrace. Nicole stood just inside the French doors and looked from Lady Scott to Lord Montagu. "Lady Scott, is there anything you need? If not, I'll leave you to your guest." She bowed and prepared to leave.

"Don't go, my dear. I don't need a thing now that my nephew is here. Please join us. You may be mother and pour out the tea."

Nicole handed the tea to Lord Montagu and his

aunt. All confidences were pushed aside for pleasantries and tea.

"My nephew tells me you have met previously under somewhat disagreeable circumstances. I hope that doesn't color your opinion of him."

"Oh no, ma'am, I'm no longer upset. I'm sure my opinion whether good or bad does not concern Lord Montagu." Nicole bowed her head and picked up her teacup.

"Miss Waltham, we started off on the wrong foot, but I hope to change your opinion. I wish to earn your respect." When she looked up, he found himself smiling. He was beginning to think his aunt had arrived at a solution to his problem after all.

"Sir, the person who never alters his opinions will soon grow stale in mind and body. A good opinion is usually earned." Nicole smiled. He was not sure if she were mocking him or not.

"*Touché*, my dear. Shall we call a truce?" Lord Montagu asked.

Nicole nodded and took a sip of her tea.

"I'm so glad you've found common ground," Lady Scott said. "Now Brandon, if you'll excuse us, it's late and we must get ready for dinner. Nicole, will you call Corbin to help me to my chambers." Nicole left to find Corbin who arrived a short time later to help Lady Scott. "Brandon you must dine with us."

"I'd love to. I can't think of more pleasant company."

Nicole left to dress for dinner. Lord Montagu was standing by the French windows when Nicole came into the sitting room. Corbin handed her a glass of sherry. She sat in the high backed chair nearest the fireplace.

Lord Montagu walked behind her chair and stood before he came to rest his arm against the fireplace mantel. He set his glass of wine on the mantel and looked at Nicole. "Tell me Miss Waltham, why are you dressed in the prim and proper black of a governess? You must know colors would become you much better."

"Sir, I'm not a guest here. I am a paid companion to your aunt, and I might add not paid to be fashionable." A look of irritation crossed her face.

Both turned as Corbin pushed Lady Scott through the doorway. "Shall we go in to sample my cook's accomplishments?" She smiled as Brandon placed a kiss on her cheek.

"Of course, Aunt. Here, Corbin, let me push her chair into the dining room." He set about making himself agreeable through dinner.

When dinner was over, Nicole saw to Lady Scott's comfort. "If that is all, your ladyship, I'll retire."

"That's all, my dear. You're looking tired. Get some rest, and I'll see you tomorrow."

Nicole retired to her room.

"Brandon, will you stay for a game of cards?"

"I'd love to Aunt Annis, but just one hand. I have to get up early tomorrow. My bailiff wants to show me where I need to spend money." He rolled his eyes.

Brandon got out the cards and began to deal.

"My boy, have you been making yourself agreeable?"

"I'm trying, but she's not very receptive to my charms, I'm afraid."

Lady Scott patted his arm. "I have faith in you. I think tonight was a good start. With enough heat, ice will melt."

Lord Montagu began visiting his aunt every day. In spite of himself, he looked forward to seeing Nicole. If he did not see her, he sought her out. At first, he had to put forth great effort to make himself agreeable, but slowly realized he enjoyed talking to her. A well-educated young woman, she could speak on any number of subjects. Nicole proved to be the first of his female acquaintances that didn't have more hair than wit. He liked it that way, yet it puzzled him to be so drawn to Nicole. Not at all his style, but for some reason, he wanted her to like him also.

In the third week of his daily visits, Lord Montagu arrived just after lunch to an apparently empty residence. He looked around the empty drawing room, then found Corbin in the hallway. "Where is everyone, Corbin?"

"Miss Waltham is in the garden picking apples. Your aunt is in the small sitting room."

"Thank you. I'll check on Miss Waltham." He headed toward the garden and searched between the apple trees. He glimpsed a wobbly ladder leaning precariously against a limb and moved closer. Two feet danced on tiptoes on the top step. Before he reached the ladder, it slid sideways and fell to the ground leaving the two feet dangling and with their owner hanging from a limb.

"Miss Waltham, hang on!" Lord Montagu broke into a run.

"I can't hang on. I'm slipping!"

He heard the crack of the limb, then saw her slipping down through the tree's fruit filled boughs. Lord Montagu sprung forward, arriving just in time to catch her before she hit the ground. Her basket flew off her arm, and apples pummeled the ground beneath the tree. Stunned, he realized her arms encircled his neck, as he looked into the depths of her gray eyes holding him in their gaze. A warm sensation spread through him, a strange emotion experienced through no will of his own. It was somewhat of a shock when it dawned on him he did not want to release her from the embrace. His mouth went dry, and he lost the power to speak. He had never felt so helpless.

He came out of his trance when Corbin called his name.

"You can put me down now," Nicole said.

He turned as Corbin's footsteps bore down on them.

"Lord Montagu, Lady Scott is asking for you."

He set Nicole down and took a dazed step backward. Lord Montagu stepped on an apple from her basket, his legs slid out from under him, and he fell painfully on his backside.

"Lord Montagu, are you all right? I'm so sorry." She wrung her hands while Corbin extended a hand to help him stand.

He looked up at her concerned countenance trying hard to maintain a frown. "May I ask why you are up a tree when my aunt has servants for that?" He stood and gingerly touched his bruised hip. He brushed himself off and waved Nicole away when she reached out to help.

"It's a beautiful day, and everyone was busy. Lady Scott sat down to rest after her walk on the terrace and expressed a wish for apples. I found a ladder and decided I would pick the apples myself. Nothing simpler?"

"If I hadn't come along, you might have broken an arm or a leg instead of me." He tried his best to sound stern. "Here, let me help you collect your bounty." He bent over and collected apples, hiding a smile hovering on his lips.

"Thank you again. Thanks for breaking my fall. Oh, your coat has a little dirt on it. If you'll give it to Corbin, he'll have someone clean it."

"That won't be necessary. I'm not staying long. My man will take care of it. However, if you would be so kind as to go into my aunt, we need to discuss something with you of importance."

"I'll straighten my dress and be with you before long." Nicole took her basket into the house.

When she made her way to the withdrawing room, Lord Montagu and his aunt were waiting for her. He stood and eyed her while rubbing the back of his neck.

"Sit, my dear. We have a proposal to discuss with you. It concerns my nephew's future, and yours."

Nicole sat, looking from one to the other with a puzzled expression. Lord Montagu walked over and stood by the fireplace with his head bent. He turned around and cleared his throat several times. "Miss Waltham, I have something to ask you. I'm not sure how to begin. The long and short of it is that I need a wife, and I am asking for your hand in marriage."

\*\*\*\*

She looked from Lord Montagu to Lady Scott and back, bereft of the power of speech. Her heart beat foolishly. She took a shallow breath and clasped her hands together. It was hard not to let her growing attraction to this rake overpower her good sense. She could not believe her ears had heard correctly. She licked her dry lips, cleared her throat, and wrung her hands. Nephew and aunt were looking at her, waiting for an answer. She had no idea what to say or how to say it. Confused by her feelings, she considered herself both insulted and flattered at the same time. She swallowed hard.

"Y...you've what? You cannot be serious. Is this a jest? If it is, it's in poor taste. Moreover, if this isn't a jest, you'll pardon my being frank. I assure you I may have fallen upon hard times, but I am not desperate enough to tie myself to a notorious rake."

"Most assuredly, I'm sincere in my offer. I wouldn't have asked you if I were not. I have need of a respectable woman to marry me who would do so with conditions and terms. You would not be the loser in this transaction. You understand I do not come professing love. This is more of a business arrangement."

Nicole's senses reeled as his cold words assaulted her. "And...you thought of me, an impoverished woman who would jump at the chance to be married to a lord of the realm."

She stared at first one and then the other with her mouth open, unable to form the words that hastily flashed through her mind for several moments. "Lord Montagu, is your brain disordered, or is there more to this ill-considered proposal than you are telling me? All I can say is that both of you must be mad, insane, or else this is a nightmare, and I shall wake up soon. Did I hit my head when I fell, or did you? I can see no other explanation for this proposal." Nicole shook her head.

"My dear, let me explain since Brandon is reluctant. Granted he made his proposal clumsily, but please give this some thought. This would be a marriage of convenience in the French style. Brandon travels to the beat of his own drum and damns the consequences. He has driven his strict, straight-laced father to distraction. When he'd had enough of Brandon's reckless ways, in death he left a will forcing him to do what he could not accomplish in life. Brandon will come into his inheritance when he turns five and twenty years of age.

"Before he comes of age according to the will, he must be married for one year to a respectable lady of quality. They cannot live independently but must be housed under the same roof no matter where for the entire year. The executor under the will must approve this lady. If he does not make such an arrangement for himself, the titles and assets would then go to his cousin, Lord Dover. There cannot be the hint of a sham or scandal during this year. The executor is charged with ensuring the letter of the will is honored."

"I don't know what to say other than what I have already said. This is insane. I'm sure my father's scandal has made me ineligible in any case." Nicole was breathless. Her hand touched her burning cheeks.

"I don't think so. My solicitor is coming tomorrow, and I plan, with your permission, to put the scheme before him. You are a lady of quality and title. Your father's disgrace should not make you ineligible.

"I know I must be part of all things you despise, but please consider what I am proposing. Is your reluctance because of my scandalous past? There is no reason to demur. This will be strictly a business arrangement. However, you can tell no one of the arrangement, or I fear all would be lost."

"No, I'm in no position to condemn anyone. My pride is not sunk so low where I must consent to such an arrangement. Why have you selected me for this...honor? I cannot pretend to understand your reasons for asking me, but surely you would be better advised to offer for a lady of your acquaintance." Nicole put her hands to her burning cheeks again. She looked wildly around the room hoping for a way to escape.

"My reputation is such that a respectable family would not consider my suit."

He watched Nicole's face turn a brighter shade of red and a growing irritation write itself across her face as plain as if she had spoken. She put a hand across her mouth and stared back at him.

"Please don't get up in the rafters over what I just said. Your situation is different. In the normal course, you would not welcome my suit either, but your circumstances have changed. Please consider what I'm proposing. You're still young. Do you have expectations of a betrothal?"

She took her hand away from her mouth and squared her shoulders. "It is most doubtful that anyone would ask for my hand, sir. I do not see how I could entertain an alliance with anyone. I am penniless. My father has caused a scandal. No, no, this is madness."

She stood and moved to a chair next to Lady Scott. Her hands fell to her lap while she stared at the floor, unable to think what to do. If she were honest, she could not say the proposal didn't tempt her. She hoped her scruples would help her overcome the temptation. She could not deny looking forward to seeing Brandon and having developed an attachment against her will.

To have the security of marriage and once again be able to enjoy the niceties of life if only for a short time were almost too much to bear.

Lady Scott's calm, soothing voice washed over Nicole. "My dear, I know there is no scandal attached to your name. Your only fault is that you have a good deal too much pride. However, no one could fault you for that. You are respectable. Nicole, please think. You do not want to be a companion to old ladies for the rest of your days.

"In my home, you are treated with respect, but it may not be so in another. Most companions are not treated any better, and sometimes worse, than a housemaid. Whether you agree or not, it does not matter. You will still be welcome here, but I urge you to accept for my nephew's sake and for your future.

"My nephew will give you the respectability of marriage. You have to stay under his roof for no more than a year, or until he receives his inheritance. Marriages of this kind are contracted in our world all the time. This is no different. You will be compensated for your time and whatever else you require within reason."

"I cannot. You must see why I could not do this." She stared off into space and shook her head.

His voice brought her back, and she turned her head at his words.

"No, frankly, I do not. Is it your wish that I professed love to you and then led you on when I meant nothing I said?"

"No, of course not. It is much better to know the way things stand from the beginning than to be irretrievably disillusioned." Nicole's voice sounded louder than she intended.

"Brandon…" Lady Scott shook her head and tried to stand from her invalid's chair.

Brandon stepped to his aunt and helped her reseat herself. "Please, Aunt Annis, let me continue." Turning his attention back to Nicole, he said, "What I'm offering you at the beginning is honesty. Am I such an ogre that little children run from me? I admit the advantages are greater for me than you, but I promise you will not come out on the short end. You aren't compelled to oblige me, but I wish you would reconsider. I find you pleasant company. I think neither of us will be any worse for coming to an agreement. Please, tell me what I may do to change your mind. Let me know your requirements."

Thinking to dissuade them from any further discussion, Nicole put an offer on the table. "What I require I'm sure you would not wish to give me. I will tell you, and then this awkward scene can come to an end.

"If I were to consider marriage with you, Lord Montagu, I require a cottage in Standon with a pianoforte. My father raided my annuity from my mother before I could put a stop to it. All I have left is twenty pounds a year. I would want my annuity increased to one thousand pounds per annum. Our relationship in private would be wholly platonic. Those are my terms." Nicole watched for Brandon's reaction with no doubt that he would turn her down.

"I find those terms acceptable. Are you sure that is all you want? The terms will be drawn up by my solicitor when he comes tomorrow and gives his permission for the marriage."

"You already thought I would consent?" Nicole felt the heat rise in her cheeks again.

"No, no, I had no idea one way or the other, but he is coming tomorrow to conduct some business for me. We might as well get this taken care of. My twenty-fourth birthday is Friday of next week. We must be married the day before in order to complete a full year. One thing I might add but cannot put in the marriage contract is your agreement that in public, we will appear to be a loving couple. Since I am going this far, there must be no question as to whether I live up to the letter of my father's will. I take it we have struck an accord?"

"Yes, we…Lord help me, we have." Nicole sighed and let her gaze bounce from Lady Scott to Lord Montague.

"Trust me, my dear, you have made a wise decision," Lady Scott said.

"I hope so, ma'am, for I know something of your nephew's reputation. I trust you have not flung me to the wolves, for I am not a notorious sort of person."

"Nicole, I know my reputation, and some of it is deserved, and a good deal more is not. You know how stories go. Someone starts it, and before long, it isn't recognizable as something I actually did."

"My dear, I would not encourage you to do this if I did not think it is in your best interest, besides my nephew's. I can't deny that Brandon does wild and reckless things, but at heart, he is not without feeling. You can trust him to live up to his end of your marriage agreement and rely on me to help you if you fall into trouble over this." Lady Scott smiled and patted Nicole's tightly clasped hands.

"Well, I must be going. See you tomorrow." Brandon turned to leave.

Nicole followed him to the door.

"Don't look so sad. I promise to behave for at least a year. After a year, you can continue to keep up the front and remain in my home if you choose. I will endeavor to be discreet. You may go your own way as long as you are prudent. You will have your cottage to retreat to if you so desire." Lord Montagu grasped the doorknob, then turned and stared into her eyes. "No one ever gets a reputation by being virtuous. I will confess my faults are many, but I'll put no demands on you. To prove to you I am serious, I am offering to you what I've never given to another: my name." Lord Montagu walked through the doorway leaving Nicole staring after him.

She continued to stare at the closed door in a puzzled daze. She could not imagine what had possessed her to agree to this arrangement. Her future was now as unpredictable as it had been before, if not more so. She sighed at the thought that someone else would shoulder her burdens at least for a year.

She bit her lower lip. She had swallowed her pride and let this temptation overtake her. She hoped she did not live to regret it. What does a rake know about keeping his promises? She must not let him know how she felt or become accustomed to his attentions. She was sure after the marriage, or when he received his inheritance, he would not treat her with any consideration. She was just a means to an end.

Chapter Three

Lady Scott turned her chair around, and Nicole looked up from her needlework on tenterhooks when Corbin opened the door.

"Lord Montagu and Mr. Pettigrew," he announced as if they were royalty.

Nicole stood and stared in disbelief at her father's solicitor and friend coming through the door. A smile spread across her face. She ran to him and took his hands in hers. "Oh, Uncle Claude, I can't believe it. It has been so long. I wanted to come visit you and Aunt Cora while I stayed in London, but circumstances took my time."

Mr. Pettigrew stood with his mouth open looking at Nicole. He took a step back holding her at arm's length. "My child, I've been trying to find out where you were. My wife wishes me to bring you to her. We've been so worried. I did my best to warn your father. He refused to listen to anyone. By the time I learned of your father's creditor's actions, it was too late to forestall them or try to renegotiate an arrangement for paying off his debts. I made the trip down to Sussex, but you were gone by then. No one knew where you went." He shook his head sadly.

"I'm sorry you made the long trip for nothing. Everything happened so fast and left us in a chaotic mess. I should have written to you, I know, but I couldn't think straight at the time. As you can see, I've landed on my feet. I'm the companion to Lady Scott. I'm so pleased to see you. We'll catch up later. I'll have Corbin bring in refreshments." Nicole hurried from the room. She needed a chance to catch her breath and overcome her embarrassment before she saw Uncle Claude again.

****

With a puzzled look on his face, Brandon looked at Mr. Pettigrew and then at Nicole as she disappeared through the door. "How do you know Miss Waltham, sir?"

"I've been Lord Waltham's solicitor since I first entered the practice of law. We attended Eton together. He was two years ahead of me, but we became fast friends. We were good friends at one time. I'm Nicole's godfather, you know. Thus the honorary title of uncle."

"Please be seated, Mr. Pettigrew. Brandon has a little business to discuss with you." Lady Scott motioned to a desk and chair across from her usual place by the window.

"Yes, I...uh...I didn't know you knew Miss Waltham. This makes everything somewhat awkward." Brandon cleared his throat. "Sir, I have asked Miss Waltham to marry me. I have only to get your approval and make sure, since you are the executor of my father's will, that Miss Waltham fits the requirements." Brandon sat in the nearest chair. After an awkward pause, he realized how his words sounded. "I...er...I wouldn't want Miss Waltham to suffer from this alliance."

"I have no objection on that point, but I wish to speak to Miss Waltham alone before I give my final approval."

"Yes, certainly. I'll show you to the library and ask Miss Waltham to join you there. After you're satisfied, please join us again." Brandon escorted Mr. Pettigrew to the library and hurried to waylay Nicole.

He intercepted her as she came rushing down the hall, taking her by the arm and pulling her into the dining room. "Nicole, Mr. Pettigrew wishes to speak to you in the library. Please consider what you say. I know he's a family friend, but do not confide in him or all is lost. He is a solicitor first, the executor of the will second, and an honest man above all else."

\*\*\*\*

Nicole nodded. "I'm not a ninny. I understand the complications this has caused."

Brandon opened the dining room door for her. She walked out and proceeded down the hall. She squared her shoulders, took a deep breath, and walked into the library.

"Uncle Claude."

He stood and took Nicole's outstretched hands. He searched her face before he spoke. "Nicole, we've been so worried. Your Aunt Helena refused to receive me. I could not find you or your father." He dropped her hands and leaned against the desk. "You could have knocked me over with a feather when I came through the door and saw you today. My dear, have you seen your father? No one knows what became of him. I don't mean to throw questions at you. I'm just a tad flustered."

"No, I've not been able to find him either. I stayed in London for a time with Aunt Helena. As you might have guessed, that had disaster written all over it. I had to take the first position offered me. I'm too young for a governess, but Lord Scott thought I would do as a companion for his mother." Nicole shrugged, walked toward the window, and stared out. "I haven't seen my father since everything fell apart. I believe he must be living rough somewhere in London. He has no other choice. We scraped together every ha'penny we could find just to get to London. There is no money left, and his friends have fled. A friend said she saw someone who resembled Father in Covent Gardens, but she wasn't sure. In London, I searched for him in shelters, missions, and under the bridges where the homeless camp. I haven't found him or anyone that knows where he is. There are so many places, missions, and abandoned buildings. I'm overwhelmed with what promises to be an impossible task. When I took this position, I had to give up my search."

"My dear, I wish you had come to us first. There will always be a welcome for you in our home. I know your aunt can be trying. The thought of you searching for your father by yourself sends a chill through me. You should not be going into such places alone. It's not safe."

"I don't know what to do next. I must find him. He's out there alone. He could be sick, or anything." Nicole closed her eyes and placed her hand over her heart.

"My dear, we'll discuss this later. More pressing is what Lord Montagu just told me. I tried not to show how shocked his words made me. He says he wishes to marry you. Is this your wish?"

"That is correct. It is what I wish. I have given my consent if you approve according to the will."

"There is no question of not receiving my approval, but is this what you want? I must admit, I do not wish this entanglement for you. He has a dreadful reputation as one of the wildest rakes in town. I have heard it rumored that he kidnapped a woman and tried to elope with her. People say he belongs to *The Hell-Fire Club*. The club is rumored to cater to every vice, even the black arts."

"I know, Uncle Claude, but I don't believe the half of it. He has promised me a respectable life if I consent to marry him. As you must know, I'm penniless. This puts me out of the marriage market. His offer, I'm sure, will be the last I shall receive. Please say you'll consent."

"Yes, no problem, if that is your wish, but I intend to ensure that the marriage settlement is fair. I will not see you come out of this worse than you went in. If you should ever need me, you simply have to ask. I look on you as the daughter I never had. You can come to me with anything." He stood, took her hands in his, and smiled at her.

"Yes, I know. Thank you. I'm sure Lord Montagu and I will deal famously with each other." Nicole tried to smile reassuringly.

The concern she saw on his face nearly brought her to the verge of tears. The need to unburden herself and tell him everything was almost more than she could bare, but she knew she must not do that. She had given her word. She cleared her throat and put on her best smile.

"Uncle Claude, Lord Montagu will have to get a special license. We are to be married Wednesday of next week. Will you do me the honor of attending in place of my father?"

"No need to ask, my child, I am honored." He beamed at her and smoothed his mustache.

Nicole gave him a hug, and they returned to the drawing room to go over the plans for the wedding.

\*\*\*\*

There was no time to have a dress made for the occasion, so Lady Scott had one of her dresses altered. Keeping to tradition, Nicole sewed the last stitch in her gown for good luck before she left for the chapel.

It had a lined low-neck bodice made of ivory silk Dupion and embroidered with orange blossoms, beaded with seed pearls, and edged in antique lace. The sleeves flounced at the elbow with ivory lace. Moderate panniers supported a skirt made of the same silk fabric and embroidery. Lady Scott's hairdresser helped Nicole pile her powdered hair high on her head in an intricate woven pattern. A long veil reached to her waist. She slipped into Louis heeled shoes of ivory satin and fastened Brandon's wedding gift of pearl and diamond earrings with a matching pearl and diamond pendant as she prepared to go to the chapel.

\*\*\*\*

Chapel bells pealed joyously on the beautiful summer's day, with not a cloud in sight to mar the occasion. Brandon, with the assistance of Corbin, helped Lady Scott out of her carriage and into the church. This was her first emergence in public since her apoplexy. She leaned heavily on Brandon's arm. Out of breath, she sank into a pew with a sigh. When he felt he could leave her alone, he took his place in front of the altar.

The vicar emerged from the vestry and nodded for

the organist to begin playing *Jesu, Joy of Man's Desiring* by Bach.

The front door of the church opened, and Nicole stepped through into the vestibule. A warm breeze rustled her veil and the hem of her dress. A beam of sunlight shone through the stained glass window following her as she came down the aisle. The sweet smell of Maiden's Blush roses from Lady Scott's garden surrounded the wedding party.

Uncle Claude sat midway in the church. Nicole reached out to him as she passed. He smiled and gave her a reassuring pat on the arm. Brandon walked halfway down the aisle to meet her. When she came near enough for him to see through her veil, he caught his breath. He had not fully looked at her before this moment, and seeing her for the first time this way disturbed him. Her small hand trembled in his. When she looked up at him, his heart beat a little faster. He could not imagine what had come over him. With her hand in his, he escorted her to the altar where they knelt before the vicar. Even as they knelt, he could not take his eyes away from her. She had never looked lovelier.

Brandon had decided to dress in a black silk suit trimmed in gold braid. Along with his suit, he wore white silk stockings with knee-length breeches and low-heeled leather shoes with large buckles. A black ribbon edged in gold pulled his powdered hair away from his face.

The ceremony finished with the vicar telling them they were husband and wife. Brandon pulled back her veil and kissed his bride. He did not expect an ordinary, chaste kiss to make him feel so strange. Holding her in his arms longer than was sociably acceptable, he did not want to let her go.

The vicar cleared his throat, and Brandon let her go. The air in the chapel seemed to have vanished, making him lightheaded. Against his better judgment, he wanted to taste those petal soft lips once again. Reluctantly, he turned, and they strolled together toward the front of the church.

Self-control and cool logic would not allow him to become entangled. At all times his affairs were casual. Since leaving the boarding school, he'd had many dalliances and kissed many ladies, but never once had he felt this way. But this was not just another affair, he had entered into marriage. Swallowing hard, he must keep the panic welling up in him at bay.

Outside the chapel, Brandon handed her into his coach, then left to help his aunt depart as well. Mr. Pettigrew rode with Lady Scott and the two coaches made their way to Lady Scott's home where the just married couple would celebrate with a Venetian breakfast.

The wedding party was a small one with the Vicar, Lady Scott, Mr. Pettigrew, Lord Montagu, and Nicole. Two house maids and Corbin stood by to serve the party. They started with a Vermouth Amaro, the bitter and the sweet. Next, they sampled the hors d'ouvres of small cold crabs mixed with a tart sauce made of egg yolk, olive oil, vinegar and mustard on a slice of *prosciutto*. The servants distributed the next course of scampi with steaming risotto, veal cutlets done in the Bologna style, ham with hot parmesan, and grated white truffles. The meal finished with a slice of stracchino cheese and fine vintage champagne.

When the breakfast ended, Mr. Pettigrew left for

London, but not before wishing his goddaughter continued happiness. "Thank you for coming, Uncle Claude. I can't tell you what it's meant to me. The only thing that would have made it better is if father could have been here."

"Don't look so sad, my dear. Not on your special day." He held her hand in his. "There now, that's the smile I'm looking for. Try not to worry. I'm sure he'll turn up. In the meantime, my wife and I look forward to seeing you when you come to London. I'm afraid I must hurry back to London. Remember if you need us, you only have to ask." Uncle Claude bowed over her hand and left.

Brandon turned to his aunt. "Aunt Annis, we'll be leaving now. Thank you for the lovely wedding breakfast. We'll be back to visit soon."

Both Brandon and Nicole kissed Lady Scott's offered cheek, then left for Brandon's home. They rode the entire way accompanied by awkward silence. Their carriage turned up the long tree-lined drive of Worthington Park, located only four or five miles from Lady Scott's home. Brandon cleared his throat and tried to speak but could think of nothing to say. Both gave a sigh of relief when the sprawling three-storied Jacobean manor came into view.

Made of stone and stucco, it had several large windows in front with four dormers. Brandon handed Nicole from the carriage, up the entry steps, and into the dark oak paneled hallway where the butler awaited them.

"Jenkins, you may wish me well. I'm a married man. Please, let me introduce my bride, Lady Montagu."

"Very good, my lord. You have my felicitations." Jenkins bowed his head.

Nicole smiled at the butler.

Brandon turned his attention to Nicole. "My lady, if you will follow me, I'll show you to your bedchamber. Jenkins will have someone bring the baggage to your apartment."

\*\*\*\*

Nicole followed in a daze. She looked around as they made their way up the grand stairway, down a hallway, and turned into yet another hallway. "This is your bedchamber and sitting room. There is a door at that end adjoining my bedchamber, but it has a lock so you should feel safe. You realize I have no designs on your person. I hope to get through this year with as little fuss as possible."

"I understand completely, my lord. We have an agreement." Nicole felt embarrassed at his words and was not sure why.

Without warning, she felt deflated. She did not know what she'd expected, but his no-nonsense words left her feeling sad. He held the door for her as she stepped into a large room painted in light blue and trimmed in pristine white. A huge window at the end of the room lit the space.

"I engaged an abigail for you. If you don't get on, feel free to hire another. I thought she would do for the time being."

"Yes, thank you. I'm sure we'll get along quite well."

"This house is a bit old-fashioned in style. Different ancestors have added on or taken away over the years, making it easy to get lost. I'm not here often.

If you need something to occupy your time, you may update and refresh the décor. All I need is an idea of the expense. The housekeeper is Mrs. Glover. I'll introduce you to everyone before dinner. We keep country hours. Dinner is served at four. I'll leave you to rest and direct the abigail in what you need." With that, he went through the adjoining door and left Nicole standing in the middle of her bedchamber staring after him.

A servant deposited her baggage just inside the open door to her suite, and her abigail came running into the room.

"Sorry, Lady Montagu. I didn't know you had arrived. My name is Mavis Timms." She gasped and curtsied.

Nicole brushed a tear away and tried to smile. "Pleased to meet you. I've just arrived myself."

Nicole sat in a chair by the window to collect herself and watched as Mavis scurried around the room. She looked very young. Nicole guessed her age to be no more than sixteen. Her blonde hair was done up in braids and fastened in rings at the side of her head. Her round, good-natured face had a sprinkling of freckles across her nose, and her eyes were as blue as a summer sky. She had a look of fresh country air about her. Nicole thought they would get along rather well.

"After we have my clothes sorted, perhaps you could show me around the manor and the gardens."

Mavis bobbed her head and undid the cords on Nicole's trunk. Nicole changed from her wedding clothes to her every day clothes while Mavis unpacked her things. Since she did not have many clothes, it did not take long to put them away.

She followed Mavis out of her chamber, trying to

remember the way so she could come back without getting lost. They first visited the drawing room. It had tall windows with exquisite Brussels tapestries hanging from the walls. Shells decorated the high ceiling and enormous chandeliers hung at both ends of the long room. The pine-paneled dining room contained a dining table that could seat twenty easily. A great window on one side let in light, a fireplace large enough to roast an ox resided on the other, and a huge chandelier over the table completed the room.

They walked out to the back garden. Nicole was drawn to the maze with six-foot high holly hedges. They walked along the path around the maze, coming upon a large manmade lake, closed off with a double iron gate and a stonewall separated it from the manor house. When she peered through the gate, Nicole saw a pavilion and several small boats. While she watched, she saw a fish jump out of the water and reenter with a splash.

Nicole and Mavis made their way back to her chamber where she lay on her divan to rest until time to get ready for dinner. She drifted into a heavier slumber than she'd meant to almost right away.

Mavis woke her. "I'm sorry, Lady Montagu, but his lordship wants you to get ready now so he can introduce you to the staff."

Nicole sat up and looked around in a daze trying to remember where she was. She blinked away the confusion and looked at Mavis. "Yes, sorry. Not myself today."

Dressed in her one evening dress of black, she put on her wedding jewels to lighten her appearance. Mavis helped arrange her hair. By the time she finished dressing, she heard the dinner gong echo through the house. Hearing a knock on her door, she stood feeling like the new girl in school. She opened the door to Lord Montagu and took his arm. He led her down the stairs where the servants were waiting in a row.

"You remember Jenkins?"

"Yes." She nodded in acknowledgement. She marveled at the butler, thinking he had to be a cousin of Corbin and Biggers. She could not think of another explanation for the likeness.

Brandon led her to each servant and told her his or her names and what they did.

Nicole acknowledged each with a nod. She was sure she could never remember all their names. At this point, she barely remembered her own. After the introductions, her new husband led her into the drawing room where Jenkins served her a glass of ratafia and Brandon a glass of sherry.

Jenkins returned a short time later and bowed. "Dinner is served, my lord."

Brandon escorted her into the dining room. She sat at one end of the long table, and he at the other. A candelabrum at each end comprised the only decorations on the table.

Since there were just the two of them, the serving maid brought a bowl of cream of leek soup to each with a boiled cod and roasted carrots. Brandon carved a ham and handed a plate to the servant to pass on to Nicole. There was an assortment of vegetables, but Nicole found she could not eat more than the sweet potatoes. The next course consisted of leg of lamb and peacock pie with yet more vegetables, along with gumballs and cheese wigs. With the main course over, the servants removed the dishes and the tablecloth. A new tablecloth replaced the first, and the desserts arrived. There were sugared fruits, sweetmeats, and several flavors of jams and jellies. After nibbling at the desserts, she drank one last glass of wine, excused herself with respect to her host, and retired to her small sitting room.

\*\*\*\*

Brandon stayed at the table, drank several more glasses of port, and wondered about what he had done this day. He could not understand why he felt responsible for the happiness of this woman. He had not given a thought to any other women throughout his life. They used each other, and when one grew tired of the other, there were no hard feelings on parting. He kept telling himself that he had in reality married someone. Something he never expected to do. One could not get out of a marriage without problems, unlike an affair. It took an act of parliament to dissolve a marriage. They had a business arrangement, and she had agreed to the terms. He rarely had pangs of conscience, yet the impression he had acted selfishly refused to leave him.

He found Nicole in the small sitting room. "Is everything all right?"

"Yes, thank you. I'm just working on my needlework. Did you need something?"

"No, no… If you want me, I'll be in the library."

Nicole nodded and returned her attention to her needlework. He closed the door softly, feeling as if he should have kept her company. She looked so small and alone. Deep in thought, he walked into the library where Jenkins brought him a bottle of claret, and then another. Jenkins offered to help him up the stairs to his bedchamber sometime later, but he refused. He finished the last bottle and fell asleep in the wing chair in front of the fire.

****

The next morning, Nicole dressed and rode over to Lady Scott's home. Although she was a relative now, Nicole looked on her as a friend. Lady Scott had made significant improvements in learning to walk again. She still needed a cane, but today she walked around her garden three times without feeling fatigued. Very pleased with her progress, Nicole left and headed home.

Jenkins stopped her as she came through the door. "My lady, we have company. Four of his lordship's friends have come for the grouse season. I put them in the library. Lord Montagu is away touring the estate with his bailiff."

"I didn't know you had shooting parties. Do they come regularly?"

"Yes, my lady, they come every year at this time."

"In that case, please have their rooms prepared and refreshments brought to the library. They will most likely enjoy ale, and I prefer a pot of tea."

"Very good, my lady."

Nicole put on her best smile and walked through the library door, not sure what awaited her. Before opening the door, she heard loud voices and laughter. When she came through the door, the laughter died. The four men hastily stood and stared at her.

"How do you do? I'm Lady Montagu. You may not know, but Lord Montagu and I were married a short time ago this summer." She walked around to each with her hand outstretched.

Each in his turn told her his name and bowed.

"Lord Turnbridge."

"Lord Wharton."

"Lord Dunmore."

"Mr. Marchand."

She saw decidedly handsome gentlemen dressed in buckskins and coats of varying shades of green and blue with silver or gold buttons and highly polished Hessians. They appeared to be the same age as Brandon. Lord Turnbridge was the tallest of the four. He had dark-brown hair, hazel eyes, and a clean-shaven face. None of the men wore a wig but pulled their longish hair back and held it with a ribbon, except Mr. Marchand who left his hair loose. Lord Wharton had light brown hair, green eyes and sported a van dyke. He was of average height and showed a penchant for flamboyant waistcoats. Lord Dunmore had red hair and wide, trusting, sage green eyes. He was of average height, and one could see in a few more years he would be fairly plump. However, he had a very pleasant appearance. The most handsome of the four by far was Mr. Marchand. He had blond hair and piercing blue eyes. His exquisitely cut traveling outfit looked molded to his form. His legs showed to advantage, and he had no need of padding to fill out his jacket.

"I'm so pleased to meet you. Lord Montagu is with his bailiff, but he should return before long. Please be seated. Jenkins is bringing refreshments. I'm sorry I was out when you arrived, but you see I didn't expect you. With everything that has happened, it must have slipped Lord Montagu's mind."

"We had no idea he married. We're sorry to intrude. I think it best if we left," Lord Dunmore said.

"Nonsense, you're most welcome."

Everyone sat in the nearest chair and stared around

the room not sure where to look or what to say.

Nicole cleared her throat before speaking. "I didn't realize a shooting party was being made up. Is there good birding in this area?"

"Yes, we have come down for the last six years and have not been disappointed. We make up a party with Sir William, whose property adjoins Worthington Park to the north and Lord Carlton's property in the west. They have beaters flushing the grouse for us," Lord Wharton supplied.

"How very exciting. I used to go with my father to shooting parties in Sussex. We had excellent sport," Nicole said.

"Pardon me, Lady Montagu, but did you say Sussex? You look familiar. I've been wondering of whom you remind me. You said Sussex. That brought it back to memory. Let me see, it must have been three years ago. I was invited to Lord Waltham's with my friend Lord Darlington to ride to the hounds," Mr. Marchand said.

"Well, what a coincidence. I thought you looked familiar also. Lord Waltham is my father. Do you remember that remarkable incident with Lord Chester?"

"Do I remember? How could I forget?" He looked around at his friends and found it difficult to control his laughter. "You know Lord Chester?"

Everyone nodded knowingly.

"He attended the hunt. As you know, he considers himself a nonpareil horseman. He wore his favorite wig everywhere he went. He had a string and tied the wig on with it under his chin so as not to lose it when he took a fence. Did you ever meet a more tiresome or vain creature?" Mr. Marchand shook his head and snorted.

"Well, he made a run at this fence, which had a tree near it with a towering branch that hung over the fence. Lord Chester took the fence, and his horse must have been feeling its oats because it sailed high through the air, clearing the fence by a good three feet. As Lord Chester passed over the fence, somehow a hornet's nest hanging from the limb snagged his wig. When his horse hit the ground, those hornets swarmed. He batted at the hornets to no avail. His horse danced around wild-eyed, and you could see it would not be long before the poor horse ran. Hornets were everywhere. Everyone around him had trouble keeping his horse from running. I was stung twice myself.

"Lord Waltham grasped the situation and rode up to Lord Chester, yelling for him to remove his wig. He refused to take off the wig and kept on batting at the hornets. They were becoming angrier with each swat. With his riding crop, Lord Waltham knocked the nest to the ground but along with the nest came the wig. Lord Chester's horse ran off with Lord Chester bouncing on the back like a child's bandalore. Lord Waltham caught up with them and reined in Lord Chester's horse. Lord Chester was stung at least twenty times and so was his horse. All the time, through what must have been considerable pain, he kept calling for someone to bring him his damn wig. Sorry, my lady. I know we shouldn't laugh, but it was the funniest thing I've seen in my life."

"It wasn't so funny when he stayed over a month with us. He complained every day about his odious wig. It almost drove the household crazy." Nicole covered her mouth to keep from laughing.

By this time everyone was laughing. The awkwardness disappeared with the laughter, and everyone began sharing hunting tales.

****

When Brandon came home, he heard laughter coming from the library the moment he stepped over the threshold.

"What's going on, Jenkins?"

"Your friends arrived a short time ago for the grouse hunt."

"Blast, completely slipped my mind."

"Lady Montagu is in the library."

"Is she indeed?" Brandon had a scowl on his face when he opened the door and saw everyone treating Nicole as if she were an old friend. He didn't know why this irritated him. He shut the door with a bang. The laughter stopped, and everyone looked toward the noise.

Nicole stood at once. "Lord Montagu, I've just been talking to your friends. It seems Mr. Marchand and I have met in the past. I must check with Mrs. Glover on a household matter. Gentlemen, I'll leave you in Lord Montagu's hands. Until dinner." She bowed and left the room smiling.

"Brandon, old man, had no idea you'd married. We wouldn't have come. We offered to leave, but Lady Montagu assured us we were welcome. Very gracious lady. Let us offer our belated felicitations on your good fortune." Mr. Marchand handed Brandon a tankard of ale and raised a toast to the happiness of the couple.

Brandon recovered his good humor and welcomed his friends with another toast. "The announcement was in the paper. It completely slipped my mind you were coming, but I'm glad you're here. A moment ago I came from going over the estate with my bailiff, and it looks to be a good season for grouse. A toast to a decent shoot tomorrow."

They refilled their tankards and raised them in yet another toast. "Hear, hear!"

\*\*\*\*

Nicole came down to dinner and found the men waiting for her in the drawing room. Brandon took her arm and led her into the dining hall. He had the long dining table leaves removed making the table small enough to seat six intimately. They ate the same menu as their wedding dinner with the addition of mashed potatoes and lots of butter. Nicole sat at one end with Brandon at the other. Mr. Marchand sat on Nicole's right.

He monopolized her attention throughout the meal. Nicole felt Brandon's eyes on her over the course of the long dinner. Nervous and confused by his attention, she laughed a little more gaily at Mr. Marchand's jokes than she normally would have. She listened attentively to his tales of the *ton,* as did everyone else around the table. His attention did not deceive her. She realized, being the lone woman there, he could not help flirting with her. Some men are born flirts, and Mr. Marchand had raised it to a new level, but he did not take her in. In her first season, she had learned to recognize mild flirtation with no serious intent.

After finishing her dessert of sweetmeats, she drank her last glass of wine and pushed her chair away from the table. The five men stood and bowed. "I'll leave you to your cigars and port. Until tomorrow, gentlemen." She looked around the room and smiled. "I hope you return overflowing with grouse. Our cook is looking forward to your success, as am I." She curtsied and left the room.

Hurrying up the stairs and to the sanctuary of her bedchamber, she could feel Brandon's eyes still boring into her. What could she have done wrong? Restless, she settled in before the fire to read her book but soon could not keep her eyes open. Startled by a knock on the door breaking the silence of the night, she looked up to see Lord Montagu striding into her room. She met his smoldering gaze.

"We have an agreement, do we not? I distinctly remember we shook on it before we married." His eyes held menace as he strode across the room closing the distance between them.

"Whatever are you talking about? If you mean our marriage contract, then yes we shook on the parts that could not be written on paper." Nicole felt a blush heat her cheeks.

"Did we not agree that you can go your way and I mine as long as we were discreet? We both agreed to live circumspectly until our one-year anniversary. Is this not the agreement?" His eyes snapped at her.

"Yes, that is our agreement. What are you thinking? Why are you in my chamber sounding like thunder? If you have something to say, just say it," Nicole said through her teeth.

He gripped her shoulder where she sat and squeezed. "You will not poach on my home territory. I will not be cuckolded by my friends. Do you understand?"

"Oh yes, I understand perfectly. I find your behavior boorish in the extreme. Not to mention insulting. I have tried to do nothing but be a good hostess to strangers I had no idea were coming here to stay. I've listened to their jokes and tales, and tried to make an appropriate response. It seems to me that jealousy and several bottles of claret have you overwrought. Although I do not understand why you should be jealous since I mean nothing to you."

"You are my wife. I have a duty to protect my own."

"I am yours in name, nothing more." She turned away, trying to shrug off his hand. He removed it from her shoulder, and she stood and faced him. She wanted to say more, but the lump in her throat prevented her speaking.

"Very well, madam! Listen to what I have to say. You will not be indiscreet under my roof or with my friends." His voice sounded as sharp as flint.

"Perhaps you have a list, so I will know who your friends are." Nicole glared at him through narrowed eyes.

"No doubt you dislike me, and what I represent. You will agree I have not treated you badly. I have given you my name, and although it may not mean much to you, it means a great deal to me."

"You...you, sir, come into my chamber accusing me of things you know I have not done. You speak of your name as if it were akin to the Holy Grail. If you thought so much of your name, your father would not have put that ridiculous clause in the will, and I would not be here. You offered marriage because you must, not from any tender feeling for me. Never fear, my lord, I will live up to my end of the bargain. When a year is up, hold on to your hat because I'll beat Woodrose's record getting out of your sight." Her eyes flashed as she snapped her fingers in his face.

He grabbed her hand and held it in a vise-like grip. "You push me too far." He continued to hold her hand, staring daggers at her.

She tossed her head and stared back defiantly, adding fuel to the fire.

He dropped her hand as if it were a hot poker and strode to the door. "I bid you goodnight, madam." He pivoted and slammed the hallway door on his way out of the room.

She heard his footsteps retreating toward his bedchamber.

Nicole raced to the adjoining door. She waited until she heard him enter his own room and noisily turned the key in the lock. She stomped back to her chair and picked up her book. Too cross to read, she sat turning the pages and staring at the adjoining door.

The door rattled, then splintered inward. Lord Montagu strode into her room. Nicole stood and picked up a figurine of two owls cast in brass and held it behind her back. Lord Montagu came at her in a rush. He grabbed her by the shoulders and brought his lips down hard on hers, sucking the life and the will out of her. At last, he let her go and stood back looking at her. He swayed a little, held up his hand, and pointed a finger at her.

"You will surrender the rights of a husband this very night."

"Sir, have you gone insane or are you merely drunk? I most certainly will not yield to you. We had a deal, and that was not part of it."

"Deal be hanged. We'll see if you're made of ice or

flesh and blood. I have the right to beat you." He hiccupped. "And I have the right to share your bed. I demand that right."

"Which right do you demand? Is it your wish to beat me?"

He looked confused and shook his head. "You know full well what I meant." His speech was slurred. His gaze scorched her as if his eyes were red-hot coals from a furnace.

Nicole took a step back trying to put as much distance between them as she could. "I have no intention of surrendering to you. I must ask you to leave my chamber."

"Or you'll do what?" Brandon took another step toward her.

"Do not come any closer. I give you warning," Nicole's voice trembled.

He moved in closer and grabbed her by the shoulders. He bowed his head to kiss her again, and Nicole stomped hard on the arch of his foot causing him to lose his grip. She struck out with the figurine she held in her hand, hitting him a glancing blow on the side of his head. Brandon crashed to the floor breaking the small table beside her chair.

Nicole started toward the door at a run, then turned and went back. With halting steps, she made her way to Brandon and knelt by his side. In her panic, she could not tell if he was breathing or not. Her heart beat deafeningly in her ears, and perspiration broke out on her forehead.

"Oh lord, I've killed him. What am I to do?" She stood, looked around the room wide-eyed with fright, and wrung her hands. *I have to find Lord Montagu's valet. Stephens will help me.*

She tried to run out her door into the hallway but in her panic, could not get the handle to work on the door into the hallway. She ran through the adjoining door now hanging by one hinge and came out through Brandon's open hall door. She looked up and down the hall before she ran to Stephen's door and pounded on it. A bleary-eyed Stephens appeared.

"Oh, Stephens, you must help me. I think I've killed your master." Nicole wrung her hands and bounced from one foot to the other.

"Wait there, my lady, and I'll get my robe." A short time later, he came back out the door and hurried behind Nicole to where Brandon lay. Brandon lay sprawled on the floor, ashen and bleeding from the cut on his head.

Stephens felt his wrist and looked up at Nicole. "My lady, he's not dead. His skin is warm, and his pulse is strong. Do you think you could help me get him to his bed? I would not like to call for help. The less anyone knows about this the better."

Nicole sighed with relief. "Oh, yes, I understand. Why are his eyes not opened? Are you sure he's not dead?"

"I imagine he has passed out. He holds his spirits well, but after the third bottle, he becomes a bit reckless." Stephens let a smile escape. "It appears the knock on his head settled him properly."

The two of them lifted and pulled until they had him in his chamber. Stephens had the head and shoulders, and Nicole had both his feet. Once they had him near his bed, Stephens put his upper body on the bed and helped Nicole swing his feet and legs up onto the bed. They stood catching their breath and listening to Brandon snore.

"If you could help me, my lady? I'll hold him up, and you remove his clothes."

Brandon moaned and was of a mind to thwart their efforts. Nicole and Stephens had their work cut out for them. Getting his clothes off and keeping him in bed tasked their physical limits. At last, Brandon exhausted his efforts and fell back on his pillow. Stephens brought in bandages and dressed the wound on the side of his head and a cut on his arm where he fell into the table.

"My lady, please go to bed. I'll stay here and look after him."

"This is my fault, Stephens. I'm sorry to have interrupted your sleep. You get a little rest, and I'll stay with him. I'm too upset to sleep. I hope he's not too angry when he wakes."

"As you wish. I'd be surprised if he remembers. Don't worry, I've seen him in worse shape. I'll come back to relieve you in two hours' time. Perhaps you'll be calmer by then."

"Yes, that seems an excellent plan. Thank you."

Stephens returned a short time later with a pot of tea. He left it on the hob to keep warm and went off to his room. Nicole paced the floor until worn out and forced to sit. Her nerves were calming, though her energy was drained. She drank her tea and watched Brandon. She felt the pulse at his wrist every little bit. It continued to beat strongly, and his skin felt warm to the touch. She reached up and pushed a stray lock of hair out of his eyes.

He turned over, reached out, and grabbed her hand tightly, pulling it to his chest. His eyes still closed in sleep, he whispered, "Don't leave me," and then released her hand before turning to the other side.

Nicole stood with her heart beating faster and stared at his back.

Stephens came back and insisted she get a few hours of sleep. She returned two hours later to relieve him. He put his finger to his lips for quiet and motioned for her to follow him back into her bedchamber.

"My lady, you're worrying for nothing. He woke up a few minutes ago, complained about a headache, and turned over to go back to sleep. Chances are he'll not remember what happened. I sent a maid for his breakfast and a pitcher of hot water. He'll be a bear when I wake him up, but I know he doesn't want to miss the first day of the shoot."

Stephens set the door back as best he could. Nicole heard Brandon growling that he had the mother, father, and grandfather of all headaches. She heard him pouring water and cursing. From the distorted sound, it must have been over his head.

She heard Stephens say, "My lord, I tried to tell you. You had the cold water pitcher. Here is the warm water."

Nicole smiled for the first time since last night. *Men are such children. I have a problem on my hands. I don't know what to do. Why did I agree to marry someone who cares nothing more for me than he does his horse? Ha, what am I saying? He, in all probability, thinks more of his horse. Nothing but ownership.*

*Where are the tender feelings of a man for a woman? Am I never to hear a man's whisper of passion that melts and stirs my heart?*

Nicole lay back propped up in bed, sipping hot

chocolate and looking out the window. A noise startled her. She looked around to see Brandon advancing toward her. Her heart thudded against the walls of her chest. She looked around for a weapon, sat up straighter in bed, and held her head a little higher. He made his way to her bed and sat on the edge at the foot of it.

"What has happened to our shared door, my dear?"

"It appears to be the work of a drunken oaf, my lord." She mustered all her strength to smile sweetly at him.

"Yes, it would appear so. I take it you were not hurt in any way."

"No, I'm somewhat capable of defending myself. My cousin stayed with us on his school holidays. Unbeknownst to my father, he taught me to fence and the art of self-defense."

Brandon gingerly touched the side of his head. "He taught you well. A carpenter will repair the door this morning. I have asked him to install a more substantial door and put a stronger lock on it. A new table will also be fetched to replace the broken one. I apologize for your visitor's boorish behavior." He bowed and left the room.

Nicole did not know what to think and realized she was more than a little irritated. She had worried all night that she had seriously injured him. This morning he walked into her room and acted as if it were an everyday occurrence. He did not seem to care that he had worried her or caused her any discomfort.

\*\*\*\*

After a day of shooting, the friends carried home many pheasants for the cook. They changed their clothes and met in the drawing room before dinner.

Brandon waited, his irritation growing with each minute, but Nicole did not join the group for dinner.

Brandon cursed under his breath and yelled for Jenkins. "Jenkins, find out what's keeping Lady Montagu? We're tired and hungry."

A short time later, Jenkins appeared in the doorway. "Her ladyship regrets she does not feel well enough to come down to dinner. She will have something in her room. She has a headache." Jenkins smiled and bowed out the door walking backward.

"I guess we are on our own tonight. Let us go in to dinner."

They talked of the day's sport, and Marchand told more tales. Nothing held Brandon's attention except a bottle of claret and the doorway he kept looking toward expectantly. Soon they retired into the library where their host's bad mood put a pall on the party. "You're not very talkative tonight, Brandon," Marchand said.

"I don't yammer on when I have nothing to say. It would do you good to keep your own counsel. Where the devil is Jenkins?"

"You rang, my lord?" Jenkins stepped just inside the door.

"Bring another bottle, and be quick about it." Brandon frowned and threw an empty wine bottle into the fireplace. The bottle shattered throwing out a burst of flame.

Marchand stretched and yawned. "Fresh air always makes me tired. We tramped all over your blasted estate today. I take it we'll do Sir William tomorrow. I think I'll turn in."

The other three nodded and got up to leave. Brandon sat there staring at the fire and poured himself another glass. When they were at the door, he managed a nod. "Goodnight, gentlemen. I'll see you in the morning."

Since he could not trust himself to go up the stairs, he resigned to another night in front of the fire in the library. He'd made a fool of himself. There had never been an occasion when he had acted in such a fashion before. The women of his acquaintance would not have turned away from his advances but would have welcomed them. Half were prettier than Nicole, but he could not recall a single face to his mind. What he saw in his mind's eye was Nicole's face. He saw her countenance the first time he had honestly looked at her in the chapel when he lifted her veil.

He remembered that first kiss. It was just a kiss—a chaste kiss at that—and yet he could not get it out of his mind. Thinking about it made his heart beat faster. He poured himself another drink. He could not have feelings for her, and would not.

What was love anyway? Just a temporary emotion. A fire that burned hot for a time, and like a bonfire, turned to cold ashes. His mother had proven that love did not last. She left him and his father to run off with her lover. No, he had lived these four and twenty years free of entanglements, and his emotions would remain unattached. He could force her from his mind and forget her as he had so many others.

No matter how many times he said it, he knew he could not forget her. Why could he not? More confused than ever, he poured himself another drink but left it on the table untouched.

Chapter Four

Nicole came down the stairs dressed to go out as Brandon came through the library door. Nicole stopped in mid stride several steps from the bottom. He looked up and stood unmoving. She had not seen him since the morning after he crashed through her door.

He revealed a stiff smile. With his hands clasped behind his back, he came into the hallway. "Going somewhere?"

"Yes, I'm on my way to see Aunt Annis. I breakfast with her during the week. She likes me to help her with her walking exercises in the mornings. I'm proud of her progress. She asks often about you and sends her love."

Nicole descended to the foot of the stairs and put on her driving gloves, then walked to the door and put her hand on the doorknob. Brandon cleared his throat. She turned around, waited, and noticed for the first time how disheveled he looked, and his eyes looked tired. That he had spent another night drinking was easy to guess.

"Nicole, I wish to apologize for my actions of the other night." He touched his head tenderly where he had an impressive bruise. "I don't want us to be on bad terms. If you'll forgive me, I want our relationship to go back to the way it was. I miss seeing you at dinner."

"I want that too. However, I will not stand by and

let you accuse me of things I have not done. For your information, I will not, as you so vulgarly put it, poach your friends. I have no wish to become entangled in your set."

"Yes, I know that. I'm sorry for what I said. I want to blame the claret, as I remember little of what I said or did."

"Ah, yes, one's memory dissolves itself nicely in a bottle or two." She crossed her arms with her brows knit together in a frown.

"From your expression, I know what you're thinking, and I'm aware that I deserve your censure. That being said, you have my promise it will not happen again. I rarely give my promise. My character is such that I hardly ever regret my actions, but in this case, I sincerely do. Am I forgiven?"

"What a pretty apology. Yes, my lord, I will forgive you for the sake of peace in our relationship. I'm sorry for the action I took, but you left me no choice. We will say no more. I too want our relationship to go back to the way it was. I would like to get through this year with the least amount of friction between us. It is my wish we stay friends when this is over. Now I must be on my way."

She walked through the vestibule and did not glance back. She sensed his gaze bore into her and followed her through the passageway. After shutting the door, she leaned against it and took a deep breath to gather her composure before stepping into her carriage. The breeze was getting colder, and the sky looked overcast and ready to rain any second. She should have turned around and gone back, but her stubbornness would not let her. Today was the last day of the grouse season, and Brandon's friends planned to leave tomorrow. She hated to see them go. They were a buffer that would have given her time to become more comfortable in Brandon's company again.

As soon as she reached Lady Scott's home, the sky let loose its moisture by the buckets full. Thunder clashed and lightning streaked across the sky. She helped Lady Scott do her exercises, and it was time to go. Nicole and Lady Scott waited, but the storm did not abate. It eased off from time to time but always returned with a vengeance. Nicole broke fast with Lady Scott; she took a midday nuncheon and waited. The storm continued unabated.

"My dear, come away from the window. You cannot make nature bend to your will. You'll just have to wait until it quits."

"Oh, Aunt Annis, I dare not. It's getting darker with every passing hour. I must head back. Lord Montagu will wonder what's become of me."

"I'm sure he realizes you can't go out in a storm as bad as this. You must pass the night here."

"Oh, no, I could not. You remember the terms of the will. We must be under the same roof." Nicole twisted and fidgeted her hands while pacing in front of the fireplace.

"I'd forgotten that, but it is just for one night. I'm sure no one will tell. It can't be helped."

"I'm sorry, but I can't take that chance. I've given my word. He would hate me if he were chained to me for no purpose. I must go before it gets any darker." Nicole bit her nails and once again stared out at the downpour.

"My dear, you sound so sad. Is everything all

right? Brandon is not treating you shoddily, I hope. I will not stand for that." She leaned on her cane, drew a deep breath, and struggled to keep standing after all the exertion.

Nicole went to her and helped her sit. "No, no, everything is fine. Please don't give it another thought. I meant... Oh, well, it doesn't matter." She let her voice fade away, then glanced out the window once more and made a decision.

She went in search of Corbin and found him in the hallway. "Corbin, please have my carriage brought round."

Lady Scott gave her an extra cloak, and Nicole kissed her good-bye. Upon opening the door, an icy gust of wind blew rain into the hall. Nicole pushed against the wind and took the reins from the drenched groom. She looked back and saw Corbin struggling to close the front door.

Every time thunder clashed or lightning streaked across the sky her horse neighed, looked around wild-eyed, and shied sideways. It took every ounce of strength she had to control her horse and keep the carriage out of the ditches. It was the longest four miles she ever traveled. Torrents of rain fell. It blurred her vision, causing her to wipe her eyes repeatedly. When lightning revealed the drive to Worthington Park, gratefully, she turned onto the tree-lined lane. Once at the stable, she handed the reins to a surprised groom who helped her out of the carriage. Exhausted and chilled, once again she braved the rain and hurried toward the kitchen door.

\*\*\*\*

The rain had forestalled the day's shooting, and

everyone adjourned to Sir William's for drinks and refreshments instead. Sir William sent Brandon and his friends home in his covered traveling coach. When Brandon arrived, he looked around for Nicole. When he did not see her, he called for Jenkins.

"Jenkins, where is Lady Montagu?"

"She has not returned, my lord. We are very worried."

"You mean she has not been here all day. Good lord, she could be in a ditch somewhere if she tried to drive home in this. You should have sent someone to search for her. I'd better see if she is still at my aunt's." He donned his great coat once again and headed through the house toward the stables with Jenkins trailing behind him.

Brandon reached for the doorknob, but before he could open it, the wind caused the door to fly out of his hand. Nicole fell through the doorway and into his arms on a gust of wind. Instinctively, he picked her up and held her in his arms. Her arms went around his neck. Pulling her closer, his hand strayed over her soft rounded curves. He caught a whiff of her perfume and felt her breath on his neck. She looked up at him with those wide trusting eyes and he found he could not move. Seeing those softly molded lips, he wanted to taste them just one more time. An unfamiliar feeling stirred within the depths of his being, and his heart threatened to beat out of his chest. A sudden gust of wind slammed the door shut. The noise brought him out of his trance. He shook his head and turned around.

Helping her stand, he looked at her pale face. "Nicole, we've been worried. I was just coming to search for you. Look at you. You're drenched. Here, let me take your cloak. Your hair, your dress, everything is soaked. Why didn't you stay at my aunt's?"

She leaned in, making sure no one could hear. "I couldn't…"

"What do you mean you couldn't?" he asked just as the reason dawned on him. "I'm sorry. Yes, I see. You must get out of these wet clothes. Jenkins, find her abigail and have her draw a hot bath for Lady Montagu. She'll also need a warming pan for her bed. She needs some dry, warm clothes as soon as possible."

Nicole started shivering and could not stop. Her teeth chattered, and her hands trembled. Brandon drew her over by the fire in the kitchen and pulled up a chair. The cook brought her a steaming cup of tea. Soon Mavis had her bath ready. Gratefully she followed the young abigail to her chamber and settled into the warm scented water. The shivering subsided somewhat when she put on her warmest bedclothes and sank beneath her covers. Her feet hugged the warmth left behind by the warming pan. Feeling warmer, Nicole dozed for a short time before jerking awake with severe chills. Every bone in her body ached; she had a fever and a sore throat. Shortly after midnight, she rang for Mavis.

"Lordy day, my lady, we must send for the doctor. I'll wake Stephens. He'll know what to do. We must notify his lordship. Something must be done." A frantic Mavis ran from the room.

****

Brandon entered Nicole's bedchamber. "What's this I hear, my dear? Stephens says you're unwell."

He touched her forehead and brought his hand away promptly. She had a raging fever. Before settling down beside her bed, he had ordered everyone to stay away from her chamber so she could rest, then sent a stable boy to fetch the doctor. He remained by Nicole's bed, bathing her head with cool water until the doctor came. No matter how much he tried, her fever seemed to be getting worse.

Through half-closed eyes, she looked at him and tried to speak. But her attempt caused a struggle for her to breathe. She coughed and held her throat. Brandon fluffed up the pillows and raised her up so she could breathe better. Again, Nicole struggled to speak but only managed to croak.

"Ssh, my dear, the doctor's coming. Just rest," Brandon mumbled while changing the cool cloth on her brow.

Dr. Peterson arrived. When he saw Nicole and heard her symptoms, he gave Nicole a dose of anodyne draught.

She looked up and put her hand on the doctor. "Doctor, I'm hurting from head to toe. Every bone aches. Heat is coming out of my feet and ears... I'm so tired."

"Yes, my dear, I know. Not to worry. We'll have you right as nine pence before you know it." The doctor patted her arm, then motioned for Brandon to follow him out of the room.

"I'm afraid Lady Montagu has influenza. There's an outbreak in the village. This is my tenth house call this night. I recommend her ladyship breathe salty water in to relieve her nasal congestion. I left a bottle of anodyne draught for the pain. It will also help her sleep."

"Doctor, she came in last evening soaked to the skin. She was caught in the downpour. Could that have caused this?"

"No, influenza takes at least four days to appear. It's extremely contagious. I saw Lady Montagu in the village about three or four days ago talking to Mrs. Hodge in that little shop beside the tobacconist. Both the tobacconist and Mrs. Hodge are ill. In answer to your question, the soaking did not bring this on, but it could possibly have made it worse. Give her plenty of fluids. I'll check back tomorrow. We must try our best to keep her from getting pneumonia." With a wave of his hand, the doctor hurried down the stairs and disappeared out the door before Brandon could ask any more questions.

Mavis came up the stairs with a pot of tea.

Brandon stepped in front of the door. "I'm afraid I can't allow you in your mistress's room. The doctor says it's influenza and very contagious."

"Yes, my lord. Begging your pardon, but my grandmother recommends Elderberry tea. She swears by it. I've made a pot. It will make Lady Montagu well sooner, and it will keep you from getting sick." She held the tray out to him.

Although Brandon did not see how mere tea could help Nicole, he took it from her. "Thank you, Mavis, and thank your grandmother."

He carried it to Nicole's bedchamber and poured her a cup. While helping her to sit up, he felt her shudder. Too weak to grip the cup, he held it to her mouth. She took a few sips, but this exhausted her. She fell asleep before she finished the whole cup. Brandon drank a cup and kept watch.

Through the night, he watched Nicole struggle through fever and pain. He piled the covers back on her when she threw them off as her fever raged. He continued to place cool cloths on her forehead through the night and into the evening of the next day. The last time he did, she put her hand on his.

"Brandon?"

"Yes, my dear, I'm here. You have influenza. I'm keeping you company. Mavis brings us pots and pots of Elderberry tea. She tells me her grandmother swears by it."

Nicole tried to smile but only succeeded in tearing at Brandon's dusty, virgin heartstrings. "Talk to me," she whispered hoarsely.

"What would you like me to talk about? Oh, I've been charged with my friends' words of regret at your indisposition. They left me with a wish that they will see you in excellent health when we come to London. They left yesterday."

"That's very thoughtful of your friends. I want you to tell me about...you. I know nothing about you...or your family."

"There's not much to tell. My mother's name was Icie. She ran away with Lord Overton soon after my first birthday. Several years later, they died in a fire in Paris. My father could not bear to look at me after she ran away. He left me here with a nanny and spent most of his time in London. As soon as I was old enough, he sent me to boarding school. I saw little of him the whole time growing up. He didn't have any time for me, nor did he attempt to make time. Regrettably, I resembled my mother's side of the family. I suppose I must have been a constant reminder."

"Sorry, both of you must have been very unhappy."

"You know, I never thought of my father as being

unhappy. Now I think about it, he must have been. He never remarried or formed a liaison that I know of." He closed his eyes remembering his father.

"I can't say I was *un*happy. I was just *not* happy. The only time I can remember being happy was when Aunt Annis visited. Sometimes Father permitted me to stay with her on school holidays. When I arrived at Eton, being the youngest and the smallest, the older boys teased me relentlessly."

"Did you not make friends?"

"Eventually, and you have met them. All four were here."

"I'm glad you've kept your friendships. Were you angry with your father?"

"At first, but later when I looked back I realized whatever his intentions were, the experience made me self-reliant. I learned to take care of myself early on."

She motioned for him to help her sit up. He plumped her pillows and handed her a cup of tea. She sighed and sipped until too tired to hold the cup on her own again. Brandon helped her finish the drink, then set the cup on her side table and freshened a cooling cloth for her head. Her flushed face and tired eyes caused Brandon some concern. Her fever raged and subsided at its whim.

"I've told you about my past. What about your past? I know nothing of your life before I met you," Brandon said.

"I was an only child, but I had a loving mother and father. There was a nanny and tutors, and then I went away to finishing school. I grew up wild and free and not very ladylike, I'm afraid. After my mother died, my Aunt Tess insisted Father send me away to learn the art of being a lady before he brought me out to society. I didn't have a season until I turned nineteen. Almost an old maid." Nicole tried to smile but started coughing and could not stop.

Brandon brought her water and gave her more Elderberry tea that had been warming on the fireplace hob. When her coughing spasm subsided, she lay back on her pillow exhausted. Brandon held her hand and watched her, not knowing what else to do.

After a short time, she said, "My cousin came to us from boarding school on his school holidays until he was old enough to travel to Italy on his own. When his father died, his mother moved to Italy. That's my Aunt Tess, my father's sister. She's as different from my Aunt Helena as night and day. She's a wonderful, kind person, but easily led. That said, I must also say she lives on a different plane than the rest of us. She follows all these mysticisms as they come into vogue.

"Being an only child, I found it lonesome not having someone to talk or play with. When my cousin came on school holidays, we played knights and castles, climbed trees, raced horses, and terrorized the countryside. We were more like brother and sister than cousins.

"He taught me to fence and planned to teach me the manly art of self-defense. That had to go by the wayside, though. I forgot to duck, weave, or keep my guard up when we were sparring, and he landed me a facer, which knocked me out. He thought he'd killed me. My father saw it happen. Needless to say, we both were eating our meals standing up for some time."

"Did you learn the manly art of self-defense?" Brandon tried hard not to smile.

"Oh no! I learned a few moves, but mostly, I found it a little too manly." She rubbed her jaw and laughed shakily, then sank into her pillow and tried to catch her breath.

"If I remember right, you had a fiancé?"

"Oh, yes. I met Lord Bedlington at my first ball. He made himself agreeable to my father and my aunt. At this point, my father gave me cause for concern. With my mind on my father and the worry he caused, the distraction must have been the reason I agreed to marry Lord Bedlington. I can think of no other reason for my temporary insanity. He showed me particular attention whenever I entered a room. He was handsome, very personable, and at times made me feel special. I was not a seasoned debutante, and I fell for his attentions. I believed he had a tender spot in his heart for me, but as it turned out, I was wrong." She stared off past Brandon.

"Were you in love with this paragon?" A frown crossed Brandon's face.

"I became infatuated at first, and he asked for my hand. He came from a good family. Everyone said it was a perfect match and congratulated me on my success. My father had no objection. In short, I agreed to marry him. His parents sent him to acquire culture on the continent, and we were to be married after his return.

"He gave me a diamond necklace with matching earrings and a gold grooming kit as an engagement present. After the engagement announcement came out in the paper, I heard a few disquieting stories but did not regard them.

"When he returned, he did not call at Aunt

Helena's or try to find me. By that time, everyone knew my father's fortune had dwindled. I had heard he returned through some friends. Since I was no longer an heiress, I had to think his interest diminished along with my dowry. If he was too embarrassed to face me, I thought I should be the one to take the first step. I sent word that I wished to see him at my Aunt Helena's home.

"It did not surprise me that he appeared relieved when I released him from our engagement. In truth, I could not blame him for not wanting a penniless bride coming on the tail end of her father's outrageous behavior. I knew how it would be, but I thought he would object a little. If not out of some affection for me, at least for show, but he did not. I offered his gifts back, and he took them without a word." She sighed and closed her eyes in sleep, still holding Brandon's hand.

"The man must be a fool," Brandon whispered.

When he heard her breathing evenly, he pulled his hand free. He had not shaved or changed his clothes since Nicole became ill two days ago. He could not leave her side. He ran his hand through his hair and paced around the room until he became tired. He sat in the chair next to her bed after he changed the cloth on her forehead. Leaning back in his chair, he closed his eyes in exhaustion and slept soundly through the night. The next morning, he awoke to the sun streaming through the window and Mavis knocking on the door.

"Your breakfast tray is on the table in the hall, my lord," Mavis called through the door.

\*\*\*\*

The following morning and the next, Mavis

brought food and more pots of Elderberry. She kept them supplied throughout the day with pots of hot tea. By the end of the fourth day, Nicole had gained a little strength and could sit up by herself. Her fever had passed, and she could hold her own cup. She agreed to drink the gruel Mavis brought and later ate a panada.

Dr. Peterson came every day to visit since her illness and smiled when he saw her sitting up in bed. "Well, my dear, you're looking much better today. Your temperature is within the normal range. It'll be safe to let your maid back in your bedchamber."

"Thank you. I feel much better."

The doctor left, and Brandon returned to her side. "Doctor Peterson assures me you're on the mend." He smiled warmly at Nicole and took her hand.

"Yes, you're off nursemaid duty. I thank you for your care."

There was a knock at the door. Brandon opened it and found Mavis standing there holding yet another tray with tea. "Come in, Mavis. Your mistress is much better. I shall leave her in your care."

Mavis bobbed and curtsied.

Brandon left the room.

Nicole smiled at Mavis. "My lady, if you can bear to sit up for a short while, I'll change your bed linen. His lordship refused to let anyone in to do anything for you. He never left your bedside."

Mavis helped Nicole to a chair, then set about cleaning and straightening the room. Nicole changed her gown, and Mavis helped her exhausted mistress back into bed. Nicole fell into a sound sleep at once.

\*\*\*\*

Brandon went to his room to change his clothes

and attend to his own toilette. It made him glad that Nicole was better, but he missed sitting by her bedside. He had never taken care of a sick person, never sensed the need. His father had not wanted him when he became ill. His mistresses would have been shocked and embarrassed to have him watch them in distress or see them not looking their best. He was always told to go away and come back when they felt better. Nicole was a practical sort of person who did not mind him helping her with any difficulty she had.

No matter that he was exhausted, his thoughts ran back and forth as he groomed and dressed afresh. I don't know where this is going. Am I in this alone? Am I a fool? We have a contract, a business arrangement. I've been out of the boarding school too long to be acting this foolishly over a woman. She's given no indication she has any feeling for me other than friendship. Funny, I think of her as a friend too, but I want more.

There are any number of women who would welcome my advances. And yet...I've lost the desire for the thrill of the hunt. I used to have a restless feeling, but that's gone now. I cannot think of a single reason why I would want to leave. Is this what marriage does? I cannot possibly be in love for the first time in my life.

Why do I like her?

I find I can talk to her about anything, which is strange since I never wanted anything from the others except my own pleasure. At the back of my mind, I have the uncomfortable feeling my life would be empty without her. How did my life get so complicated?

He shook his head and started down the stairs.

Indecision disturbed his peace of mind. He needed a ride and a visit with his aunt. He did not reach the door before Stephens, Jenkins, and every servant he passed asked after Nicole. She had won over his entire staff, even Jenkins.

****

Over the next couple of weeks, Nicole regained her health. She came into the drawing room one evening to find Brandon standing in front of the fireplace looking pensive. "Ah, I'm glad you're here. It has come to my attention that you have a limited wardrobe."

"Yes, my wardrobe is small but serviceable. I'm able to add accessories or take them away making my outfits appear different."

"This will not do. I will not have you looking dowdy. You are my wife, and as such, you must be dressed as well as anyone of our set. I cannot have it appear as if I'm being miserly. There will be enough talk as it is. I think tomorrow we will go into Southend. I'm told there is a seamstress there, Madame Fortier. She does excellent work and is up on all the latest fashions. After the first of the year, we will go to London for the beginning of the season. You'll need any number of gowns and accessories."

"A new wardrobe sounds wonderful, but I do not have the funds to spend on new clothes. You increased my allowance, but I have hired two servants to keep the cottage, and there are expenses. I'm sorry. When we go to town, I do not have to go out if I might embarrass you."

A frown of annoyance crossed Brandon's face. "Nothing you could do would embarrass me, I'm sure. However, I did not ask you to pay for this. I will buy everything you need. This is not up for discussion. You may think you are disguising your outfits, but you will not deceive any of the old cats of society.

"You must have several gowns, outfits, etcetera, so you do not wear the same one over and over. When we go to town, there will be many invitations. You will be required to attend with me. Was it not in our agreement that we appear the happy couple in public?"

"Yes, that is our agreement. Let it be as you wish." She nodded stiffly. As Jenkins came through the door, she asked her husband, "Shall we go into dinner?"

Brandon took her arm and led her into the dining room.

\*\*\*\*

The couple arrived at Madame Fortier's salon early the next day.

"Lord Montagu, what a pleasure to have you in my salon again. It's been a long time. This lovely lady must be Lady Montagu. I read the notice of your nuptials in the paper," she said with a smile and bow. "Please follow me."

Brandon nodded and cleared his throat when Nicole looked at him with a question in her eyes. He motioned for Nicole to follow Madame Fortier. She led them to a salon where a servant treated Nicole to a ratafia and handed a sherry to Brandon.

With her hands clasped in front of her and a broad smile lighting her face, she looked at Brandon. "What may I do for you, Lord and Lady Montagu?"

"Lady Montagu will require shifts, lappets, beads, negligees, riding habits, ball gowns, morning gowns, evening dresses, etcetera. As you might guess, she needs a complete wardrobe for the London season."

Madame could not have smiled any broader. She clapped her hands together, and models paraded before them in the latest styles. She showed them swatches and made several suggestions. There were silks, linens, sprig muslins, velvets, and lace. Madame held the swatches up to Nicole's face, and either tut-tutted or nodded. Asked to choose while having so many materials pushed in front of her made Nicole's head swim. She sat exhausted, but Brandon and Madame Fortier continued making choices for her. It did not appear as if Brandon was a stranger to women's fashions. He had definite ideas on how he wanted her dressed.

"You have chosen well, Lord Montagu. Lady Montagu has a delicious complexion. Except for white, all colors become her, even black. I'm thinking of a riding habit in black velvet trimmed in silver...yes, yes. I will need Lady Montagu to return for a fitting in four weeks' time. After the adjustments are made, the wardrobe will be completed before the New Year, and you leave for London."

Ensconced in the coach on their way home, Nicole put her hand on Brandon's arm. "Lord Montagu, this is too much. You have spent a fortune. Please go back and at least tell her to deliver half."

"Nicole, I want you dressed suitably. I will not discuss this. Please indulge me." He turned his head and stared out the window.

Nicole did her best to discourage his buying spree. She remembered her coming out. Her aunt had taken her shopping and bought a comparable amount of clothing and accessories. When her father had seen the bill, he almost had an apoplexy. She knew well the cost of such fine raiment. She could not shake the sense that she had received something under false pretenses.

After a quiet life in the country, she dreaded the round of parties, routs, opera nights, soirees, and picnics. She would have to face all the people who knew what her father had done. She had given society much fodder for their gossip mill with her broken engagement and her current marriage to a known rake. Could she hold her head high? Did Brandon realize he would come in for his share of gossip as well? Considering his reputation, perhaps gossip and innuendo did not matter that much to him. Nicole tried to tell herself it did not mean that much to her either, but her pride refused to let her.

****

The days faded into December, and they started on a round of party invitations from the gentry in the neighborhood. Lady Scott surprised everyone and gave a Christmas Eve party. She invited everyone she knew, and Brandon and Nicole were to spend the night. The party proved a success and lasted until after two in the morning. When the last guest left, Lady Scott, Brandon, and Nicole sat in the drawing room too exhausted to move.

"Now, I remember why I don't give parties anymore. It is too fatiguing. Did you enjoy yourselves, my children?"

"Yes, my darling, you have out done yourself. It's late, and I know you must be worn out. Shall I call Corbin to take you up?" Brandon said with concern etched on his face.

"Don't you dare. The poor fellow is worn out. He's not as young as he used to be. Give me a few more minutes to catch my breath. You and Nicole can help me up the stairs. I'm quite improved." She winked at Nicole.

To everyone's surprise, she negotiated the stairs very well. She stopped halfway to catch her breath, but made it the rest of the way to her chamber. At her door, she kissed Nicole and Brandon goodnight.

Brandon walked Nicole to her bedchamber. "Wait here. I'll be right back."

Nicole stepped back in her room to pick up something and returned through the door as Brandon made his way back. "Here, I have a present for you."

"And I have one for you." She handed him the small gift wrapped in silver paper.

Nicole tore into her brown paper package and found a square, flat, navy blue velvet box. Carefully, she opened the box and saw its contents. "Why, Brandon, this appears to be…but it could not. Is this my mother's necklace and earrings? How can this be?" She gazed at him wide-eyed with her hand over her mouth.

"Aunt Annis told me your jewels were seized and sent to auction. My original idea was to find as much of your mother's jewelry as I could and buy it from whomever purchased it at auction. As it turned out, your father converted most of your jewelry to paste except this necklace and earrings. My man found the auction house, and the box of jewelry. He thought your necklace didn't look like paste. Someone had placed it in the box with the other costume jewelry. The manager of the house sold it to him for the price of a fake. He took it to a jeweler and had it cleaned and appraised. It is the original necklace and earrings."

"My father gave these to my mother on their

wedding day. Before she died, she gave them to me. I never thought to see any of her jewelry again. Oh, my, what can I say? Thank you is not enough." Nicole's eyes brimmed with tears.

Brandon took his handkerchief and gently dabbed at her eyes. "I did not mean to make you cry." He ran his finger around her cheek and under her chin.

Nicole looked up through her tears and tried to smile.

The lump in his throat made it difficult to swallow. He brushed a kiss across her cheek. "There, that's better. Let me open my present."

He tore the paper from his present and found a small silver box. He opened the box to find a meerschaum pipe with the bowl in the shape of a wolf's head. "This is exquisite. How ever did you find the pipe?"

"The woman in the little shop next to the tobacconist has an odd assortment of items. I saw your pipe collection in the library. When I saw the pipe in her shop, I knew you must have it."

"If I had known she carried this, I would have bought it for myself. Thank you, Nicole. You're very thoughtful." He kissed her on the cheek again. They stood looking at each other, neither knowing what to do next. Mavis moving around in Nicole's chamber brought them back to the present.

"May I help you get ready for bed, my lady?"

"Uh…yes, thank you, Mavis. Goodnight, Brandon. Sleep well and Happy Christmas."

\*\*\*\*

"Pleasant dreams, my dear." Brandon strolled back to his room lost in thought.

Exhausted, Brandon sat by the fire and poured himself a glass of canary wine. He wondered for the hundredth time what he had gotten himself into. It seemed so simple at first. Convince the solicitor he intended to conform to his father's will, marry Nicole, and keep out of scrapes and scandals until the end of a year's time.

What could be simpler?

Why did she have to be so pleasant?

There was something about her that drew him. She had an inner calm and a quiet dignity. She never complained. There were no hysterics. No case of the vapors.

My aunt likes her, the servants like her, and she has won over most of the stuffy people in the area, including the mayor and his wife. Blast and double blast, I like her! What's to become of us?

\*\*\*\*

Christmas day they went to church with Aunt Annis, returning to Worthington Park in the afternoon. Snow clouds amassed overhead, and the temperature dropped below freezing. Soon snowflakes blanketed the landscape. After several days of arctic temperatures, the countryside froze to an icy landscape. After dinner, Nicole came into the library and found Brandon in his favorite wing back chair, staring at the fire.

"I'm going out for a while," she said

"Is it not too late for going out? I didn't realize you had an engagement."

"Oh no. I'm going skating in the park in the village. The pond is frozen. I hear there will be carolers. Do you skate?"

"I used to, but I haven't since I was in school."

Brandon tried to hide his excitement.

"If you can find your skates, why don't you come with me? I think it'll be fun. Besides the carolers, I've heard they'll have tea and hot chocolate and bonfires."

"Jenkins," he yelled.

As if eavesdropping outside the door, something a good servant must never be caught doing, Jenkins entered the room placidly. "Yes, my lord."

"Do I still have skates?"

Jenkins looked puzzled then turned and went through the doorway. A short time later, he returned with a pair of skates.

"I'm not sure I remember how. What the devil, let's go." He took Nicole by the arm, and they made their way out to the waiting horse-drawn sleigh.

The whole village had turned out to either watch or skate. The enormous pond had a bridge that divided it in half but towered above the pond letting the skaters glide underneath it. There was a small island in the middle of the pond with a pine tree growing out of it. The young skaters chased each other around the island. Several flambeaux placed around the pond radiated light for the skaters. There were three bonfires around a shed at one end where skaters stopped to warm and get a cup of tea or chocolate. They saw several people they knew.

Nicole waved to the vicar as he skated by them where they sat on a bench to lace up their skates. She stepped onto the ice first and skated in a small circle, warming up while waiting for Brandon. He stepped on the ice a little more cautiously, and she took his arm. They skated hand in hand several times around the pond. When Brandon was more confident, he skated faster, then came over a bump in the ice and lost his balance. Flailing in the air, he grabbed handfuls of nothing and fell hard, flat on his back. Nicole could not help laughing at the comical sight.

She skated over to help him, but pulling him up caused her to lose her balance. Her feet flew out from under her, and she landed beside him on her backside.

"Ha! Not so funny now, is it?" Brandon looked at Nicole and grinned. They turned their heads and looked at each other before breaking into laughter like children.

The vicar came by and skated around them surveying the damage. He stopped and helped both of them stand.

"Lord Montagu, I haven't seen you in church of late."

When they were standing again, he put one on each arm and guided them around the pond.

"I'm not much of a church goer. I come during the holidays, and I came on my wedding day." Brandon beamed at Nicole.

The vicar let go and maneuvered them side by side, taking the inside position of the circle they were skating. Brandon took Nicole's hand, and they skated around with the vicar.

"Lady Montagu comes every Sunday. She has been playing the organ while our organist's broken arm heals. I try not to make my sermons too long or boring. The music is exquisite. You could not help but enjoy our choir. If you close your eyes you might think you were listening to angels sing." The vicar grinned from ear to ear and winked at Nicole.

Before Brandon had a chance to reply, the vicar

was floating away on the ice. "See you in church," he called out while waving good-bye.

By the time they decided to partake of the available refreshments, the carolers had arrived and were serenading the skaters with *Greensleeves,* followed by *Deck the Halls.* Snow continued falling. Brandon felt more confident and took Nicole around at a faster pace. He twirled her around, and she beamed with pleasure. The temperature fell further and not even the bonfires sent out enough warmth. Soon the skating party came to an end. Brandon and Nicole made their way home tired but happy.

They entered the doorway to find Jenkins still there waiting for them. "Jenkins, do you skate?" Nicole asked.

"Yes, madam, in my younger days."

"The pond is frozen, and the skating is delightful. This cold snap cannot last," Nicole said.

Jenkins looked at Brandon much puzzled. "Yes, Jenkins, you may have tomorrow afternoon off if you wish. As my lady says, the skating is delightful." Brandon smiled and watched Nicole start up the stairs.

He hurried up the stairs after her and caught her at her door. "My lord, I had a lovely time. I'm glad you came with me. With the snow and the carolers, it's magical."

"Yes, I enjoyed it too. I can't remember when I've had a more enjoyable evening. Thank you for inviting me. You make me feel young again. Sometimes I forget how it was to be a callow youth. Thanks for reminding me." He took Nicole's hands in his and kissed each in turn. "Goodnight."

Nicole bowed and went into her room. Her

thoughts ran away as soon as she closed the door. Why does a shock run through me every time we touch? I'm such a ninny. I know he does not care a fig for me. If only he did...but I can't think like that. I'm too straitlaced for intrigues and scandals. Will I grow old and spinsterish with no one to warm me? Will there be nothing to look forward to in my future? Oh, why did I agree to this marriage?

She sat in front of her dressing table combing her hair and staring into the mirror without seeing her reflection. Mavis came, but she did not notice until she took the brush from her hand and started brushing her hair. She helped Nicole change and get ready for bed. Nicole lay for several hours with melancholy thoughts still bouncing through her head. When she could not stand another minute of self-pity, she slapped her bed linens and sat up.

"I will not be sorry for myself. I'm a grown person, a married woman. Something I did not expect to be. I have a cottage. When my year is up, I will retire to the country and fill my days with good works. I will not let marriage or a man define me. I am my own person. With the respectability of marriage cloaking me, I can travel and do anything I wish. Yes, I can." She snapped her fingers and nodded. She lay back on her pillow with new determination giving her peace of mind, and sleep overtook her the instant her head hit the pillow.

Chapter Five

After the first of the year, they set out on the road
to London and the social season to come. Brandon sent
two coaches ahead loaded with servants and baggage.
His groom went in advance of the party with a change
of horses and to make sure The Blue Moon tavern and
inn at the halfway point had rooms ready for them. One
night's rest and they were on their way to London.

The weather turned stormy with a wintry rain
dampening the streets as they entered London.
Grosvenor Square came into view, and Nicole could not
help thinking of the house her father once owned on
Half Moon Street not so far away. The carriage stopped
in front of a fashionable residence in the midst of
Grosvenor Square. It had five bays, three main stories,
and an attic. She guessed there was a basement kitchen.
A central garden for the use of the occupants could be
seen across the street from the house.

Jenkins opened the door, and Nicole stepped into
an elegantly furnished residence that unlike the country
estate had no need of updating. She followed a maid to
her bedchamber. Most of her wardrobe had already
been unpacked. Mavis unpacked the rest. Staring out
her window while Mavis worked, Nicole leaned her
head on the glass and listened to the raindrops beat a
rhythm on her windowpanes. She turned her head,
looked across the paved courtyard to the mews, and

watched the grooms lead the horses into the stable. Feeling oddly melancholy and tired from her journey, she stayed in her chamber until time for dinner. Thankfully, they did not have to go out. There were no invitations yet as the season had scarcely begun. The full swing of London's social season started at Easter.

Nicole began searching for her father as soon as the weather turned. A nervous Mavis accompanied her on these treks. She knew of several missions and went to them first. She left a sketch of her father in the hopes someone might recognize him and let her know where to find him. Each place of refuge for the homeless told her of other places to search. From nine in the morning and until three or four in the afternoon, she traveled from one mission or alms house to the other.

She left each morning with a smile and a quick step and returned late in the afternoon tired and downcast. She worried Brandon might see her coming or going and try to stop her. Even if he wondered where she went, she felt sure he would not lower himself by indulging in gossip with the servants. His pride would not let him take the chance she might catch him following her. Why should he exert himself on her behalf? After all, he was not concerned with what she did or did not do. Their agreement said they could go their separate ways as long as each was discreet.

She gave out the last of her sketches and returned this afternoon, barely able to put one foot in front of the other. Jenkins brought a pot of tea to the small sitting room. Her feet hurt, and her spirits were at their lowest. As she sat staring out the window, she wondered if she had a chance of ever finding her father. Was he even in London, or was he indeed dead, as she feared? In his present circumstances with no money or friends, he was not equipped for living rough in every kind of weather. She drank the tea and rested her head against the back of her chair ready to doze off when Jenkins's knock roused her.

"My lady, I have a Lord Fleetwood to see you. Shall I send him away?"

Nicole jumped up and clasped her hands together. "Did you say Lord Fleetwood? Oh, my, can it be?" She flew through the open door and ran past Jenkins in her excitement. He trailed calmly behind her, as though he found nothing strange in her behavior.

Her heart leapt for joy when she glimpsed a painfully thin young man of average height standing in the foyer with his back to her. She recognized the slope of his shoulders and the wild, curly brown hair no quantity of pomade could tame. She stopped before she reached him. "Horus, is that you? Is it truly you?"

He turned around and smiled at her. She flew into his arms, causing him to stumble backward. When he regained his balance, he pushed back and held her at arm's length, giving her the once over. "Let me look at you, Nikki. What is this I hear you're a married woman and your husband is Lord Montagu, of all people? I came round the moment I read your letter."

"It's true." She took his hand and led him toward the hall. "Come with me, and I'll explain. Jenkins, please bring Lord Fleetwood some refreshment."

\*\*\*\*

Brandon caught the entire scene from the balcony overlooking the foyer. He came down the stairs and met Jenkins coming back from the sitting room. "Who is our visitor?" he asked sharply, causing Jenkins to give a start.

Jenkins drew in a breath and regained his composure. "Lord Fleetwood, my lord. He appears to be a friend of her ladyship." Jenkins smiled and bowed.

"He does without a doubt. Thank you." He strolled into his library with his head down and cracked his knuckles in frustration. He planned to wait, give them time to settle in, and then surprise Nicole and her guest.

\*\*\*\*

With Lord Fleetwood comfortably settled on the settee beside her, Nicole could not help but beam widely. "How long have you been home?"

"I've been back three days. I didn't get your letters until I had been home two days. The last one arrived this morning. They traveled a day behind me all over Europe. What's this you said in your last post that you had married this Montagu person? I didn't finish the letter. I had to see for myself. 'Pon rep, he has a shocking reputation. Did you know?"

"Yes, certainly I knew. I'm not so green as that. I'm so glad to see you. What have you been up to? Tell me what marvelous adventures you've had, and I'll tell you mine."

"Mine can wait. Nikki, out with it. What has been happening while I've been away? I read your letters, but I can't believe it. I've only been gone six months. How could all this happen in such a short time? I can't make heads nor tails of what you told me. You're married to a notorious rake. Uncle Charles is bankrupt and disappeared. Last I read, you had not found him."

"Yes, we're as poor as a church mouse, I'm afraid. I haven't been able to find him. I'm so glad you're here. You can help me hunt. Two eyes are better than one."

She took several sheets of paper out of their hiding place. "Look here, I made a list of places to search. My list grows with every place I visit. If we divide it in half, we can cover more territory. I don't think he can be in the hands of moneylenders, but we must make sure. I made a list of them in case we might find him there."

"Nikki, slow down to a trot. Do you mean to tell me you visited these places alone? I wonder at Lord Montagu letting you do this. Does he even know?"

A scowl crossed Nicole's face effectively erasing her smile. "This is my business, my father. If need be, I'll go through fire to find him. Nobody will stop me. I must find him. I must find him…one way or the oth—" Nicole broke off with a catch in her throat.

"Calm yourself, Nikki, take a breath. You must realize it's dangerous what you're doing. I'm worried about you; that's all I meant."

"My abigail comes with me. I don't know what else I can do. I must locate him before it's too late." Tears were brimming in Nicole's eyes.

"Here now, we'll have none of that, my girl. I'll help you, but you can't be going into these places with just an abigail." He put his arm around her and dabbed at her eyes with his handkerchief.

The door flew open and Brandon strode into the middle of the room.

Nicole and Horus stood quickly, like errant children.

"I didn't realize we had company. Permit me to introduce myself. I'm Lord Montagu, the lady's husband. Whom do I have the pleasure of addressing?" Brandon eyed the stranger scarcely concealing his anger.

"Brandon, this is Lord Horus Fleetwood. I told you about him. He's my brotherly cousin." Nicole could not understand why she blushed or felt guilty.

The menacing look on Brandon's face relaxed a little. "Please, be seated. Ahem... I understand from Nicole you have been on the continent."

"Yes, I've recently returned, and I see it's in the nick of time I did. Did you know that Nikki has been going out alone to missions and low places looking for her father?"

Brandon looked at Nicole with a frown. "No, I didn't. Why didn't you tell me that's what you were doing?"

"First of all, I did not go alone." She gave Horus a look of exasperation and rushed on. "I had Mavis with me. Everyone has been kind and helpful. I haven't felt threatened at any time."

"Now that I'm back, I'll go with her until I must return to my studies at Oxford."

"That's kind of you, but I was thinking of something else. Mr. Pettigrew has said if we needed someone to help find Lord Waltham, he has a reliable agent that will help us. I think that's a more acceptable and an efficient way of finding Lord Waltham. We'll ask him to go with you and save Nicole the trouble of tramping over London."

"I say, excellent idea since I know Uncle Charles. This fellow will have a better idea just where to search." Horus nodded at Nicole.

"That's settled. I'll have someone here at, say, nine. Please, won't you dine with us tonight at seven, Lord Fleetwood?"

"Call me Horus since we're family. I'd be delighted. I'll just go round to my digs, change, and be back around seven." He kissed Nicole's hands, bowed, shook hands with Brandon, and left whistling an old familiar tune.

When the door closed on Horus, Brandon turned to Nicole. "Nicole, you're not in the country anymore. You can't travel around London's worst parts with just an abigail. What were you thinking?"

"I was thinking I must find my father. I didn't think I needed to ask your permission."

"That's not what I meant. I've seen you leave and return too tired to put one foot in front of the other. If I had known, I most certainly would not have allowed you to go."

"You have no right to dictate to me." Nicole started to leave the room with her head held high.

Brandon took hold of her arm as she passed by and turned her around to face him. "Nicole, do you not understand the dangers of what you've been doing? I can't protect you if you do these foolhardy things."

"Did I ask for your protection? You barged in and took over, ignoring me. He is my father."

"I'm not ignoring you. My thought was to help. You're my wife, and you are under my protection, like it or not. Is there something more? Are you meeting someone on these little trips of yours?"

With her free hand, she delivered him a stinging slap. "How dare you? You have no right. We have our accursed agreement, which says you go your way and I go mine. I do not check up on you…make you account for your time. Tell you that you can't go to your gaming hells or your mistress's house." When she finished, her chest was heaving and her fists were clenched at her side.

Both stared at the other, refusing to blink.

At last, Brandon broke the standoff. "Damn the blasted agreement!"

He left the room, slamming the door as he went.

Nicole stood unable to move with a lump in her throat. She sat abruptly in the nearest chair. Tears came, and she cried until there were none left. Straightening her dress and hair, she hurried from the room and up the stairs, hoping no one had seen or heard.

\*\*\*\*

Horus arrived a few minutes before seven and Jenkins led him into the awkward silence of the drawing room. Brandon stood by the fire staring into its depths with an untouched glass of sherry in his hand. Nicole sat on the sofa reading a book but not turning a page. They both looked up with relief when Jenkins announced Horus.

Horus sat beside Nicole. Brandon came away from the fireplace and attempted to make himself agreeable. Horus started by telling Nicole news of her Aunt Tess and finished with a few tales of his trip on the continent. It turned out, he and Brandon had been to the same places and were acquainted with a few of the same people. The ice broken, dinner turned out to be a pleasant affair. They were finishing dessert when Jenkins entered.

"My lord, there is a person to see you. He says his name is Jack Pepper from Mr. Pettigrew. I put him in the library." Jenkins bowed out of the room.

"Our man has arrived. Shall we adjourn to the library?" Brandon led the way.

They found Mr. Pepper looking at the rows of books. He turned as the three entered the library. A small, neat man with dark-brown hair and eyes, and a day or more's stubble on his face, he was dressed in the brown clothes of a laborer. He held his cap in his hand. It was easy to understand how he could blend into any situation.

"Thank you for coming so quickly, Mr. Pepper. Please be seated. As I told your employer, it's expedient that we find my wife's father as quickly and discreetly as possible. My…er…We made inquiries, but we've found out little in the way of leads. I'll let my wife tell you."

Nicole felt a blush burn her cheeks. She took a deep breath and attempted to swallow her pride before telling a stranger about her unfortunate father. "My father's name is Lord Charles Waltham. He left me on the endmost stop into London from Sussex. That was the last time I saw him. He has no money and no friends. I believe he's living rough somewhere. We asked at missions, and they gave us a list of other places to try. I have the list here." She handed it to Mr. Pepper.

She looked at Brandon, daring him to say a word before she began again. She squared her shoulders and continued. "Before I left London last year, someone suggested I try under various bridges, and I did. There was a man standing at a distance in a group of men. I was so sure it was my father. I ran toward him and called out, but he didn't turn around. Instead, he left the group at a fast pace. He headed for an old, rundown brick building and went through the door.

"I tried to follow him, but another man stepped in front of me. He spoke like an educated man and told me

I could not go in there. It was a dangerous place.

"I explained I thought I had seen my father, and he said he would get word to the man if he was my father. I told him my name but did not give him my address. I said I was staying at my Aunt Helena's and planned to wait for him in the park across from her home. I was sure my father would know which park I meant. Every day between one and three I went there and sat waiting, rain or shine, until I left London. He never came. I marked the bridge where I thought I saw him on my list.

"Oh, Mr. Pepper, do you think you can help us. My cousin Lord Fleetwood will come with you to help, and I made you several sketches. I left a sketch at each mission I visited, too." She handed the sketches to him and waited while he looked at them.

"Lady Montagu, you're a brave lady to go to these places you marked. There are grown men who hesitate to go to a few of these establishments. However, this is an extensive list. I'm glad you marked off where you've been." He looked at Lord Fleetwood. "Is this a good likeness, sir?"

"Yes, spot on. Ni...Lady Montagu was always very clever."

"Excellent. We'll get started tomorrow night. Evening is the best time to make inquiries. Homeless people tend to move around during the day and return to roost at their favorite places for the evening. Lord Fleetwood, write your address here if you will, and I'll pick you up tomorrow night around ten. Begging your pardon, sir, but if you could dress differently. Dressing in a nondescript way draws less attention to our persons."

"Oh, I understand." Lord Fleetwood looked at his silk stockings and gold edged buckles and smiled. "You can count on me to be as plain as a Quaker."

"Uh…Lord Montagu, I must tell you that this is not the first inquiry we've had for Lord Waltham. The first time we did not have a sketch, and the client refused to go around with us. Since we only had a description, we were not able to find him."

"Who was this person making the first inquiry?" Lord Montagu asked.

"I'm sorry, I'm not at liberty to say. My continued employment requires discretion. He did not go through Mr. Pettigrew, but another solicitor that I work for. I wanted you to understand that we tried and failed previously, but with Lord Fleetwood and the sketch, we'll have a much better chance this time."

"Excellent. Thanks for telling us. I bid you a pleasant night." Brandon rang the bell, and Jenkins escorted Mr. Pepper out.

"Don't look so worried, Nikki. I wonder who the other person was? Probably another bill collector. But no matter; we'll find him. How can we not with Mr. Pepper and yours truly?" He patted Nicole on the arm and stood to leave. "Well, I must be going myself. I'll come by tomorrow morning around eleven and pick you up for a drive? There are several lovely parks in and around London. A pleasant outing in the fresh air will do you good."

"Yes, I'd like that. Thank you."

Horus left. Brandon and Nicole sat in silence.

"Nicole, I am always apologizing to you. I'm sorry for what I said."

"An apology is not needed. I should have told you

what I've been doing. It has been brought home to me that I should not be going alone to these places. I'm just so worried. I didn't think. Oh, my, what if he's d—" Nicole choked and put her hand to her mouth.

Brandon moved to sit beside her. He took her hand and searched her face. "Don't think dark thoughts. We can't assume anything until we find your father. Mr. Pepper, I'm sure, is a competent man, and he has a good reputation. We'll find him. Now dry those tears." He smiled at her reassuringly and dabbed at her eyes with his handkerchief while pulling her closer. His arm went around her, and she leaned in with a sigh.

"Thank you. I'm exhausted. I think I'll go to bed. We're getting dozens of invitations. I left them on the table in the hall. If you want to attend any of them, let me know and I'll write our acceptance. Goodnight, Brandon." She stood to leave.

Brandon stood as well and linked her hand in his arm, then walked her up the stairs to her room. At her door, he kissed her cheek. "Pleasant dreams, my dear." He turned and walked down the hall to his chambers.

Unable to move, Nicole stood watching him go.

The click of his door closing and resulting emptiness of the hallway released her from her awe, and she entered her room. Leaning against her door, she brought her fingers to her cheek and gingerly touched where he had kissed her. She chastised herself for smiling as she touched the spot and for the foolish beating of her heart, then shook her head to clear it of silly thoughts and let Mavis help her get ready for bed.

\*\*\*\*

"Horus, thanks for taking me out. It's a gorgeous morning. The birds are singing, and all's right with the world."

"I thought we would start with Kensington Gardens. I think it is by far the more beautiful of the Royal parks with its landscaped garden, round pond, formal avenues, and a sunken Dutch Garden."

"Kensington is my favorite too. I especially like Bridgeman's Serpentine Lake over there. I love strolling through the fountains and sculptures.

"How clean the air smells here, and how peaceful. You picked a perfect day to take me round." Nicole kept turning around in her seat to get a better view.

"From Kensington we can go on to Hyde Park. I brought a picnic lunch. We could have that by the Serpentine Lake."

"That sounds perfect. I don't know how you can choose between the parks. They're both beautiful and peaceful."

"I never go past Green Park without thinking about where The First Earl of Bath, William Pulteney and the First Earl of Bristol, John Hervey had their famous duel. I wish it were open to the public."

"Oh, Horus, don't talk of duels on such a beautiful day. My, what a beautiful lake. Did you ever see so many fowl? There are swans, geese, all manner of ducks, pelicans, and is that a cormorant?"

"Yes, it certainly is."

Horus turned the carriage around and started back. He came out of St. James Park and into St. James Square.

"Drat it," he muttered under his breath.

"Why did you say that? What a charming square with those lovely red brick homes. Oh, look, there's Brandon." Nicole pointed at a red brick house where

Brandon stood on the steps, knocking on the door.

Horus swiftly pushed her hand down.

"Nikki, don't point and quit looking. Bend down. Don't let him see you."

"Brandon's going into that house. The woman who answered the door, I think I know her. That's Lady Bennett. I met her at Lady Hamilton's soiree last week. She talked to me. We had an entertaining conversation. She's an exquisite creature. Why did you scold me just now?"

"Lord, Nikki, what a babe you are. Do you not understand who she is?"

"No, who is she if she isn't Lady Bennett?"

"Oh, she's Lady Bennett all right. That's the point."

"I'm not seeing what you mean. What are you saying?"

Once away from the square, Horus pulled the carriage to a stop, sighed, and gave Nicole a serious look. "What I'm saying is she isn't a proper person to be acquainted with, especially in your circumstance. Her husband is dead. He left her in very comfortable circumstances. However, she likes to gamble, and she plays deep.

"She needs help with her debts, and uses her…uh…*assets* to gain the necessary funding. I really shouldn't be talking to you about this. One of us ought to have the grace to blush. Let's just drop the matter."

"Oh, Horus, don't be so stuffy. I thought we could talk to each other about anything. Are you saying she takes a lover from time to time?"

"I can't look at you when you say things like that. I hope your face is the color of scarlet."

"Oh, stuff and nonsense. What are you not telling me?"

He glanced sideways at Nicole, then stared straight ahead and sighed. "My information might not be reliable, but from what I've heard I think it's true. When I left town, she was Brandon's mistress. I assume she still is."

"Oh, I see. I didn't realize. Thanks for telling me. I'm tired suddenly. Take me home please." Nicole's world stopped spinning.

Horus started the horses moving again.

****

Brandon, Nicole, and Horus went to Vauxhall Pleasure Gardens to watch the fireworks and listen to a concert. Soon after they arrived, a whistle blew and lamplighters went to their stations. A second whistle blew and the cotton wool fuses were lit causing the flame to make its rounds to over a thousand lamps. After the lighting display, they ate a supper of assorted cold meats, salads, and pastries. Brandon and Horus drank a rum punch while Nicole had cider.

After the concert, Horus and Nicole stepped out of their supper box and strolled along the lighted walk leading to the water's edge to watch the fireworks while Brandon remained, drinking rum punch. Enjoying the stunning display, Nicole glanced back at Brandon to see if he saw it also. Her glance fell, then lingered on Lady Bennett sitting beside him, looking up at him with her hand on his. Nicole came to her senses and hastily turned around. Her enjoyment was at an end. When the fireworks were over, they returned to their seats to find Brandon sitting alone.

On the way home, Nicole ignored Brandon staring

at her while wondering if he realized she'd caught him with his mistress.

"Did you not enjoy the fireworks and concert? You seem sad."

"Yes, I did. I'm just a little tired." She leaned back against the well-cushioned carriage and closed her eyes, putting an end to any further conversation.

****

Brandon escorted Nicole home the next night after an opera, to find Horus sitting at the top of the stairs in his shirtsleeves. He ran down the stairs to meet them. "Nikki, we found him! We found Uncle Charles. He's upstairs with Dr. Parsons now. Sorry, Brandon, I had no other place to take him."

"It was proper to bring him here. You said you had the doctor with him? How is he?" Brandon handed his coat to Jenkins.

"He's not himself. Nikki, I—"

Nicole tossed her cloak to the floor before Jenkins could catch it and raced past Horus. "I must go to him."

Both gentlemen started after her.

Horus caught her at the bottom of the stairs just as her foot landed on the first step. "Nikki, the doctor's with him. He's not himself. We had a rough time getting him here. Mr. Pepper finally had to deliver a right to his jaw to knock him out. He fought like a fiend, even after he saw me. I don't think he even recognized me.

"Brandon, with your permission, Mr. Pepper will keep guard outside the door until the doctor comes back tomorrow. The doctor gave him a sedative, but it is slow in taking effect. We secured the shutters from the outside, so he can't open the windows and jump out.

"I collected his trunk from Aunt Helena. We have clean clothes for him. When I brought his trunk in, the fight just left him, or it could have been the laudanum. When the laudanum started to work, he went to sleep. That gave Stephens a chance to cut his hair and trim his beard. While he was calm, we cleaned him up as best we could. His calm didn't last long. We had to call the doctor again. I'm sorry, Nikki."

"Stuff and nonsense. He's here now. Thank you, thank you. Thank you, Brandon. I know you didn't plan on this inconvenience to your household."

"Not a problem, my dear, we'll see him through this crisis. I'm sure the doctor will settle him down in no time."

Horus went upstairs to talk to Mr. Pepper. Brandon and Nicole waited in the drawing room for the doctor. Nicole paced the length and breadth of the room wringing her hands and looking toward the door with every sound.

"How did Horus get his name? It's an unusual spelling," Brandon asked.

Nicole turned at the sound of his voice, still wringing her hands.

"Uh…Horus…yes. You remember I told you my aunt was into mysticism. When Horus was born, she was into everything Egyptian. Horus is the god of the sky. A man's body with the head of a hawk. You may not have noticed, but Horus does remind you of a hawk with his sharp features, piercing blue eyes, and beaked nose. I don't know if she saw that in him as a baby, or he grew into his name."

"You have an unusual family. I think I will enjoy getting to know them."

Nicole nodded distractedly. Footsteps on the stairs sent her rushing out to find Dr. Parsons standing in the foyer.

"Lady Montagu, how nice to see you again. I'm sorry we must meet under these circumstances." He bowed over her hand, turned to Brandon, and nodded. He looked back at Nicole. "My dear, don't look so serious. Your father is sick, but nothing that time won't heal.

"I feel sure he is suffering from another bout of melancholia. He's extremely underfed and has a rattle in his chest that concerns me. With good food and rest, we shall have him better in no time. I recommend taking him away from London. Some place quiet where he can rest and recover. Away from his former vices."

"Yes, that is my intention. I have a cottage waiting for him in the country. How soon do you think we could move him?"

"I'll be back to check on him tomorrow and every couple of days after that. If he continues to improve, there's no reason why you could not move him in a couple of weeks. If necessary, I can recommend a nurse, but we'll discuss that later."

"Thank you, Dr. Parsons." Nicole struggled to speak past a catch in her throat, and her eyes brimmed with tears.

The doctor put his hand on her shoulder. "Now listen to me, child. I've known your father since before you were born. You must not make yourself sick worrying over him. Before this happened, he was fit with a strong constitution. He's not that old. There is no reason why he can't make a full recovery. He's not dangerous, just confused." He patted Nicole's shoulder.

"You get a little rest, my dear. Doctor's orders." He smiled at Nicole and bowed over her hand.

"May I see him now?"

"Go on up. Mr. Pepper is with him now. He is in and out of consciousness."

Nicole turned and ran up the stairs taking them two at a time. Horus came down the stairs at a slower pace that showed his exhaustion. Brandon told Jenkins to bring refreshments to the library.

When Horus came into the library, Brandon poured them both a glass of sherry. "You must be worn out. Why don't you stay the night? I'm sure Stephens can furnish you with the necessary."

"Thanks, I will. You might need me later. It's been a long evening and night. For that matter, a long-drawn out couple of weeks." Horus raised a toast. "To relatives lost and found."

****

Nicole knocked timidly on her father's door. "It's me, Nikki. May I come in?"

She pushed the door open a crack despite no response, peered in, and saw her father lying on his back, staring at the ceiling. Without a sound, she pushed the door open farther and entered the room.

"Papa, it's me, Nikki. How are you?"

When he turned his head at the sound of her voice, she realized he had been crying.

"Papa, please don't cry. You're safe now. I'm here. You most likely don't know, but I married Lord Brandon Montagu. This is Lord Montagu's home. I have a cottage of my own as part of the marriage settlement. When the doctor says it's all right to move you, I'll take you to the cottage in Standon." Not knowing what else to say, she stared at her father and wrung her hands.

She rushed to fill the silence with anything that came to mind. "You remember Standon, the same village mother was born in. It's a lovely little cottage called *Butterfly Cottage*. It gets its name from the previous owner who planted all kinds of flowers that attract butterflies. Biggers is there. He'll take care of you, as he always has. Papa, please say something."

"I'm sorry, Nikki. I've ruined my life and yours. Why did you bother to find me?"

"How can you ask such a question? I love you. I want to take care of you." Nicole took his freezing hand in hers. "You took care of me all those years ago. Now it's my turn. Please, get well."

He looked up through tears silently tracing a path on his time worn cheeks. He closed his eyes and turned his face to the wall.

Nicole kissed his cheek, then let go of his hand. "I'll leave you now so you can rest. I'll be back in the morning." With her hand on the doorknob, she turned and stared at her father's back. "Papa, why didn't you come to me in the park? I left word with that nice man under the bridge."

"I did, Nikki. The man we call the professor gave me the message. He used to be a don at Oxford but took to drink and lost his position. I came and watched you from a distance. I came every day until you stopped coming. Call it pride or embarrassment. Whatever you will, but I couldn't make myself walk over to where you sat."

"I'm sorry I didn't see you. I've missed you so much these many months. Please don't leave me again.

Goodnight, Papa." She slipped from the room nodding at Mr. Pepper on her way out.

Nicole ran to her room, undressed, and fell into bed. She cried herself to sleep. When Brandon entered her chamber, she woke up but pretended to be asleep. She did not want to talk. He stood over her, and she watched him through half-closed lashes by the light of the moon shining through her window. He placed a kiss on her cheek and pulled the blanket over her arms. He stood by the bed for some time and watched her. Abruptly turning, he strode out of her room through the adjoining door.

****

By the end of the week, Lord Waltham improved enough to eat dinner with Nicole, Brandon, and Horus. At the end of the meal, Nicole left the men to their cigars and port. She left orders that her father was not to smoke cigars or drink wine, but allowed him a small glass of ratafia and nothing stronger.

When the men came into the small sitting room, Lord Waltham sat beside Nicole. "Papa, Dr. Parsons has given us permission to take you to the cottage tomorrow. Do you feel up to the trip? If not, we can postpone it until you do. There's no hurry." She glanced at her father with concern.

"You worry too much, my dear. Yes, we can leave tomorrow. It'll be nice to get a breath of fresh country air. I'm feeling much stronger, and my cough is not as bad as it was. It'll be good to see Biggers again. Nikki, play something for us. It's been ages since I've listened to you play."

Horus said, "Yes, Nikki, play something. Brandon, have you listened to her play?"

"No, I didn't know she played." He looked at Nicole with a puzzled frown.

"I try to practice when you're not here. As my father can attest, it's no fun listening to someone trying to learn a new piece." She laughed, made her way to the pianoforte, and shuffled the sheet music sitting on the music rack.

She played Haydn's piano sonata No. 46 in A flat major, catching her audience with the opening movement *Allegro Moderato*. Her fingers flew across the keys with the playful melody. She glanced at her audience when she played the second movement, *Adagio*, with its slow melancholy melody complemented with a series of trills. From the look on their faces, they were enjoying the sonata as much as she was. The *Finale Presto* took nothing away from the piece. When she finished, everyone stood and clapped.

"Bravo, Nikki, you haven't lost your touch." Horus beamed from ear to ear.

"Exquisite, my dear. You could have been a concert pianist. I don't know where you get your talent. I can't carry a tune. In fact, I've often been told I hum off key," Lord Waltham said.

"Nicole, I'm awed. I had no idea you could play so well. For the better part of an hour, you played the most beautiful music I've ever heard, and with such feeling. You must be exhausted. Here, come sit with us, and I'll have Jenkins bring you a glass of wine."

Nicole sat by the fire, sipped wine, and listened to her family argue over bare-knuckle fighters.

"I don't believe Ryan has a chance over Johnson. Johnson is the better man in every way. I say it'll be over before it's begun. Did you hear the purse is to be six hundred guineas?" Brandon said.

"That I did, but I think Ryan can take him. I'm so sure, I've put twenty pounds on Ryan to win."

Horus and Brandon continued their good-natured arguing. Nicole gazed at her father. He did not participate in the heated discussion but appeared interested. Before long the conversation moved on to horses and hunting. Nicole soon tired of their friendly bickering and bid her companions goodnight.

They set out for Standon the next morning. The weather cooperated, and their coach arrived without mishap three hours later. A picturesque two-story cottage with a thatched roof, stucco walls, and heavy timbers came into view. It was the best time of the year when the flowers were just bursting into bloom, and the bushes were getting greener all around.

Nicole stared out the window of the coach. "Oh, Brandon, it's charming. The last time I was here, the workmen had everything at sixes and sevens. Dust and piles of lumber everywhere." She threw open the door of the carriage and jumped out before it came to a complete stop. She turned round and round, trying to take in everything at once. After the coach came to a complete stop, she took her father by the hand and drew him toward the cottage path.

"Papa, do you like it? I hope you'll be happy here." She linked her arm in his and smiled up at him, leading him toward the door.

Biggers opened it and beamed at the travelers. Biggers bowed stiffly to Lord Waltham. "My lord, your chamber is ready. The journey must have tired you. I'll show you to your apartment, and you can have a nice rest before dinner."

They disappeared up the stairs. Nicole came back outside and strolled around the garden. She wandered amidst the greenery and put her finger out for butterflies to land on. Soon they were landing in her hair and on her shoulders. When she was covered in a blanket of butterflies, she whirled around, and they took flight. She glimpsed Brandon watching her from the dining-room window, then shake his head and smile. Waving, she continued her tour of the grounds.

In the drawing room, Nicole found pieces of furniture from her previous home. At one end, in front of the large bay window, stood a piano. She moved toward it. Her hands tenderly touched the wood. She opened the lid to the keys and fingered the ivory.

She turned with a jerk when Brandon entered the room and closed the door. "Sorry, didn't mean to startle you. Well, do you approve?"

"Certainly, I do. How could I not? You even furnished it with furniture from our old home. How…?"

"I sent Biggers with my man to the auction houses again. The pianoforte is new. It came from Vienna. I don't know anything on the subject of pianofortes, but I've been assured it is a fine instrument."

"Oh, yes, I've not seen a finer one. The maker has an excellent reputation."

A door opened and Biggers entered. "My lady, your maid awaits you. I'm sure you are tired from your journey. Dinner will be ready at five."

"Thank you, Biggers. I am tired." She nodded at Brandon and left to explore the second floor.

The country dinner consisted of pheasant pie, cold roast beef, and an assortment of vegetables. For dessert, the maid brought in a trifle. Nicole gave permission for

Biggers and the maid to leave. Brandon, Nicole, Horus, and her father moved into the drawing room for wine and tea.

Nicole kept glancing at the piano every little bit, her fingers were itching to try it out.

"Nicole, would you like to favor us with some music on your new pianoforte?" Brandon said.

She smiled, and he grinned back. She stepped over to the piano and looked around. "I'm afraid there's no sheet music."

"Nikki, play that piece. You know the one I mean. It was called...*Unforgettable*. It had such a haunting melody. How could I forget the name?" Horus said.

"Yes, I can do that. I'm surprised you remember it." She sat at the piano and played a melancholy sonata that somehow reminded her of autumn and falling leaves.

Brandon moved closer and leaned against the piano. When she finished, he said, "What is the name of the piece again? I don't think I've ever heard it before this. It's very beautiful."

"You wouldn't have heard it before. The name is *Unforgettable*. I wrote it myself."

"What an unusual name. Why did you name it *Unforgettable*?"

"For some reason, this melody kept running through my head. I couldn't get it out of my mind. As soon as I wrote it on paper and played it, I felt at peace. It quit nagging at me. It was too hard to forget, so I named it *Unforgettable*." She beamed at Brandon.

The evening ended early as Nicole, Brandon, and Horus planned to leave early the next morning to get back to London. The season was in full swing with everyone throwing soirees and routs. Nicole had nothing to mar her enjoyment of the season any longer. She'd found her long lost father, and that was all that mattered. The gossip she'd feared had not been too marked, and at several soirees she'd been welcomed by old acquaintances. She felt she could relax now and enjoy the season. The only meeting she dreaded was seeing her ex-fiancé. His wife had entered her confinement in the country, and she hoped he stayed with her at least until the baby was born. An attentive husband would not leave his wife and newborn child, but she doubted Bedlington had such refinement of feelings.

## Chapter Six

Brandon stood looking up the stairs in wait for Nicole to make her appearance. They were invited to Lady Wigam's ball. Hers was the most sought-after invitation of high society and promised to be the highlight of the season. The ball was sure to be packed tight with everyone who was anyone. It was rumored His Royal Highness, the Prince of Wales planned to attend. Most partygoers planned to arrive around ten o'clock, directly from the opera.

Brandon looked up when a door closed and watched Nicole descend the stairs. He thought he had never seen her look more stunning than on her wedding day, but had been wrong.

Her pastel blue, beaded gown had a ruche skirt made of silk Dupion over an azure silk, brocade underskirt and elbow length sleeves with frothy silver lace. A band of silver ribbing ran up the front edge of the gown and around the square neckline. Her low-cut bodice revealed the rounded swell of her breasts. She wore shoes with jeweled heels and buckles. The diamond and pearl necklace and earrings Brandon gave her as a wedding present complemented her costume to perfection. Mavis had piled her intricately woven powdered hair high on her head. She carried a cloak of black velvet lined with the same pale blue silk of her gown.

She took his breath away.

Brandon stepped to the foot of the stairs and waited, then took her hand and led her to the door. She stopped before the door and turned around several times for him to see her costume.

"Do I look presentable?" Nicole grinned from ear to ear.

"Fishing for compliments, my sweet? You know you will be the most gorgeous woman there. Madame Fortier was right. With your complexion and hair color, pale blue suits you." He grinned and bowed low, brushing her fingertips with a kiss.

When he looked up, she blushed a most becoming shade of rose. He helped her into her cloak, and Jenkins held the door for them. Outside the door, a light town coach pulled by four matched Cleveland Bays danced on the cobblestones waiting to take them to the ball.

****

Nicole looked over her husband's cloth-of-gold costume with approval. His gold lace cravat held one large diamond in its folds. He wore a waistcoat of gold brocade with gold lace at his sleeves. A gold ribbon held his powdered black hair in place. His shoes had raised heels and jeweled buckles. Gold silk lined his black velvet cloak. On his hand, he wore a single gold signet ring.

When they arrived at Lady Wigam's, a liveried footman helped Nicole step from the coach. The enormous mansion was ablaze with light. Beautifully arranged flowers added color to the already impressive decorations. Exotic palm trees and orchids decorated the stairs and entry. After being announced to their hostess, they made their way up a massive staircase toward the ballroom.

Although Brandon had been here many times and knew his hostess well, this was Nicole's first time. The lights and fashionable people dazzled her. She and Brandon drew their share of attention. Several heads turned, and Nicole sensed their eyes on them as she and Brandon made their way to the dressing room. Nicole felt her face heat up under their scrutiny and held onto Brandon's arm a little tighter. Brandon patted her hand reassuringly.

Nicole looked up at her escort. "I'll remove my cloak and check my costume. Where shall I meet you?"

"I'll wait for you in the ballroom. Remember the first dance is mine."

She watched Brandon walk away.

After shedding her cloak, she found Brandon and his friend Robert Marchand at the entrance to the ballroom. They stood talking until Nicole reached them. The musicians began playing a minuet just as Nicole entered the ballroom. This made her step a little lighter and put a smile on her face. A gargantuan chandelier hung at each end of the ballroom. The candlelight highlighted the gold veins in the marbled floor of the ballroom. The room appeared to be gilded in enchantment.

Brandon led her onto the dance floor where they performed the intricacies of the dance to perfection. Dancing so close, her hand in his, she felt happy. Her cares were forgotten with the lilting music.

The music ended too soon for Nicole. Brandon bowed, and Nicole curtsied. They walked off the floor, and he found an empty chair for her, then went off in search of refreshments. Nicole looked around the room at each one of the magnificently dressed people. A few she knew and waved to, or they stopped by to greet her. Several of the people she knew by reputation, but had never met.

Merry laughter and smiles accompanied the music. She watched elaborate bows from distinguished men and delicate curtsies from striking women. The gossip mill had not run as cruelly as she feared. There were whispers when she and Brandon entered, but no one snubbed her. Their hostess even walked over to her and passed a few minutes of polite conversation. This small gesture sealed her acceptance into society. She relaxed and enjoyed herself.

Rapt in the excitement of the moment, Nicole jumped when startled by a voice from her past. "I didn't expect to find you here, my dear."

Nicole turned around and looked into the eyes of Lord Bedlington. She stood, and he came closer.

\*\*\*\*

Brandon, on his way back with a glass of ratafia for Nicole, came up short when he saw Bedlington talking to Nicole. His anger rose by degrees the closer he came to them. Before he could reach Nicole, Marchand stepped in front of him and pulled him aside.

"What's that scoundrel doing with my wife?"

"Don't you know who that is? You knew they were once engaged."

"Yes, naturally, but she looks upset." Brandon peered around Marchand, then stepped out and started toward Nicole again.

With his hand on Brandon's arm, Marchand whispered in Brandon's ear, "Stop and think. You cannot go over there. If you cause a scene, Lady Wigam will never invite you again. Do not embarrass your wife. Let Nicole handle the situation. What do you have against him? They were engaged once. You can't expect him to snub her."

"He's a scoundrel and a coward. I met him for the first time in Paris. It must be at least two years now." Brandon could not take his eyes off Bedlington. He kept looking around Marchand until Marchand cleared his throat to get his attention. "Oh, yes, well, Father sent me to France to ride out another scandal. One scandal too many, you might say. That was when he altered his will the last time."

"Was that the time you tried to elope with the headmaster's daughter?"

"No, that was earlier, when I was seventeen. As you know, my father caught us before we reached Gretna Green, and she claimed to be there against her will. In truth, *she* talked *me* into eloping. But no, this was another time and another scandal. I was twenty-two this time. I'd been in a duel and had to leave post haste. He was expected to die but pulled through.

"At any rate, Bedlington and several others, including myself were playing cards in a notorious gaming hell in Paris. I can't even remember the name now. I caught Bedlington cheating and called him on it. He denied it and called me out.

"We each named our seconds, set the time and place. That same night, someone brutally killed a woman of the evening. The *gendarmes* investigated and received an anonymous letter saying someone saw me in the company of the lady. There was no truth to it, but the *gendarmerie* arrested me and kept me in jail until my companion of the evening came forward and vouched for me the next morning. I missed the appointed time for the duel. Bedlington went around before he left Paris saying I didn't have the courage to confront him. Luckily for him, he left before the *gendarmes* released me."

"I'll say, he didn't know how lucky he was," Marchand said with a grin.

"I investigated on my own. The stationary came from the place where he stayed. I never found any evidence, but I believe he had a hand in that woman's death. He's a loose screw and a dangerous man besides being a coward and a cheat," Brandon said through his teeth.

Staring in their direction, he grasped the stem of his wine glass much too firmly and snapped it in several pieces. When Marchand pointed out that his hand was bleeding, Brandon turned and set the shattered glass on a nearby table. He took a handkerchief from the sleeve of his jacket and wrapped it around his hand until the bleeding stopped.

Marchand leaned in. "Brandon, stay here. You do not want to create a scene. You know what you're akin to when you lose your temper. I swear the devil takes a step backward. You don't want your wife's name bandied about either. You know those old society cats are just waiting for a juicy piece of gossip. Let me work my magic." He winked and sauntered unsteadily toward Nicole.

\*\*\*\*

Although Bedlington did not touch her, Nicole felt trapped. He stood closer than he should, imprisoning her between him and her chair.

"Nicole, it's been a long time. How have you been?

I've missed you and our early morning rides through Hyde Park. Thinking of those stolen kisses always sends a shiver through me. In spite of what has happened, my wish is we are still on good terms. I don't want to lose you as a friend."

"Thank you. I value your friendship also. It seems we were not destined to be tied together since you have married someone else, and so have I. Your wife, Cordelia, was a friend of mine at finishing school. I understand she is in the country. I look forward to renewing our acquaintance when she returns to town."

"You understand why our engagement had to be terminated. My father wished to refurbish our country estate, and money was in short supply. It was my duty to marry well, but I have not forgotten you. How could I? I had not worked up the courage to ask you to release me when I received your note. Thank you for making it so easy for me. Now I find you have married such a one as Lord Montagu. Why did you agree to marry that scoundrel?"

"Robert, I will not discuss my husband with you. I advise you never to broach the subject again if we are to remain friends. Now I must go." Nicole tried to walk around Lord Bedlington.

He took hold of her elbow and held her where she stood. Her heart beating faster, she looked around for Brandon. "I want you to meet me. I know you can get away. Meet me in Kensington Gardens tomorrow where we can chat with no ears to overhear. I think we may come to an arrangement. No reason our spouses should curtail our friendship."

"I'm sorry, Robert, but that is not possible. Please release my arm. Lord Montagu is bringing me refreshments and should be here soon." She stared around the ballroom, her heart beating so loud she thought everyone must hear it.

The last thing she needed was Brandon finding her talking to her ex-fiancé. Not that he cared other than a male protecting his territory. She feared what was sure to happen when Brandon found Bedlington talking to her. She put a trembling arm around her waist, finding it difficult to breathe imagining the confrontation. Someone jarred Lord Bedlington and caused him to lose his grip on Nicole.

"I say, a thousand pardons, my good man. Clumsy of me." Marchand swayed somewhat, looking at Lord Bedlington through half-closed eyes.

"There you are, Lady Montagu. Been looking all over for you, my dear. Promised me the next dance, and I've come to claim it."

"Yes, sorry, I forgot. The musicians are beginning to play, shall we?" Nicole held out her arm to Marchand. He smoothly took her arm and led her to the dance floor where he danced perfectly without falter.

When the dance finished, Nicole laughed and curtsied. "You rescued me. Very clever of you. How ever, did you know? He frightened me. I can't think why, but I was never gladder to see anyone."

"From your expression, I could tell you did not enjoy talking to Lord Bedlington. Watching him take hold of your elbow and not let go gave me cause for concern. I had to think of something quick before Brandon caused a scene. He saw what I saw. It isn't a good idea to tell Brandon what Bedlington said," he whispered over her hand as he bowed low.

She curtsied and with her head bowed. "Yes, I

understand. And again, thank you."

He straightened up and smiled. "Glad to be of service."

Brandon met them and claimed Nicole for the next quadrille. "What did that bounder want?" Brandon growled when he had Nicole close enough to whisper against her ear.

"I'm not sure. It was a strange conversation, but nothing to worry you or me. Mr. Marchand spirited me away nicely." She tried to smile and ease Brandon's mind.

She could not look him in the eye. She hoped Brandon did not notice her hand trembling in his. When she searched the room, she did not glimpse Lord Bedlington and assumed he left. After the dance ended, Nicole retired to the dressing room to check her hair and regain her composure. Brandon and Mr. Marchand left for the game room to play dominoes.

With her nerves calmer, Nicole made her way to the dance floor and enjoyed watching the dancers glide across the marble floor. Her dance card was full, and soon Lord Wharton claimed her hand for another minuet. Horus arrived shortly after midnight and asked to dance with her next if it was not a *gavote*. After their dance, her energy waned, and she asked Horus to bring a glass of Negus to her table.

Nicole watched Lady Bennett walk through the ballroom. She drew the attention of a few of the women there, but mostly it was the men who watched her weave in and out of the partygoers, very much at her ease. She strolled so casually along the room making it appear she had no control over her sexual allure. She gave the impression of being fragile, but underneath,

Nicole suspected she had a heart of stone. Her charm wrapped around her carelessly as if it were a mantle. From the moment she entered the ballroom, the men stopped whatever they were doing and watched or spoke to her. It was hard not to admire her cool confidence. Nicole turned back around to watch the dancers, disappointed that she'd had to see Lady Bennett again. Although she lived on the edge of polite society, she had received an invitation through her many connections for an affair as large as this one.

Lady Bennett was dressed exquisitely in a stunning ball gown of gold and rust, beaded, and embroidered in gold roses over a gold silk petticoat. An elegant powdered wig covered her dark hair. Someone had gone to great pains to skillfully apply her makeup so as not to give the impression of too much or too little. A renowned beauty, her unlined face made it difficult to determine her age.

Nicole was not aware Lady Bennett had worked her way to stand behind her until she was tapped on the shoulder. She turned around, looking past the fan the lady held, to stare into the pale, wintry blue eyes of Lady Bennett.

Lady Bennett had the disconcerting knack of looking at one with widening eyes and tilted head, in an appraising way. Nicole returned her stare, causing the lady to clear her throat and glance around the room uncertainly.

"How do you do, my dear? We meet again. Lovely ball and such a squeeze. I can't remember when I have danced so much."

"Yes, it is delightful. Nice to meet you once again," Nicole said, trying to be polite.

"Pardon me, Lady Montagu, but it looks as if you're more fortunate than I with your youth to recommend you. All too soon, youth fades along with a woman's charms. It doesn't appear to happen to men. They become more charming with age. However, you have succeeded where I have failed. But no matter, I have his heart, and that is more than enough."

"I'm sorry, but I do not follow the point of our conversation," Nicole said while trying to look puzzled.

"Can you not know who I am?"

"If I'm not mistaken, we met at Lady Hamilton's. You're Lady Bennett, are you not?"

"You know perfectly well of whom I speak. Do you think I intend to allow such as you to steal his love from me?" Although to the people around them, Lady Bennett appeared to be talking to Nicole in polite conversation, her tongue dripped with venom. Her hard eyes bored into Nicole.

Prepared to feign ignorance and brazen it out, Nicole stared back at her. "Whose heart do you imagine I have stolen, madam? Maybe I am stupid today, but I still do not know what you're talking about. I believe you have me confused with someone else. If you'll excuse me, I'll join my friends now."

Lady Bennett grabbed Nicole's arm. "You know without my telling you that Brandon is mine. We have been as one in everything. You shall not have him if I have any say in the matter. When a man has been enjoying haute cuisine, he will not settle for milk toast. I promise you, I've forgotten more ways to please a man than you will ever know," she hissed in Nicole's ear

"I thank you for enlightening me." Nicole jerked

her arm free, bowed before turning, and walked away with determination in a casual search for refreshment.

As soon as she was out of sight of Lady Bennett, she put a trembling hand to her face and looked around wildly for an escape. She found French doors leading onto the terrace and stepped through them. On the deserted terrace, she caught her breath and tried to calm the beating of her heart. She wandered over to the fishpond, lost in thought. Strains of music wafted on the evening breeze, and she swayed while listening to the calming tones. When the music stopped, she took another deep breath, collected her shattered nerves, and decided to return to the ballroom.

She gasped when a familiar voice called to her across the terrace. "How fortunate I am tonight? We meet again. Now we can have that talk."

"I have nothing more to say. Please excuse me." Nicole started back toward the French doors.

Lord Bedlington stepped in front of her and kept moving until he had backed her to the edge of the pond. "I wanted you to know that Montagu has never been faithful to any of his mistresses. The stories I could tell you should not cross a lady's ears. You only have to say the word. Leave the preparations to me. You will not be sorry. I can take you on an intimate trip through the joys both a man and a woman can share." He held her face in his hand and bent to kiss her.

She tried turning her head to avoid his kiss, but he held it in his grip. He brushed her lips with his and let go of her face.

"Sir, never do that again, or I shall be forced to tell my husband. As to your other proposal, I hope my ears deceived me. I do not want to credit you with offering me carte blanche. I'm sure I didn't hear you correctly. Please excuse me. My cousin is by the refreshment table waiting for me."

"You have not mistaken my words. Why should we not enjoy a dalliance? The marriage was forbidden us, but the pleasures of marriage can be ours for the taking."

Nicole longed to slap his face. She looked at his sly fox eyes and felt a chill run through her body. With the heel of her shoe, she stomped hard on the arch of his foot. When he bent and grabbed for his foot, she pushed hard against his shoulder, deftly slipped around him, and hurried through the French doors. Her nerves frazzled anew, she could not tolerate any more. Horus came across the room with a glass of Negus in his hand and beckoned to her.

"Nikki, where have you been? You sent me for this foul refreshment and ran off." Horus glanced past Nicole through the French doors. "Nikki, why is Bedlington coming out of the fish pond? He looks to be soaking wet." He broke into laughter and handed Nicole her drink.

"I guess it was too much to hope he drowned. Oh, Horus, have you seen Brandon? I need to go home."

Horus's laugh caught in his throat. "Nikki, are you sick? What's going on? Did Bedlington insult you? You're as pale as a specter. Last time I saw Brandon, he was in the game room. Let me take you to the dressing room, and I'll get him for you." He held onto Nicole's arm with concern etched on his face.

"I can't explain now. Come to me tomorrow and I will, but now I want to go home. Oh, I wish I had never come." Tears were forming in her eyes, threatening to spill at any moment.

"There now, old girl, we'll have none of that. Think where you are. Do you want to start tongues waggling? Dry those tears. I'll find him. Ah, here he comes now." Horus waved to Brandon.

Nicole hurriedly brushed the tears from her eyes and pushed a stray curl from her face. "Brandon, I'm not feeling well. Please take me home. Horus can take me if you'd rather stay."

****

"No, I'm ready to go myself. I'll have the coach brought around. Horus take her to the dressing room for her cloak and then meet me out front. Don't leave her side." He watched her walk away. She had been in such high spirits earlier. He wondered what had caused this. Through the French doors he saw someone talking to a servant. There was something familiar about the man's backside. Brandon did not have time to get a better look. Nicole's indisposition made him uneasy, and he hurried away. With a pang of conscience, he wondered if he should have sought her out sooner.

When they arrived home, he escorted her to her bedchamber door, there holding her hand unable to let go. There were things he wanted to tell her, but standing there, staring into those luminous, innocent eyes, he could think of nothing. His only thoughts were of an innocent wedding kiss spinning his world out of control; he had not recovered from it yet. He wanted to taste those petal soft lips again, to hold her warm and pliant in his arms, and freely give her his heart.

"Goodnight, my lord. It was an enchanted evening. I hope I'm not the reason you left so soon."

"No, I was ready to go home. Are you feeling

better? You're not as pale. What was wrong? Did someone insult you?"

"No, no, I took a strange turn. It could have been something I ate or too much wine. I'm fine now." She gave a half-smile, and her words did not convince Brandon.

She turned to open her door. Brandon put his hand on her arm and turned her back, then took her in his arms and held her snugly against his chest. When she looked up at him, it took his breath away. His heart beat in rhythm with hers. He kissed her gently at first, sparking feelings he did not know he possessed. His passion flared. The white-hot fire coursing through his veins shocked him, spiraling his emotions out of control. He felt Nicole yield, then kiss him back with ardor.

When he could stand it no longer, Brandon broke the weld and stepped back to catch his breath. He stared into her trusting face, then, without a will of his own, pivoted abruptly and left. He left Nicole staring after him, though he could not understand why his feet had betrayed him. At any other time, he would have satisfied his hunger, but could not. He could not take an action that promised to change his life forever. They had an agreement. He wondered what he had been thinking over the course of a sleepless night fighting with his bed covers and staring a hole through the adjoining, unlocked door.

****

Exhausted by the events of the evening, Nicole fell into a deep sleep. She could take no more—the last thing she wanted to do was think.

Nicole awoke after the noon hour to find a

concerned Mavis hovering nearby with a worried look on her face. She sighed when Nicole opened her eyes. Feeling dull witted with a headache, Nicole stayed in her room. When Horus arrived soon after three, he found her on the divan in her room with a cold cloth on her temple.

"Lor, Nikki, what's the matter with you? I've never seen you take to your bed for anything. Are you on your death bed?"

"Horus, you don't know what a night I had. I can't wake up. I want last night to disappear from memory." She told him of her conversations with Lord Bedlington and Lady Bennett.

"I knew when I found out he was courting you, he was a wrong'n. Before I could get you alone to tell you what I knew, your engagement came out. You're better off with Brandon, believe me. Besides, I like Brandon. This Bedlington is a dangerous man. I have no proof, you understand. It may be malicious gossip, but it's a feeling I have from stories and from people I trust.

"As for Lady Bennett, I'd take what she said with a grain of salt. Word on the wind is she expected Brandon to marry her. Nikki, don't worry. I've seen the way Brandon looks at you. Maybe he doesn't know it yet, but he cares for you. I think you care for him as well."

"Oh, Horus, I can't believe this will end well for me. I don't know what to do about my heart." She could not hide her despair from Horus. He was more akin to a brother than a cousin. He understood her.

Horus moved next to her and put his arm around her shoulders. She trembled on the verge of tears. With great effort, she gained mastery over her emotions.

Horus left her shortly before Brandon came home. She dressed and met him for dinner, looking much better.

She noticed Brandon watching her and waited curiously for what he had to say.

"Nicole, you appear much better today. Your color is better, but I fear you're worn out from our busy social life. We must have been to twenty balls, thirty dinners, and countless routs, soirees, and concerts. We both need to stay home for three or four nights and rest up for the next round of entertainment. It's very tiring being a model citizen. I haven't raced my phaeton through the park, participated in a duel, or gotten into a drunken brawl."

Brandon and Nicole both laughed.

"There, that's better. You have a nice smile."

"Yes, I can understand where being a model citizen might be stressful to one of your bent." She laughed once again and glanced across the table at Brandon from under her eyelashes. "Yes, I'm sure a few days' rest is what I need. I think I'm worn out." She sighed wistfully, looked back at her food, and tried to eat.

The question on his mind was written on his face as plainly as if he had said it aloud. Her greatest wish was to avoid telling him Lord Bedlington's conversation and hoped he would leave everything as it stood now.

"What was Bedlington saying to you that upset you? Don't say it wasn't important. I saw the look on your face, and I saw him hold you back when you tried to leave."

"It's over now. I cannot hope to avoid him. He will be invited to the same parties we are. I will do my best to stay out of his way. I don't want to discuss it. Let me just say this much: He made a suggestion I didn't like, and I made it plain I did not appreciate his remarks."

"If I had known, I would have settled it with him. I will not stand for you being insulted."

"Please, don't call him out for this. We must have no scandals, or everything we have done will be for naught. It was a misunderstanding. I have settled it. I don't believe he will bother with me anymore. Please just forget it."

"If it happens again, you must tell me, and I'll take care of it," he growled. He stared at his meal a long time before pushing his plate away.

All confidences suspended, awkward silence droned on through the rest of the meal. He ordered more wine. The scowl never left his face.

Nicole pleaded a headache and left the table for her bedchamber. Brandon did not look up from his glass. She was not sure he even heard her and hurried to the solitude of her chamber. The door closed behind her, and she leaned against it, taking deep breaths to settle her fractured nerves. She settled before the fire to read, but all too soon, heavy eyelids caused her to doze, and the book to fell to the floor. Several hours later, she heard Brandon enter her chamber but pretended to be asleep, not wanting to lie to him or answer any more questions. Watching him stand over her where she lay on her divan, from under her lashes, she continued to feign sleep. He backed out of the room and closed the door softly.

Three days later, they rejoined their social engagements. Nicole did not see Lord Bedlington again. Someone said his wife had delivered, and his father-in-law requested his presence in the country immediately. It was said his father-in-law frowned upon the way he had neglected his daughter at this important time by coming to London.

The days turned into months and with August, the glittering season drew to a close. Everyone left the hot and humid London for their country estates. On the ninth of August, Brandon turned five and twenty years old and received his inheritance. The year at an end, everything they hoped for was coming to fruition.

Instead of being glad, Nicole had a feeling of being in limbo and was more or less depressed. Brandon, on the other hand, became more animated as the time drew near. In two days' time, they had an appointment to go to Mr. Pettigrew's office, sign the papers, and receive his approval along with his inheritance. Nicole feared her enjoyment and the security of her easy lifestyle was at an end. She could not imagine what would happen if Mr. Pettigrew did not give his approval, and Brandon found himself tied to her for no purpose.

Chapter Seven

Brandon paced the solicitor's office.

Nicole sat with her hands tightly clasped, waiting and wondering what new turn fate had in store for her. Their agreement at an end, did he plan to turn her out or keep up this pretense? She could not decide what she wanted. Never seeing Brandon again caused a sadness to wash over her.

The door opened, and both sets of eyes turned in anticipation.

Mr. Pettigrew's clerk came through the door. "Mr. Pettigrew will see you now."

Brandon held his hand out to Nicole. Together they stepped into Claude Pettigrew's office.

The solicitor stood with a smile on his face and came around his desk to shake hands with Brandon and to bow over Nicole's hand. He motioned for them to sit, then leaned against his desk and looked them over.

"Well, well, it has been a year and two days since I attended your wedding. I'm happy to say you have not caused any scandals, gossip, or done anything your father would not approve. Our investigators have been diligent. They interviewed your servants and friends. Before you object, we have been the soul of discretion. No one realized they were being interviewed or to what end.

"The most important part of this unique will was

the stipulation that you marry a lady of quality, remain under the same roof for a year, appear together in public, and refrain from causing a scandal for the equivalent time period. I'm happy to say you have fulfilled these requirements." He stood and shook Brandon's hand. "The only thing left is to sign the papers."

As if on cue, the clerk came through the door. "Please follow me, Lord Montagu."

"Nicole, you may stay here with me."

Brandon turned to Nicole with a questioning look.

Nicole nodded and smiled reassuringly. After he disappeared through the door, she turned back to Mr. Pettigrew. "Uncle Claude, how have you and Aunt Cora been?"

"Never been better, my dear. She asks after you. Please visit more often. Cora loves seeing you."

"I'll try to visit more. The season is such a whirlwind of balls and parties. The running around and late nights are especially tiring."

"Before Lord Montagu comes back, I must ask if you're happy. I do not mean to belabor the point, but your happiness is upper most in my mind. From outward appearances, he is a changed man. I hope this continues."

"Uncle Claude, don't worry. I'm happy. Lord Montagu has given me a pleasant life." She tried to smile cheerfully.

"That takes a load off my mind. I wasn't sure I did the right thing in sanctioning your marriage. Forgive me, my dear, but he has a dreadful reputation, and this gave me cause for concern. He appears to have changed, and this makes me very pleased for you."

"Please don't worry, Uncle Claude. I'm happy with the way things have worked out."

"Good, good." He rubbed his hands together and smiled. "Ah, here they come back. Remember, if you ever need me, you only have to send word."

Nicole stood in wait for Brandon. Mr. Pettigrew came around his desk and escorted them to the outer office. Nicole turned, waved good-bye, and closed the door. Back on the street, Brandon was smiling from ear to ear.

"Well, I did it. I out foxed the old fox. He'd turn over in his grave if he knew he'd lost again." Brandon chuckled and rubbed his hands excitedly.

He turned his attention to Nicole. "Nicole, I'll get a hack to drive you home, unless there is somewhere you want to go. I think I'll walk for a while and stop in at my club. Not to worry, I'll be back in time to take you to Lord Wharton's for my friends and my collective birthday celebration dinner."

He handed her into a hack and waved good-bye. Nicole looked out the window and watched him saunter along the street without a care. She stared gloomily around her.

*That's a fine turn of events. He did everything by himself with never a thought to my contribution. I wonder what I'm expected to do now. Does he want me to stay or is it best if I go?*

*I wish Horus were here. Maybe I could determine the best thing to do with his levelheaded help, but he won't be back for another week.*

*I wish I didn't have to go to this dinner. I'm tired of smiling and pretending to enjoy his friends. Maybe the best thing is to leave while he's away with his friends on their birthday celebration trip. He won't miss me…*

*…but my heart feels as if it may break in two at the thought of never seeing him again. I at no time meant to lose my heart.*

*I must be insane to care about this rake.*

*What am I going to do with the rest of my life?*

\*\*\*\*

Brandon was lost in thought for the entire walk to his club. While he sat thinking over a cold luncheon, he ordered another glass of wine, then left it on the table untouched. With the year at an end, he had no idea what to do with himself next. Everything he wanted was his except for the most important thing in his life. What was he going to do concerning Nicole?

He'd had no problem with any woman he wanted in the past. They more or less came to him. He always dallied with women who knew how to play the game. When it ended, as it surely must, there were no hard feelings. Nicole did not play games. He knew this, and it puzzled him that he wanted her more than any woman he had yet to meet.

They had a marriage of convenience with each agreeing not to interfere in the others' intrigues. The thought of another man touching her made him see nothing but red. This trip for him and his four friends had been planned for several months, and because each would be turning the same age within a week of each other. They planned to celebrate by visiting Germany, Austria, and Switzerland as they had done when they turned eighteen. He could not back out now but had no desire to go. Maybe when he returned he would have his feelings sorted.

He did not look up until a shadow crossed over his

table. He stared up, into the icy calculating eyes of Lord Bedlington.

"Lord Montagu, I did not expect to find you here. Our paths have crossed once again." Without being asked, he sat in the chair opposite Brandon.

Brandon raised his eyebrows at Bedlington and stared at him from under half-closed eyelids. "I understand congratulations are in order. I hope mother and child are well."

"Yes, I left them in the country. A person can only take so much rustication. You've been married for a year. When will I be able to congratulate you?" Bedlington sneered. He picked up Brandon's full glass of wine and drank it in one gulp.

The only thing stopping Brandon from landing a right to Bedlington's jaw was the fact they were in Brooks and the club's committee members frowned upon that sort of thing. Holding his temper in check, Brandon clenched his fists but kept them close at his side.

"Well, I must be getting back. Excuse me." Brandon stood, never once taking his eyes off Bedlington.

Bedlington stood leisurely. A slow unpleasant smile crossed his face as Bedlington reached out and put a hand on Brandon's arm to stop him from leaving. Brandon looked at the hand and back at Bedlington, then shook it off.

"I bid you good day, sir."

"We need to talk. I've not said everything I want to say, Montagu."

"You've said more than enough. We don't have anything more to say to each other, but I will give you a word of warning. Stay away from my family and me. If I ever see you touch one of us again, I'll finish what you started in Paris." Brandon watched Bedlington turn a shade paler and an angry vein stand out on his forehead.

"You have something that belongs to me. I intend to get it back."

"You are mistaken. I have nothing that belongs to you. When you cast something aside as if it were of no importance, you lose all claim," Brandon said through clenched teeth.

"We have not finished the game. I will not give up until I have her," he hissed.

"You go too far. Speak one more word, and I will have you name your second. You will not weasel out as you did in Paris. Now if you will pardon me, I must be going…*home*…to my *wife*." He turned to go, his temper barely under control.

To his dismay, everyone in the room was watching. He hoped they had not eavesdropped on the conversation. He had tried to keep his voice low but in his anger, had no idea how loud he'd spoken. The last thing he wanted or needed was more gossip, and Nicole's name bandied all over town.

Head down and lost in thought, he wandered through familiar streets in the city, arriving back home just before sunset. He climbed the stairs to his chamber, dressed for the evening, and waited downstairs for Nicole. A door closed overhead, and he gazed up as she appeared at the top of the stairs.

She looked stunning as usual. A black silk dress with silver piping and embroidery was the perfect backdrop to her mother's diamond and emerald necklace and earrings. Her hair was powdered and woven in an intricate pattern. Her grace and beauty confused Brandon even more with each step she took toward him.

He held out his hand as she reached the bottom step and escorted her to the waiting town coach.

"With both of us dressed in black, we make a solemn couple. You would think we were on our way to the gallows," Nicole said.

Brandon laughed and settled back in the carriage. "Yes, one of us should have put on some color."

As their coach passed near Covent Gardens, Brandon spied a flower girl outside the opera house. He had the coach stop and came back a short time later with a single red rose. He fastened it in Nicole's hair.

"There now, one of us has a bit of color, although you needed nothing to complete your costume. The rose is more like painting the lily."

In the light from a flambeau, he watched Nicole blush becomingly and gingerly touch her rose at his compliment. She turned to him and smiled. He smiled back, unable to look away until the coach stopped again.

\*\*\*\*

Lady de Grey, Lord Wharton's sister, greeted Brandon as an old friend and smiled at Nicole. There were twenty guests, and everyone knew everyone. Before going into dinner, Lord Wharton raised a toast to their trip and the celebration of their combined birthdays.

The guests went into the dining room and sat at an elaborately decorated table. Through the center of the table was a miniature representation of a formal garden complete with hedges, flowers, and a diminutive gazebo.

The servants served the first course of soup, fish, fricassees, vegetables, and ragouts followed by a course of roast beef, venison, and ham that Lord Wharton carved generously for his guests. After over two hours, the servants came and removed the dishes before putting on a new tablecloth for the dessert course. All manner of fruits, nuts, cheese, sweetmeats, several flavors of jellies, and syllabubs were served. The servants kept filling the wine glasses throughout the meal, and at the end of the dinner, refilled everyone's wine glass one last time.

When the glasses were empty, Lady de Grey rose and the other ladies followed suit, then retired to the drawing room. The gentlemen remained to drink and talk. A string quartet surrounded the dining room with soothing music. Several of the men stayed to listen while others wandered off to play cards.

The string quartet finished their concert and started to pack away their instruments. Nicole left the drawing room and wandered toward the game room looking for Brandon. She heard the sound of voices and stopped beside the doorway. She listened to Brandon and Marchand talking. She knew it was wrong to eavesdrop but could not help herself. When she heard her name, she moved closer to be able to see and hear with no one knowing.

"Are you sure you want to come with us. You have a wife and the rest of us are free birds, you might say. I don't imagine she'd approve if she knew what we got up to away from the social conventions."

"My wife need not concern you or me."

"No need to take offense, old man. I remember the clause in the will, and that you had to find a wife. We should all be so lucky. Your luck held as usual."

"What do you know regarding the will?" Brandon took a step toward Marchand.

"Don't you remember what you did when the lawyer read the will? You went on a three-day bender. When we finally found you, you told us everything."

"Yes, you're right. I guess I forgot. It's coming back to me now."

"I know I wouldn't care to leave someone as exquisite as Lady Nicole to her own devices for at least six months. With Bedlington hanging around and that cousin of hers dancing in attendance... Well."

"What are you saying?" Brandon narrowed his eyes, on the verge of losing his rapidly rising temper. He took another step forward.

"Brandon, old man, I meant nothing by it. I merely wondered at your wanting to go with us. That's all; nothing more."

"Why shouldn't I want to go? I do as I choose and so may my wife. Nothing has changed since the last time we went on this trek. Everything is the same. Exactly the same." Brandon said the last words without the same conviction as his first assertions.

Out of the corner of his eye, Brandon caught a fragment of silver trimmed black skirt flounce past a corner of the doorway and heard a swish of silk. He knew then that Nicole had heard everything they'd said. His face heated up in a blush. He could not understand why...even as a schoolboy, he never remembered blushing.

He stifled a yawned. "It must be getting late. I had

better collect my wife and go. When next we meet in two days' time, it will be on board a ship to Holland." He waved good-bye and left in search of Nicole.

He found her in the drawing room, sitting by herself and staring out of a window into the night. At his footsteps, she turned around. "Are you ready to go, my dear?"

"Yes."

She raised her head and searched his face. He took her hand. She stood and walked with him to get their cloaks. The ride home was filled with an almost palpable strained silence they both knew well by this time.

Brandon started to speak, but when he turned to Nicole, she appeared to be asleep in the shadow of the coach's bench with her head resting on a squab. When they arrived at the house, she let the footman help her out of the carriage and went into the house without saying a word. Before Brandon could catch her, she started up the stairs.

****

"Nicole, wait. Don't go yet. Come into the sitting room. I want to talk to you."

Without comment, Nicole turned and walked solemnly into the sitting room as one in a trance. She thought he was about to tell her what he planned to do with her. She sat with her hands clasped and waited.

Jenkins brought in a tray with two glasses and a bottle of champagne.

"I know it's late, but we haven't celebrated together what we've accomplished." He poured her a glass of champagne and one for himself, then held his glass high. "'Tis to thee I drink."

Nicole raised her glass. "To your health," she said woodenly.

"I just remembered we have not celebrated our wedding anniversary. The very reason we can raise our glasses in a toast. I'm sorry, Nicole. Forgive me for taking you for granted. I've always been selfish. I'm sorry for ignoring you and your contribution to our marriage and my fortunes."

Nicole set her glass on the table untouched. "No reason to be sorry. I'm tired. I think I'll retire to my chamber."

She stood to leave, but Brandon moved in front of her.

"Don't leave just yet. Please stay and talk to me. I know you heard what I said in the card room. I should not have said those things to Marchand, and for that I'm sorry."

"No need to apologize. We have an agreement. Now that you have accomplished what you wanted, what's to become of me? Shall we keep up this pretense? Shall I leave? What do you want me to do? I need to know."

"I don't want you to leave. I want you to stay. I've gotten used to having you around, and I enjoy escorting you. It will sadden me if you choose to live apart."

"While you're gone, I'll think over what you said. At this point, I don't understand why you want me here. The reasons to go out number the reasons to stay. I'm not a member of your fashionable set or—"

Brandon drew her into his arms and trapped her lips with a hungry kiss. At first, she resisted, but his demanding, passionate kisses left her weak and wanting. A warm feeling spread across her as she melted into his embrace. The fires of passion kindled into a white-hot flame, and she kissed him back eagerly.

His hands cupped her tender breasts, and his touch sent electrical impulses through her being causing her nipples to respond in tender peaks. He pulled her hard against him and held her tightly. He traced kisses over her eyelids, down the narrow hollow of her neck, and onto the rounded swell of her breasts. When his manhood pressed hard against her thigh, she wanted to cry out. He picked her up and carried her upstairs.

"Brandon…are you sure?"

"I've never been surer of anything in my life. You are mine to love and to cherish. Another will not have you. No one will taste your virgin honey except me. I do not want another. Only you."

\*\*\*\*

They arrived at her bedchamber, and he laid her on her bed. A sleeping Mavis woke and scurried out of the room. Nicole stood. Brandon undid the stays of her dress. Her dress fell around her like melting wax from a candle. He watched the candlelight play off her milky white skin and sparkle in her eyes. Her sheer chemise revealed a supple silhouette that drove his desire beyond control. Once again, he took her in his arms and kissed her passionately demanding fulfillment.

He shrugged out of his clothes, picked her up, and laid her on the bed. He lay beside her and undid the pins holding her hair in place. "Nicole, this past year I have not bed another, nor have I wanted to. I have led a monk's existence.

"The torment of watching you, being with you, and touching you, but never enjoying the pleasures of your body has been more than I can stand. I come to you and claim the rights of a husband. Is that repugnant to you? Do you not desire me as well? Come to me with your whole heart and let us start afresh."

"Oh, Brandon, I want that more than you can imagine. I too want the pleasures you speak of. I crave the warmth of your body as a flower yearns for the warmth from the sun."

He caught his breath, his need of her coursed through his veins, and he pulled her closer to him. He held her in his arms warm and pliant. The agony of waiting and controlling the fire that threatened to scorch him was almost too much. He ran his hand tenderly down the full length of her naked body. She pulled his head to her and kissed him with the same longing he craved. Their bodies strained together. Nicole's sweet, soft moan of pleasure filled his ears. Unable to restrain himself, he took her and felt her yield to him. The intensity mounted until both were satisfied. Their passion spent, they collapsed out of breath. Brandon held on to her as if he were afraid she might take flight.

Once again, passion flared between them, and once more, Brandon claimed Nicole with his passion. They met again the next night and continued to ride the wave of excitement and self-discovery that did not diminish but intensified with each molten embrace.

****

Nicole woke early and with her eyes closed, reached out for Brandon, but he was not there. A few moments later, he came to her side of the bed and sat on the edge, bent, and kissed her waiting lips.

"I'm sorry, my love, but I must go. I promised my friends. If we had not planned this trip for so long, I wouldn't go. I'll be back before you've had time to miss me."

"I wish you didn't have to go. You haven't left, and I already miss you. Please be careful and come back to me as soon as may be."

He kissed her one last time and hurried through the adjoining door. Nicole dressed in her wrapper and stood on the balcony, watching Brandon go down the stairs. At the door, he turned and looked up at her. She blew him a kiss, which he pretended to capture and put on his cheek. Another wave and he disappeared through the door.

****

Nicole went back to her bed, but sleep did not come. It was chilled and empty without him beside her. Her arms longed to wrap around him once again. She moved onto his side of the bed and smelled his scent, sending her senses reeling. The tears started to fall and when the tears stopped, she fell into a fitful sleep. She spent the day in bed. Mavis moved around the room on tiptoes.

She felt better in the morning and went shopping, then came home around noon to find Horus waiting.

"Horus, you're back early. I'm so glad. I've missed you."

"My business was finished in record time. I'm getting good at dispersing my mother's suitors. I've sent yet another of her so-called counts packing. I don't know where she finds these men. When they find out I control the purse strings, it's amazing how fast they disappear. Enough of my problems. I take it Brandon has left on his celebration trip."

"Yes, he left yesterday. We're packing and moving

to Worthington Park by the end of the week."

"You're looking happier than I've seen you in a while. Do you want to go for a walk in Kensington Gardens tomorrow?"

"Yes, I'd like that. You must dine with me this evening. I don't plan on going out. I'm tired of the partying."

"Love to. I'll be here around six." Horus bowed and left.

The next day Horus came by for Nicole at midmorning. Together they strolled through the gardens enjoying the scenery and saying hello to friends. Nicole sat in the shade of a large tree to rest while Horus walked farther on and spoke to a few of his friends.

She twisted with a start when a familiar voice hailed her from behind. "My dear, I'm so glad I found you. Your butler said you were here. He said you're moving to the country. I must apologize for what I said the last time we met. I didn't understand the situation. Now I do, and I must thank you," Lady Bennett's smile did not reach her eyes.

"Lady Bennett, whatever do you mean?"

"You don't have to pretend with me. I know everything now. I knew Brandon did not want to abandon me after all we have meant to each other. He told me about the will. We will be as one again. I'm meeting him in Germany and going on with him and his friends. This trip will be most amusing, and I have you to thank for it. Well, I must fly. I have packing to do." She flounced off to her waiting carriage.

Nicole sat where she was too stunned to move. Horus came up to her and started talking, but she found it hard to concentrate on what he was saying. "Nikki, what's wrong? Look at me. You were so happy a minute ago. Why the change?"

"Oh, Horus...I've b-been a f-fool." She choked with tears brimming in her eyes.

"Nikki, hang in there. I'll get a hack. You can't cry in the park. It just isn't done." He handed her his handkerchief while looking around.

A short time later, he came back and ushered her into a hack. When it stopped at her address, she opened the door and ran into the house before the groom could come around to help her.

Horus hurried in after her.

Nicole collapsed on a settee in the sitting room.

"Nikki, out with it. What's wrong?"

The tears were coming in earnest now. Horus sat beside her and put his arm around her shoulders until her tears began to wane. He moved back and took her hand. "Nikki, what did Lady Bennett say to you? I saw her talking to you, but I couldn't get over there before she left."

"Oh, Horus, I've been a fool to think he cared for me. He was just using me. Putting a claim on his property. How could I be so stupid? We had an understanding. I knew he was a man of the world and a rake besides. Why did I place my trust in him? Why! Why!" Nicole could not stop the tears falling once again.

"Nikki, I don't understand what you're saying. You told me the terms of your marriage, but I still don't understand. What did she say to you?"

"Oh, Horus, don't you understand? I let him make love to me. I believed every word he said. What a pathetic simpleton I must be. Do you remember that old story concerning the farmer who found the poisonous snake?" She took a deep breath to get her emotions under control.

Horus looked at her with a puzzled expression.

"You must remember. It went something like this. A farmer found a wounded snake, and it asked him to take it in and nurse it. He took it and nursed it. When it was restored to health, the snake bit him. He said why did you bite me? Now I will surely die. The snake said you knew I was a snake when you took me in."

"It can't be as bad as that. He is your husband, in any case."

"Lady Bennett said she's meeting him in Germany and traveling on with him and his friends. She knew the terms of the will. She t-thanked me for h-helping them." Nicole broke off into sobs.

"Oh…I see. I'm sorry, Nikki. What do you want to do? I'll help you any way I can. You know that. But Nikki, I think you should talk to Brandon first before you do something rash."

"And have him tell me another lie? No, I've decided. I'm going to Standon. I'll not live another day under his roof. Will you hire a carriage for us? We'll leave tomorrow morning and go to Papa. Will you do that for me?"

"Whatever you wish, but Nikki, are you sure you can believe Lady Bennett?"

"She spoke freely concerning the will and the trip. Brandon told no one except me, and I only told you. If he had not told her, how could she know? He was so afraid Mr. Pettigrew might find out we had an agreement. I may have been naïve before, but the veil has fallen from my eyes."

With her bags packed and Mavis trailing behind, she said good-bye to Jenkins the next morning. "Jenkins, I want you to go to Worthington just as we had planned. I will not be going with you. My cousin is picking me up, and I'm going on to Standon. I don't expect to see you again. This is thank you and good-bye."

"But, my lady—"

The rattle of a coach on the cobblestones interrupted, and she ran back upstairs to get her bandbox, leaving Jenkins to supervise the loading of her baggage. The servants came out to say good-bye. Once everything was packed and secured, the somber party was on its way to Standon.

Shortly after they left London, the rain started. The gloom of the day matched Nicole's mood. Muddy roads made traveling difficult. They had to stop several times to rest the horses or make repairs. At one point, Nicole and Horus had to walk up a hill while the driver worked on getting the carriage unstuck and moving again.

Several times on the trip, Nicole wanted to turn around and go back. She told herself if she could have Brandon part time, it was better than not at all, but her pride refused to let her accept love on those terms. If she closed her eyes, she could imagine him on the ship with the wind blowing his black hair across his face. She wondered if he missed her. Her musings left her on the verge of tears. She shook her head to clear it of all thoughts of Brandon, but that did not work too well.

Chapter Eight

Biggers opened the door to Nicole and Horus. "Lady Nicole, Lord Horus..." He looked from one to the other before stepping aside for them to enter.

"Biggers, I've come home to roost. Can you manage my trunk? Just put it in my chamber. Where is my father?"

"Uh, yes, my lady. He's in the small sitting room. Will Lord Montagu be coming later?" He looked around Nicole to the coach.

"No, he will not! Lord Fleetwood is staying the night and will leave in the morning. I'll just go to Father and tell him I'm home to stay." Biggers had a puzzled look on his face. He looked to Horus for an answer, but Horus merely shrugged.

Nicole turned and walked away with her head held high.

She walked through the door of the small sitting room and saw a smile cross her father's face. She rushed to him, and they hugged. "Papa, I hope you don't mind, but I've left my husband and come to bear you company." She brushed a tear from her eyes and took a deep breath.

"My child, I don't mind, but what do you mean you've left your husband? Permanently?"

"Yes, I don't want to explain. Please don't ask me any questions." She tried to smile when she looked at her father, but the tears fell instead.

He put his arm around her and patted her shoulder. "There, there, child. You're home, so dry those tears. Biggers and I could use a little livening up. We're getting set in our ways. Mighty dull they are, too. I've missed you."

Nicole laughed in spite of herself. She kissed her father on the cheek and went off to her apartment to rest before dinner. Her troubled mind refused to let her rest, though. She did what she always did when life weighed too heavily on her. She sat at her piano and played feverishly for over two hours. The strains of music filled the whole house and filtered out to the surrounding houses.

Nicole wandered around the cottage without a direction in mind after Horus left the next morning. She in due course found her way out into the garden, sat on a bench under a large maple tree, and leaned against the trunk. Her heavy eyelids closed in sleep. As she drifted off, she felt a tug on her dress sleeve. She opened her eyes to a small girl with large expressive eyes staring at her.

"How do you do?" She waited for the little girl to speak. "May I help you?"

"Were you the one playing the pretty music yesterday?"

"Yes, I'm sorry if I played too loudly. Did you enjoy the music?"

"Yes, very much. Could anyone learn to play the way you did?"

"Yes, but you have to have talent, and you have to have lessons. Do you want to learn to play?"

"Yes, my mother said to ask you if you'd teach me.

We can pay."

"Well, I suppose I could. I haven't given it much thought. Let me consider it. Where do you live?"

The little girl pointed to the house next door. "I'll come and talk to your mother tomorrow. Is that satisfactory?"

"Yes, my names Laura Palfrey." She curtsied before skipping away.

Nicole had not thought of teaching music, but that could be a way to earn more money. She decided to give it a try and had Biggers pass the word around the neighborhood. Several people came wanting lessons. A few could pay with coin while others bartered with produce, meat, or other needed services.

When the rector learned she could play the piano and the organ, he asked her to fill in for their organist when she had to visit her mother in a nearby town, or was sick. When the church put on a fête to raise money for much needed repairs to the church, the rector persuaded her to give a concert in the town hall. At first, she refused, but since it was for a good cause and her father did not object, she agreed to do it. The tickets sold out promptly, and the rector talked her into a second concert.

While giving Laura a lesson, strangers knocked at the door and interrupted them.

"My lady, a Mr. and Mrs. Armand de Custine to see you," Biggers announced.

"Please show them in."

A man and a woman came into the drawing room. The gentleman and lady were properly dressed for visiting. Madame wore a beautifully brocaded silk dress of canary yellow. Monsieur wore a coat and waistcoat made of brown silk and lined with silk and buckram. He was short with dark hair and eyes. His wife was a bit taller and had blonde hair. They looked around the room before their eyes came to rest on Nicole.

Nicole stood and put her hand on Laura's shoulder. "That concludes our lesson for the day. Come back on the morrow, and we'll finish." She watched Laura go through the door before her gaze returned to her visitors.

"Please excuse our intrusion, Lady Waltham, but we listened to you play last night and were enchanted. Because of your expertise, we have come to see you. My name is Armand de Custine, and this is my wife Charlotte. We run an exclusive seminary for young ladies just outside of Paris, in the Montparnasse district. Our school is in need of a music teacher. We understand from the rector that you speak fluent French, which is one of our requirements. If we could persuade you to travel to France, we will pay a premium. We are in desperate need of a music teacher. You only have to stay with us for one year."

"Accepting employment out of the country is not something I want to do, but I thank you for your offer." Nicole tried to discourage her guests and bring their visit to an end. As she was to find out, they did not discourage easily.

"We do not wish to offend, but we desperately need a music teacher. If we do not make available musical instruction, we will lose a large part of our students. Our young ladies are from the noble houses of France. Therefore, you can understand why musical instruction is necessary. You need stay for only one year, or until we can find a suitable French woman.

"We are here visiting your charming country. We will visit friends in York and be returning this way in two weeks. Please consider our offer. If it is convenient, we will visit you on our return. Your good rector has friends in the French embassy. He said he will be happy to write a letter to assure you of our excellent reputation."

"Monsieur de Custine, Madame, I will think over your offer, but I do not think teaching in a school is something I want to do. Another concern is the growing unrest in your country. There have been disturbing stories in the newspapers lately." Nicole walked toward the door with the couple.

"It is nothing to worry over, I assure you. Just a few rebel rousers from the lower classes. Nothing to be concerned with, or to do with our school. The *gendarmerie* will soon have everything under control. *Au revoir, mademoiselle.*"

During the night, a thunderstorm crashed over the quiet village of Standon. Lightning streaked across the sky, and the winds blew furiously. Anything not tied down flew about, to and fro. The sound of thunder crashed overhead and lightning lit Nicole's chamber. She awoke with a start. A resounding explosion shook the house. She smelled smoke. Fully awake now, she jumped out of bed when the limb of a tree came through the wall sending ripples throughout the house. It stopped short of landing in her bed. Her screams brought the whole house to her chamber.

When the storm subsided, Biggers went outside with a lantern and surveyed the damage. He returned and reported to Nicole and Lord Waltham. "My lord, the large tree that stands between your house and the one next door has been rent asunder by the lightning. It now lies in two pieces with the larger piece attached to your house. It has been a flame, but the rain put the fire out."

"Biggers, what are we to do? The roof, wall, and whatever damage to the house must be repaired. I fear it will be frightfully expensive." Nicole wrung her hands and looked from Biggers to her father.

"There is a carpenter in the village that does roofing and odd jobs at reasonable rates. I will have him check over the damage and let us know the cost. In the meantime, I will put a tarpaulin over the damage." Biggers bowed and left the room.

"Nicole, do you have any money? I have none." Lord Waltham turned the palms of his hands up to further emphasize his lack of funds.

"I have a few pounds, Papa, but I don't think it will be enough. I'm afraid I must take the position offered me at the French school."

"My dear, could you not ask your husband for the money? The news out of France causes me concern."

"I could ask my husband, but I will not! Things are such that I never want to speak to or see him again."

"Why not ask Horus? I'm sure he will help us out."

"Papa, I must take care of us by myself. Horus has done so much for me already. I could not ask more. No, I will find a way to pay for the repairs, and if that means going to France, then that is what I will do."

"My daughter, your pride will be your undoing." Lord Waltham walked away, his shoulders stooped and shaking his head.

Nicole sat and tried to think of another way to pay for the repairs, but nothing came to mind. She had to face the depressing fact she must leave her comfortable cottage and go to France.

When the morning came, she went to the rector and asked him to verify the credentials of Monsieur de Custine. He received a letter back from his friend in the ministry assuring they were who they said they were and gave the news to Nicole.

The carpenter Biggers contracted made the repairs. As a favor to Biggers, he did the work almost at cost, and Nicole gave him what money she had except for three schillings. He agreed to wait for the rest owed him. At the end of two weeks as promised, Monsieur and Madame de Custine arrived in Standon and came directly to visit Nicole.

She was in the drawing room playing her own composition, *Unforgettable,* when Biggers came to her. "Lady Nicole, Monsieur and Madame de Custine to see you."

Nicole sighed and shrugged. "Please show them in."

Monsieur de Custine came across the room all smiles with his hand out. "Lady Waltham, how beautiful the music you were playing just now. Such a haunting melody. Please tell us you have changed your mind and will accept our humble offer."

"Yes, I have decided to accept. I'm embarrassed to ask, but because of circumstances beyond my control, I will need an advance on my salary."

"But, of course, mademoiselle. We were planning to give you an incentive to come with us. We will give you fifty English pounds. Does that satisfy your requirements?"

"Yes, Monsieur, I thank you. When must we

leave?"

"We planned to leave tomorrow morning for Seaford where we will board a ship to Dieppe. Is that acceptable?"

"Yes, I will be ready." Nicole saw her new employers out.

Before leaving, they gave her the fifty pounds and required her to sign a contract saying she intended to stay in their employment for one year and the terms for paying her.

When they left, Biggers came into the drawing room. "Biggers, I have been paid an inducement for going to the school. Please add this to the household fund. I will have to keep ten pounds out for my expenses. This will tide you over until the next installment of my allowance and finish paying for the repairs. As much as I hate to do it, I will have to let Mavis go, for I cannot take her with me or afford to keep her here."

"Do not worry, my lady. We will make do. Our needs are few."

"I'll go pack now. I promise to write to you often when I have an address. Don't say anything to Papa. I'll tell him after dinner." Nicole left the room hurriedly with her head bent. Once in the hall, she hastily brushed a tear away. Squaring her shoulders and holding her head high, she meandered up the stairs to her chamber.

****

Monsieur de Custine collected Nicole early the next morning. They left with a tearful Nicole waving good-bye to Biggers, Mavis, and Lord Waltham. Soon they were on their way to London.

"We will stay the night in London, and then on to

Seaford where we will stay overnight, but the next day we will be in Dieppe. Have you been to France before this, Lady Waltham?" Madame de Custine said.

"No, I have never been off English soil. I have longed to travel, but circumstances have not permitted it. I must ask a favor. My maiden name is Waltham, and my married name is Montagu. I do not wish to go by my title. Please just refer to me as Mademoiselle Waltham."

"As you wish, my dear. I admit we did not know what to call you. Since everyone in Standon called you Lady Waltham, we did too. We also checked your credentials and your character before we came to you with our offer." Madame de Custine patted Nicole's hand and smiled.

"Good, I'm glad we understand each other. Is Paris far from Dieppe?"

"It is nearly forty leagues, I believe. We shall take it in easy stages. It should take us three days to reach our school."

The de Custines passed the time talking on the subject of their school and their students from the best families of France. They talked so much that Nicole felt she knew them before she reached the school. After boarding the ship to Dieppe, Nicole stayed topside. With a heavy heart, she watched England disappear from view.

Madame de Custine came up on deck and stood by Nicole. "Are you getting your sea legs? I hope you will not be seasick."

"Yes, the sea air is very invigorating. I barely noticed the movement of the ship. Oh, look, could that little speck be Dieppe?" Nicole asked and pointed.

"Yes, I believe it is. Such a charming seaside resort. You know the English and Dutch navy destroyed it in 1694. The architect Ventabren rebuilt it in 1696. He designed it in the French classical style. It gives it a very distinctive appearance for a seaport and makes it a tourist destination."

"Oh, how lovely. Too bad we do not have the time to explore." Nicole stared as the Dieppe skyline came into view. Madame de Custine nodded and smiled. "Maybe during a school break we will come back, and I will show you the town."

It did not take long to load their baggage onto the de Custine's waiting coach and be on their way to Paris. Nicole watched the stunning countryside pass by her window. When they passed through a town, it was not so pleasant. The coach belonged to Monsieur de Custine, and it had a coat-of-arms containing the *fleur de lis* on the door. The people came out of their homes and shops to glare at them. Several people shook their fists as they passed, while others shouted. Nicole understood and spoke fluent French, but it was polite drawing room French. The words shouted at them, she guessed, were profanities. She asked her employers, but they shrugged it off as of no consequence. This did little to alleviate Nicole's fears.

The streets of Paris were not much different from the towns. People with scowls on their faces watched them passing on the streets. They shouted the same words as in the country at them as they passed by. To Nicole's relief, they reached the quiet avenue of the school. The school was a five story stuccoed building painted a pale yellow with cobalt blue shutters. A covered walkway led to the house next door. She guessed it was the home of the de Custines. She discovered the students were housed on the other side of the de Custine's residence. The teachers and Nicole would occupy the fifth floor of the school.

The next day, Nicole began teaching her students. Some were interested and did well, while others came because they were required. In the evenings, Nicole and the other teachers gathered for their evening meal.

"Everyone is so quiet. Has something happened?" Nicole said.

"I went into Paris yesterday to do some shopping. Everyone is talking about the tribunal and the guillotine. While I was there, I heard the chop of the guillotine repeatedly. The crowd cheered with each fall of the blade. I hurried back here. My parents want me to come home. I have requested Monsieur de Custine release me from my contract." The teacher stared around the room wide-eyed.

"I was talking to Madame de Custine this morning, and she said it's not safe to leave our compound. When I asked about the unrest, Madame turned very pale and hurried away," another said and nodded with pursed lips.

Everyone looked from one to the other around the table. Nicole almost jumped out of her chair when Monsieur de Custine entered the room. "I'm afraid I have bad news. I must request you not leave our compound for a while. I have been advised it isn't safe. Don't be alarmed; the *Gendarmerie* will protect us from the rebel rousers." Monsieur de Custine smiled and left before anyone could ask questions.

Nicole felt closed in as if she were a prisoner. She walked in the courtyard of the school to get her exercise but did not leave the compound. After she had been there a month, Monsieur de Custine called a meeting of the teachers.

"It is my responsibility to inform you that the parents of our students request they return home at once. There will be no more students after tomorrow; therefore, your services will no longer be required. Our students are leaving as we speak. Please, I must ask you to leave at once.

"The state of affairs with our government has become dire. Our beloved King Louis tried to flee with his family to Montmédy and request the protection of the Austrian government, but he was captured at Varennes. He will be returned to Paris. Tensions are such that it is dangerous to be in Paris just now. When conditions improve, I will recall you." The teachers looked at each other and then around the room before making a panic induced dash for the door.

"Mademoiselle Waltham, please stay behind." When the other teachers left the room, Nicole turned to Monsieur de Custine with worry written across her face. "I have your transportation papers. Everything is in order. I will accompany you to Dieppe and make certain that you are able to book passage to England. We will leave first thing in the morning. Do you understand?"

"Yes, monsieur, but surely this unrest will be settled. Has something happened, something you are not telling me?"

"Yes, I'm afraid so. The government is rounding up members of the aristocracy along with common criminals and putting them in prison for crimes against the state. I'm afraid it is not safe for you to remain. I tried to get to your consulate, but protesters surrounded it. Please go and pack. If it is possible to hire a coach, we will leave tonight. I can't take my personal coach. It has a coat-of-arms on the doors. We do not want to draw undue attention to ourselves. I fear for your safety and my own."

"Monsieur, you assured me this was not serious. I came on your guarantee."

"I swear to you I believed what I told you at the time. I find it hard to believe what has happened. We are a civilized people. How can this happen, mademoiselle? I'm at a loss. You must hurry and pack. We will leave as soon as a coach can be found." Monsieur de Custine turned away, shaking his head.

Nicole left the room in a daze. By the time she reached her chamber, she was out of breath, and her legs were too weak to hold her. She packed her meager belongings. Every so often, she looked out her window for reassurance the police were not at their gate.

She did not dare undress lest Monsieur de Custine call her to go. The darkness closed in around her. The gardener came to help her take her trunk to the main floor and left it on the side porch. She returned to her room and lay on her bed, but sleep did not come. Every time she closed her eyes, Brandon's face danced before her. She felt his arms around her and his kiss on her lips. The image faded and left her cold and empty. Even after she knew the relationship between Brandon and Lady Bennett, she still loved him. She tried to hate him, but could not.

Agitated, she stood and walked to her window to lean her head against the cool glass. Her attention was drawn to a commotion farther along the street. A mob of people was coming with torches and sticks. The crowd filled the street from side to side. She grabbed her reticule, cloak, and raced down the stairs, and across the walk to the residence of Monsieur de Custine. She pounded on their door until a maid let her enter. Monsieur and Madame came running into the hallway.

"My goodness, you're as white as a sheet. What is the problem, mademoiselle?" Madame de Custine said.

Out of breath, Nicole sat in the nearest chair with her hand on her chest. "There's a mob coming toward the school. What are we to do?"

Monsieur de Custine hurried to the window and turned around with an expression of horror written on his face. "Come quickly, we must go to the cellar. Lock the doors and windows." He called to the maid, but she did not answer. Nicole looked out the dining room window and glimpsed the servants running away.

With Nicole's help, the de Custines bolted the doors, and they all rushed to the cellar. The house became deathly silent. They listened to a banging on the door, then quiet again.

"I smell smoke. Are we on fire?" Nicole whispered.

Monsieur de Custine opened the cellar door without a sound and crept up the stairs to the main floor. He hurried back to the cellar and bolted the door again. Looking around unable to speak, tears shone in his eyes.

He choked and held onto his wife's hand. "Words fail me... The school is on fire. They are burning our beautiful school." He burst into tears.

Madame de Custine put her arm around him to

offer comfort. They waited, afraid to move. The sound of Monsieur de Custine's sobs covered the muffled sound of the crackling fire next door.

After several hours, the tramp of footsteps sounded on the floor above them. Sounds of furniture being over turned and glass breaking went on for what seemed a lifetime. Madame de Custine put her fist in her mouth to keep from crying out. The tramp of feet coming toward the cellar stairs made them turn toward the cellar door and stare without daring to breathe. Someone beat on the door. The three occupants of the cellar stood completely still as if they were statues. Madame and Monsieur hugged each other. Nicole stood by their side wide-eyed with a sinking sensation. The pounding on the door became heavier. Abruptly, the door split open and men rushed through carrying clubs and sticks. They grabbed Nicole and the de Custines. The angry men dragged them up the stairs and out into the street.

The mob held Nicole in a circle. Their bodies pressed around her making it difficult to breathe. The leader took the de Custines a short distance away, and from what Nicole could see, they held them in a heated discussion. The interrogators kept looking in her direction and pointing. She noticed the de Custines shake their heads until, after over an hour, Monsieur de Custine nodded yes. Madame stared at him, grabbed his arm, and shook her head from side to side. Soon the leader and the de Custines came back to where the crowd held Nicole prisoner.

"Mademoiselle Waltham, if that is your name, you will be held as a suspected spy and taken for further interrogation."

"Monsieur, I'm an English citizen and a music teacher. How can you accuse me of being a spy? I demand to be taken to the English consulate."

"You are not in a position to make demands. Besides, a spy would say that very thing. No, Citizen de Custine has confirmed his suspicions that you are a spy. You will be taken to the College du Plessis where you are to be held until further notice."

"No, no! You cannot do this. I'm an English citizen. Madame de Custine, please tell them." Nicole pleaded in vain.

Madame de Custine dropped her eyes unable to face Nicole.

Soon two tumbrels came with other prisoners in them. A man deposited Nicole in one tumbrel along with her scorched trunk. The overflowing cart left no place for her to stand comfortably. The prisoners pushed her tight against the side of the wagon, and the rough wood rubbed her side raw with every movement of the wagon or its poor human cargo.

Chapter Nine

The journey was hard on all the prisoners. There was no room to sit. Everyone stood and jostled against each other. The *Garde Nationale* escorted them to their destination with foot soldiers and soldiers on horseback. Along the way, people came out of their houses and yelled obscenities, threw stones, or whatever was handy. A sharp stone hit Nicole on the arm and tore her dress. She tried to staunch the blood with her handkerchief. The continuous jostling of the wagon and the prisoners made it difficult to stop the bleeding. She looked at the crowd following them. The looks on their faces said more than words that compassion did not rest in their hearts.

To make matters worse, it rained, and a freezing wind blew against the uncovered wagon. Although the distance was not far, they stopped so often that it was sometime in the early morning hours when Nicole and the other prisoners arrived at the College du Plessis, not far from the Conciergerie.

A large woman jostled against Nicole and pushed her into the side of the tumbrel. "This is the worst possible prison to be detained in. It is the waiting room for *Madame Guillotine*. Many enter here, but few leave in an upright position," she whispered.

"I have done nothing wrong," Nicole said in a low voice.

"I too have done nothing wrong, but it does not matter, citizen."

"You do not appear too concerned. Does this place not scare you?"

"How could it not, citizen, but I have a friend in the warden here." She winked at Nicole. "I have hopes of being transferred to another detention center. I will not be here more than tonight." She leaned in farther and favored Nicole with a smirk.

A sleepy warden came out to greet them after the men pounded on the door to the courtyard of the prison. He refused to accept the prisoners at first, citing an overcrowded condition. After much arguing, he agreed to accept them. Once inside the courtyard, the guards helped them from the wagon, then took them through several gates into another courtyard.

Nicole stared wide-eyed at the guards surrounding them. They appeared to be drunk with their slurred speech. They ogled the women as they came by and made rude gestures. A few were bare-chested, while others had their sleeves rolled up, and every one wore red caps on their heads. The men were large and well muscled. Their whole demeanor was menacing. Her heart sank as she watched the *Garde Nationale* leave them to the mercy of their jailers.

An adolescent girl grabbed hold of Nicole with a trembling hand and held on to her dress for protection. Several other young girls held onto Nicole's new friend so the young girls formed a circle around Nicole. One of the burly jailers stood before the group and read the list of prisoners. By the time he finished deciphering the writing on his record sheet amid asking for assistance in reading the names, it was mid-morning. At last, a guard led them to a large, airless, windowless room with only wooden benches or chairs to sleep or sit on. Nicole and the young girls collapsed on the benches and overflowed onto the floor.

"Mademoiselle, what are they going to do with us? The guards scare me. Did you notice the way they looked at us when we came in?" One young girl said with a tremor in her voice.

"So far we are merely suspects. The warden has not entered our names into the jail book. They will most likely divide us up and send us to the different detention centers. Try not to worry. If we stay together, we should be all right." Nicole tried to assure the girls while trying to convince herself.

"What is your name and where are your parents?"

"My name is Louise Ricain. I don't know where my parents are. They took them in another tumbrel, and I have not seen them since I lost sight of it." She sank to the floor in despair. Her shoulders trembled and soon the tears came.

Nicole knelt by her and held her, trying to comfort her as best she could. "My name is Nicole Waltham. Please have courage, little one. Try not to think the worst."

At last, the guards brought them a bucket of water to quench their thirst. After they had been there several hours, the keeper of the prison came and looked over the prisoners. "My name is Monsieur Haly. So far, you are not entered into the jail book. This house is for the public accuser, Monsieur Fouquier-Tinville. I keep anti-revolutionists here. Tomorrow you will learn of your destination."

Everyone tried to speak to him at once. When it

became Nicole's turn, she tried once again to make her accusers understand. "Monsieur, please, I am an English citizen. You have no right to keep me here. Please send word to the English consulate."

Nicole watched him sneer and turn away. He had not heard a word she said, or if he had, did not care. She collapsed on her bench with a vague uneasy feeling that everything was going wrong quickly. She raised her head and watched the guards drag her young friends away. Their cries rang in her ears long after the door closed. She tried to listen as the warden spoke again. Monsieur Haly signaled the men to bring in the prisoner's belongings.

Nicole did not bring a mattress or have the money to rent one. Her jailer took her to a cell, which must have been used at one time as a linen closet. It was about five feet by five feet. Her bed was a mound of straw with a much-used blanket over it. She soon learned she must share her cell with another woman, and only relaxed when the other woman turned out to be a nun, Sister Jeanne. Since neither woman was tall or fat, they managed to fit in by sleeping head to toe and angling their pallets. The straw smelled of body odor from former prisoners and vermin droppings.

After her jailer deposited her trunk outside the door of her cell, a guard bent over her and leaned in close to her ear. "Mademoiselle, when you are called before the warden, he will confiscate jewelry, clocks, scissors, or any money you have. You may keep fifty francs, no more. Hide what you can."

"Thank you. We are very hungry. Is it possible to get something to eat?" Nicole wanted to say more, to ask questions, but he disappeared.

She hid what little money she had—all one hundred and twenty francs she'd managed to save. By taking her scissors, she made a slit in the veneer of her trunk, and hid one hundred francs. After resealing the veneer, she surveyed her work. Her trunk was so damaged that another scratch did not stand out. She kept her last twenty francs in her reticule. If the guard was correct, the warden would let her keep that much. She did not know when she might need money.

The warden called her to his office while her trunk and room were searched. While she waited outside the warden's door, Commissioner Lefevre entered and slammed the door. It did not close properly, and Nicole listened to most of what he said. "What is going on here?" There was a moment of conspicuous silence. "I'm looking over the records of all the prisons and detention centers, and yours has the lowest death rate. You are not here to save these people. We are here to purge France of undesirables."

"But Commissioner, I have done nothing unusual. If less people die here than any other prison, it's not my fault."

"If I find you are giving unnecessary medical attention, you'll lose your head for your troubles." He spun around and left the room, slamming the door even harder.

After the search of her cell and trunk, the warden called Nicole into his office. With a frown on his face, he stared at her. "Mademoiselle, you are very poor. I will allow you to keep your twenty francs. After much deliberation, it has been decided that you will be entered into the jail book as an agitator and suspected spy."

"Monsieur, I am an English citizen. I have made no complaints nor have I stirred up trouble. I have submitted to your wishes. Please listen. These accusations are false. I am a music teacher, nothing more. Monsieur de Custine approached me in England and offered me this position. I did not request it. This is the first time I have been to Paris or France."

"Mademoiselle, I find this hard to believe. You speak French fluently, with a Parisian accent. You will remain under the rule of Monsieur Fouquier-Tinville. We will not discuss this again. It is out of my hands. If you had money, your food could be brought into you from a nearby bistro. Since you do not, then you will have to eat the standard prisoner's fare."

"Monsieur, please, I do not care what I eat. Please listen to what I'm saying. Yes, I speak French, it is true. An émigré in my village taught me French. She was from Paris. I also speak English. Why do you not listen and believe me?"

"Ah, citizen, obviously, you have a story to tell me. I don't believe it, and I do not think the committee will either."

Nicole watched his cold smile when he talked to her. He enjoyed the misery he dished out. Depressed and fearful of what lay in store for her, she waited for the guard to take her back to her cell.

The prisoners could mingle with the other prisoners during the day. The guards watched them from their position at the stairwells. At dinnertime, a guard took them to the mess hall in the basement.

"You can expect no more than one meal a day. It is the prison's responsibility to keep you alive, not fatten you up," their guard advised.

"You'll each be given a wooden bowl and spoon. Take good care of them. You'll not be issued another."

"What about a knife?" someone yelled from the back of the room.

"There will be no knives. Those are too dangerous for the likes of you." The guard thrust his head forward and stared around the room, daring anyone to speak before leaving the mess hall.

The prisoners lined up and stood waiting until the first group finished their meal so they could sit at the table. Weak from hunger, Nicole found it hard to stand. She looked around the room at the filth no one bothered to clean. She wondered why there was not more disease. Turning to Sister Jeanne, she saw the disgust in her eyes as she examined the table and peered around the room.

"This table has not been cleaned since it was put into use. It is sticky with spilled wine and goodness knows what else. I did not expect table clothes, but cleanliness is not too much to ask," Sister Jeanne whispered in Nicole's ear.

Soon a dirty individual brought in the prisoners' food. Nicole looked at her soup with revulsion.

"Mademoiselle, you must eat. You have to keep up your strength. Close your eyes and pretend it's something delicious," Sister Jeanne whispered across the table.

"But, sister, it is nothing but a bowl of warm water with lentils and something that looks like grass and sprouted potatoes trying its best to pass for soup. Horses are fed better." Nicole's eyes became large as she watched an unprovoked swirl in her soup. "Lor, there something moving in my soup. It's a cock roach!"

Nicole started to jump up from the table.

Sister Jeanne reached over and held her hand so she could not stand. "My dear, remove the cockroach. It will not go well if you complain and draw attention to yourself. You have to eat. I'm afraid we will get no better fare. They do not care if we live or die. Now be sensible. Sit there and eat as much as you can, and try not to become sick." Sister Jeanne reached across the table with her spoon, removed the cockroach, dropped it on the floor, and crushed it with the heel of her shoe.

Nicole swallowed hard, closed her eyes, and tried not to smell as she brought the spoon to her mouth. "Beggars would turn up their noses at this."

"Understand, mademoiselle, you are not at home. Do not give our keepers any trouble. Make do as best you can." Sister Jeanne put a finger to her lips.

Sometimes they dished out an inedible stew called ratatouille. Most of the time, Nicole found something such as hair or insects in whatever soup or stew they served. Too many days, she went away hungry. She lost weight. Her once perfectly tailored clothes now hung on her. She tried to keep upbeat, smile, and not complain. There were spies among the prisoners who tried to get other prisoners to say something that could be used against them at trial. She kept to herself and talked to a few people she considered friends. Most nights she cried herself to sleep and prayed to contract one of the diseases going around the prison and die. She felt dying from a disease was preferable to the guillotine.

At night, the guards locked everyone in their cells. She found it hard to sleep. They were told a guard would come if they needed help, but this never happened. She listened to people crying out in pain nightly, and no one ever came to help them. She tried to stuff pieces of cloth in her ears to shut out the noise. Every morning she awoke more tired than when she went to bed. The maddening monotony of her days dulled her senses until she could not think past her despair.

At dinnertime, the warden called the prisoners to attention. "Citizens, because of the crowded conditions, I have been advised by our doctor that to prevent the spread of disease you will take the open air for two hours every day. The women and children will go in the morning, and the men will go in the afternoon. You will go out rain or shine."

Nicole listened in dismay to yet another hardship, but the thought of seeing daylight again cheered her. A twelve-foot high wall surrounded the garden where they walked. The drains were bad and smelled with every puff of wind. There was one gate. It had a barred square in the middle, but a small piece of wood covered it. She noticed several of the women lingered by the gate, probably secreting messages out and in without their guards noticing.

Sister Jeanne came to stand beside Nicole. "Mademoiselle, pray for courage. Do not let them see your distress. You look so sad today. I fear they enjoy our suffering, and it will be used against you when you go to trial. To have compassion for your fellow man is a punishable offense."

Nicole tried to smile reassuringly at the nun. "Thank you, sister. I'm trying to keep my courage up, but it is hard in these conditions. At least we get to walk in the garden. Even overcast the outside is preferable to the closed in spaces of our prison. Just now, I was thinking of my home and my father. I wish I could tell him good-bye." Nicole's eyes teared up, so she wiped her eyes and tried to change the subject. "Do you notice the smell of sulfur? It is everywhere we go."

"Yes, they use it to treat the soldiers who have the itch." Sister Jeanne stared off in the distance, and her eyes filled with tears.

Nicole looked where she was staring and put her arm around Sister Jeanne's trembling shoulders. The sister stared fixedly and could not seem to take her eyes away from the chapel across the courtyard.

"I once said my prayers in that very chapel. Such beautiful stained glass and woodwork. They use it to store flour and armaments now. It is a sacrilege.

"I raised my voice in praises to the Lord in there. Now listen to the soldiers singing the songs of the Revolution as they are coming out. They have defiled the house of the Lord." Sister Jeanne shook her head as silent tears coursed across her wrinkled cheeks.

Nicole turned her away from the sight of the chapel and urged her to continue their walk so the guards would not notice them.

"Sister, what will you do when you are called before the tribunal? I have heard some of the priests and nuns have submitted to the tribunal. They were pressured into denouncing their God. If you do not, you will be sent to the guillotine."

"Mademoiselle, I hope my courage holds fast to my Lord. I cannot, nor will I, deny Him. I have pledged my life to His work. If it's His will, then I will die at peace as will the others of my order."

"Sister, pray that I have your steadfast courage

when it is my turn." She hugged Sister Jeanne and together they walked back to their cell.

Nicole collapsed on her pallet too tired to sit. She stayed in her cell and refused to go down to mess. She could not face another revolting meal served by an even more disgusting kitchen helper.

A knock at her cell door woke her. When she answered the door, she saw the daughter of Madame de Duras standing there.

"May I help you?"

"Mademoiselle Waltham, my mother wishes to invite you to dine with us. Will you come?"

"I will gladly come, thank you."

She followed the girl through the hallway to the stairs and up to the attic where Madame de Duras, her daughter, a niece, and a young son lived. They were cramped under the rafters of the house and could only stand fully in the center of the room. However, they had the means to buy food and have it brought in.

"Mademoiselle, please sit at our table and share our meal. I have watched you, and I see you getting weaker. You must eat to keep up your strength."

"I don't know how to thank you. Your kindness humbles me. It has been so long since I tasted edible food." Nicole's eyes filled with tears.

"It is nothing but simple peasant food, but it's well-prepared and tasty."

"Madame, it's a feast to me. Again, I thank you." Nicole set to eating the delicious food. Because of her near starvation condition, she could only eat a little of everything set before her, but the little she ate filled her for the first time since her incarceration. Before she left, Madame de Duras gave her chocolate for her breakfast the next morning.

When she returned to her cell, she found Sister Jeanne waiting there for her. "I trust you had a nice repast."

"Yes, I'm sorry you were not invited."

"I could not have accepted, my dear. My place is with the common man. There is always a chance I may render a service or be of help to a poor soul. Don't worry about me."

"I cannot help worrying. You have lost weight since your arrival as I have. Madame de Duras gave me enough chocolate for our breakfast. I hope you will share this little treat with me."

The sister smiled at this small kindness.

Nicole leaned on the doorframe and looked around at her fellow prisoners talking in the hallway. She listened to them for a while before turning back to the sister. "Something puzzles me. Since we are prisoners here whether with justification or not, I thought everyone would try to be polite and compassionate to one another. Instead, there are petty jealousies, lies, and gossiping. There are even spies trying to make us say something to be used against us."

"My dear, human nature does not change just because you are in prison. If anything, it intensifies. People who are kind will always be kind, and people who are selfish will continue to be."

Nicole started to say something else to the sister, but her eyes were closed and her lips moved silently in prayer. She sat on her pallet and prepared for sleep. Hours before the usual unlocking of their door, a guard came and told Sister Jeanne to get ready to go.

"Where are you taking her?" Nicole said.

"This does not concern you. Your turn will come soon enough."

"No, please do not take her. She has done nothing."

Nicole followed behind the guard until a second guard shoved her back, causing her to stumble and fall. "Mind your own business, citizen. You'll get your chance," he barked and snorted mockingly.

When the guard who had warned her to hide her valuables made his round before they locked the prisoners in for the night, she motioned discreetly for him to come to her. "Sir, please tell me. What has happened to my cell mate, Sister Jeanne?"

"I'm sorry, mademoiselle. Your friend and her entire order of fifteen nuns stood before the Revolutionary Tribunal this morning. They were told to deny God, admit to filling the people's heads with fairy tales, and submit to the council. The nuns refused. The tribunal found them guilty and sentenced them to death. They were executed by the guillotine this afternoon."

Nicole gasped and collapsed on her pallet. It was not unexpected news, but it shocked her just the same.

"They lined them up and paraded them one by one. I should not tell you, but you have asked. They dressed them in red shirts as if they were a murderer and marched them step by step to their fate. I'm sorry, but you will not see your friend again. If it gives you a little consolation, at the foot of the guillotine, the nuns knelt and renewed their vows. One by one, they went to their fate singing *Veni Creator Spiritus*. I cannot get the last nun's voice out of my head. It haunts me still, mademoiselle." He shook his head to clear it of unbidden thoughts.

"You will get a new cell mate tomorrow. They are

nice people. The warden wanted to put three ladies of the evening in with you as punishment for displaying distress over Sister Jeanne. Someone talked him into putting Madame Vivien and her niece in with you."

"Thank you for your kindness in telling me. I feared that must be your answer."

"Mademoiselle, do not let them see you sad or in tears. Those are considered punishable offenses."

"Yes, I know. Sometimes it's hard to be stoic. Monsieur, why do you keep this job? You are not like the rest of the guards."

"I have a wife and four children. My family has to eat. I do what I must." The guard nodded and hurried away.

Nicole closed her door. A short time later, a key turned in the lock. She fell on her pallet and hid her face in the blanket to muffle her sobs. She cried hot, salty tears for her friend and herself.

The next day Madame Vivien arrived with her niece. She glanced around the room and then back at Nicole. "I'm sorry, Mademoiselle Waltham, to be sent to you. Your cell is so small."

"Think nothing of it. We'll manage somehow." Nicole looked around her room.

In the middle of the afternoon, they heard the gates of the prison open and at least one carriage, perhaps two, come into the prison courtyard. Madame Vivien looked at Nicole with terror in her eyes. "They have come for prisoners. They did the same for my husband. He was killed, but I say he was murdered the next day by firing squad. They led him away just past my window. It was boarded up, but I watched him through a crack as he went to his death. I could not tell him good-bye." Tears fell at the thoughts of her husband.

Nicole put her arm around the lady's trembling shoulders and tried to console her. "Madame, you must have courage. Do not despair until you are sure they come for you. You could worry for nothing. You'll make yourself sick with worry, and you're frightening your niece."

"I know I'm a weak creature. We have suffered so much and yet there is more to come. We were housed with the women of the Rue de Chartres. You cannot believe what my niece's innocent eyes have seen. Such vulgar women, and such indecent language. One woman was insane. She attached herself to us, and we could not get rid of her. She followed us everywhere and kept patting my niece's head. I don't know why the woman fixated on us, but now that she is gone I miss her. The poor tortured creature died two days ago."

"Perchance, she found comfort in your company. There is so little kindness here. You have your niece. She must be a comfort to you."

"Mademoiselle, swear on your Bible if they take me away you will look after my niece."

"Yes, certainly, you have my word." Nicole hugged her and tried to ease her mind.

The chances of any of them leaving this place alive were slim to none. She too had lost hope. She read her Bible to occupy her time and put on a brave face before her keepers and her cellmates. With every knock on her cell door, panic gripped her heart. She expected to be sent before the tribunal at any moment.

## Chapter Ten

Brandon stood on the ship's deck and watched England disappear from view in the early-morning fog. He regretted his decision to come with each rise and fall of the ship. His friends had been planning this trip for over a year. He felt obligated to come. The unfinished business at home nagged at his mind.

He did not want to leave Nicole with their new understanding, but stubbornly, he came nonetheless. Every time his mind's eye saw her standing on the balcony throwing a kiss at him, it made him want to touch his cheek where he pretended her kiss touched him. He could not help but smile at the thought.

*What is she doing now? Does she miss me? Will she wait for me to return, or will she turn to another? Is my heart safe in her keeping?*

His hand hurt. He looked at the death grip he held on the rail at the thought of another taking his place.

Marchand said from behind him, "What are you doing up here? We have an excellent game going in the lounge. Come, let's pass the time until we make Amsterdam."

Brandon nodded and followed his friend. They played cards long into the night over port and cigars. Brandon's mind was not on the game, but he won more times than he lost. He had the devil's own luck with cards, as he always had.

He left the game in the early-morning hours and made his way up on deck. The invigorating breeze tousled his hair and cleared the cobwebs from his mind. The breeze blew away the cigar smoke and sobered him. While his friends slept well into the morning, he stood on deck and watched Amsterdam come into view.

They disembarked and found a conveyance to take their entourage of valets and baggage to a nearby inn. A hired guide and coaches assisted the four friends on their way the next day. Their first stop, Flanders, and then on to Innsbruck where they had their agent hire a hunting lodge. To pass the time, they hunted and rock climbed during the day. At night, Brandon's friends went into the village to drink and carouse with the local pub's *frauleins*. Brandon went with his friends to enjoy the home-brewed beer but left before closing time. This had gone on for two weeks. Brandon's intemperate friends began to irritate him as the days wore on.

On yet another cloudless, moonlit night, Brandon mounted his horse a little unsteadily and headed home alone. He fell into bed and a fitful sleep. During the night, he sensed movement in his bed and stirred. Something bumped up against him, and arms wrapped around him. A slow hand made its way across his stomach and slowly down his thigh.

"Nicole," he called drowsily. He turned on his side and put arms around the person in his bed, pulling her to him. His hand ran over unfamiliar curves.

Brandon jerked awake when he realized it could not possibly be Nicole. He jumped out of bed, and the room spun around. He grabbed hold of the bedstead to steady himself.

"What the devil? Who's there?" He lit a candle and

surveyed the attractive *fraulein* in his bed. "What are you doing here?" He tried to shake the beer and sleep from his foggy mind.

"Your friend sent me. He said you were lonesome. Does Olga not please you?"

"What…good Lord…yes, yes, you're pleasing to the eyes."

She stood, moved her unclothed body shamelessly around the bed, and stood before Brandon. She put her arms around his neck and brought his lips down to hers. Stunned, he kissed her back before he had time to think. When realization dawned, he shoved her away from him as if she were hot. He wiped his hand across his mouth and stared at her.

"Come back to bed where it's warm. You'll be lonesome no more. Who is this Nicole that haunts your dreams? I promise to make you happy. Forget her." She sat on the bed and patted the space beside her. "Come to bed, Englishman."

Brandon all of a sudden realized he had no clothes on either and hastily put on a robe. "I'm afraid there's been a mistake. I do not require your…er…services. You're very attractive, but I have a wife. I'm sorry for wasting your time, but I must ask you to leave. Here let me give you this." He shoved enough money at her to cover her unused services and trouble.

"Englishman, everyone has a wife. It is nothing to worry over. She's not here. I am here to make you forget. Come to bed and let us enjoy the pleasures of the night. Olga's very good in bed." She stood and moved closer to Brandon.

Brandon moved a step away from her outstretched hand.

"*Fraulein* Olga, I love my wife. I don't want to forget."

"Bah, your wife will never know."

"But I'll know," Brandon drawled as if he could not believe what he was saying.

"Then why are you here?"

"I've been asking myself that same question this entire trip. Please, I've given you money for your time. I'm sorry your time has been wasted. Do you have a way home?"

"No, I did not expect to go home before the morning."

"While you're getting dressed, I'll have someone bring a cart round to drive you back to the village. Once again, I'm sorry." He hurried out of the room, relieved to be away from temptation.

After Olga left, Brandon made his way to the drawing room and the liquor cabinet. Wide-awake and wondering what to do next, he poured a drink and set the bottle on the table near a chair. Just a short year ago, he would have jumped at the chance to bed one such as Olga. She was beautiful and attractively endowed. He could not shake the unfamiliar feeling of guilt. Puzzled, he knew he had done nothing wrong, but still he felt guilty.

A short time later, Marchand came into the drawing room. "Brandon, what are you doing here?" He stood back and smiled at his friend. "Is there anything to drink?" He continued to rummage around a cabinet.

"Are you responsible for the lump in my bed?"

"You are strangely reluctant to partake of the local talent. Not the Brandon of old who never met an attractive wench he didn't want to bed. Marriage has dulled your taste for, shall we say, adventure. I thought you might need a push." He grinned and poured himself a drink.

Brandon jumped up and strode toward his friend. "I don't need your help. I can handle my love life by myself."

"But I think you do need my help, my lad. Before you lose your temper on me, let me explain." He took a step backward while holding his hand palm up between him and Brandon. "It's obvious you're not happy. We're doing the same things we did when we were eighteen, and it is not very satisfying, is it? Strange to say this, but I don't find it very satisfying either. I sent the beautiful Olga to give you a push in the right direction."

Brandon shook his head and sank into the nearest chair. He poured himself another drink but let it sit on the table. "I don't understand. You're not making much sense. I don't know what's wrong, but I wasn't even tempted by the *fraulein*. I gave her money and sent her home," he said with a sheepish grin.

"Oh, Brandon, Brandon, my poor besotted friend. You've fallen for the oldest trick in the book. You fell in love with your wife. It's unheard of in our circle." Marchand slapped Brandon on the back and chuckled.

"I didn't mean to fall in love, but I'm painfully aware of the fact I did. I can't imagine my life without Nicole. You're right. I find this drinking and carousing boring. Well, Mother Marchand, what do you suggest I do?"

"I think you need to take one of our coaches and head back the way we came. We'll hire another. Go find the sweet Nicole and make love to her. Have a house full of little ones, and I'll be their doting surrogate uncle. Quite frankly, if she had a sister, I'd go with you."

Brandon smiled for the first time on the trip. "What of the others? What will they think? I hate to go off and leave you after we planned this trip for so long."

"Go, leave the explaining to me. No one will fault you. We're still friends, we'll still come for the birding at Worthington, and we'll still envy you your good fortune in finding Lady Montagu." He gave Brandon a friendly smile and a handshake.

That morning at first light, Brandon left Innsbruck and headed back to Amsterdam. The roads were rutted and rocky. Once out of a village, no more than a couple hundred feet put him in a thick forest with just a trail to follow to the next village. Two weeks later, he arrived in Amsterdam. He had to wait two more days before he could book passage back to England. It was the better part of three weeks when he entered Grosvenor Square. He arrived in the late evening, disturbing the peace of his caretakers, Edna and Don Dicks.

Dicks opened the door and stood there with his mouth gaping. "My lord, we didn't expect ye so soon. The house is in sheets." He stood in the doorway staring at Brandon and scratching his head.

"May I come in, or must I camp on the doorstep?" Brandon tried not to smile at Dicks' confusion.

Dicks opened the door wider and stepped aside. "Sorry, my lord, I'm dull witted this evening. It was the surprise of seeing you there on the doorstep. Everyone left for Worthington Park except for Lady Montagu."

"Is Lady Montagu still here?"

"No, my lord, she left with Lord Fleetwood for

Standon. My lord, will you be staying long?"

His hopes dashed, he felt let down and disheartened. Hearing that she left with Lord Fleetwood did nothing to lighten his mood. "No, I'll leave on the morrow. Please have your good wife make my room ready and find something for me to eat. Stephens is seeing to the baggage. He'll be here before long."

Dicks bowed, and Brandon made his way to the library. Soon Dicks came in and laid a fire in the fireplace before removing the dust covers. The chilly, damp room warmed. Brandon sank into his chair and watched the flames lick the logs. He felt oddly depressed. He knew Nicole had left for what he thought was Worthington, but he expected to find her here, just as he had left her. The sleep still in her eyes, her hair tussled, and waving good-bye.

*Why did she go to Standon?*

Stephens brought him a light supper of vegetable barley soup and crusty bread with a tankard of ale. "When you're finished, my lord, your room is ready. If there's nothing else, I'll retire myself."

"Thank you, Stephens. There's nothing else."

Before he finished his supper, there was a knock on the door. He heard Dicks talking to someone, and then hurried footsteps came across the floor to the library door. Without knocking, Dicks entered. "My lord, a Lord Bedlington to see Lady Montagu. I have told him she isn't here, but he insists. He stepped through the door before I could close it."

"Thank you, Dicks. I'll take care of it." Brandon strode into the hallway ready for battle. He glimpsed Bedlington with his back to him. Upon seeing his tall, haughty backside, he was irritated that much more.

"Bedlington, what are you doing here?"

Lord Bedlington turned around and found Brandon advancing toward him. "I, uh, I came to see Lady Montagu. I did not expect you to be home. The last I heard you were away on the continent."

"Obviously, I have returned. As Dicks told you, Lady Montagu is not here. I might ask you what you're doing here. Who told you I was out of town?"

"Why Lady Bennett. Who else? She told me over a hand of *Belote*."

"So you just decided to visit at this late hour, even after I told you to stay away." Brandon moved in closer. His eyes never left Bedlington. "I explained the consequences in Brooks if you continued this game, as you call it. Choose your weapon," Brandon ground out. By this time, he was standing toe to toe with Bedlington.

"You can't be serious. Here and now! In your house?"

"Why not? It's private, and any blood is easily cleaned up on the marble floor. If you won't choose, then I'll choose for you." Brandon's eyes narrowed as he stared at Bedlington.

"Have it your way. I choose swords." He smirked and crossed his arms over his chest. Brandon knew Bedlington considered himself an excellent swordsman. He had expected him to choose as he had. Brandon rarely dueled with swords. Pistols were more in his line. However, either way, he had never lost.

"Dicks!" Brandon shouted. "My sword case."

His words echoed off the walls of the townhouse. Dicks came on the run with the sword case. Brandon opened it and offered it to Bedlington to choose first.

Bedlington chose and then moved away, never taking his eyes off Brandon. He tried the sword out with a few practice lunges and appeared satisfied. He smirked a wolfish grin at Brandon.

Before beginning, they both removed their boots and coats. They brandished their swords to get the feel of them and each man moved warily around the foyer. As they moved around the room, they watched each other as a hawk watches its prey. The candlelight played off the metal of their swords and reflected the hatred for each other in their eyes.

They saluted with their swords.

"*En garde!*" Brandon called.

The sound of clashing swords reverberated throughout the silent house. Each man parried and thrust, looking for an opening. In the still atmosphere, their breathing could be heard along with the soft padding of their feet on the marble floor. Brandon feinted, and Bedlington lunged to find he had missed once again. Brandon scored a hit high on Bedlington's arm, but it angered him more than hurt him. Like an angry bull, the nick spurred him on. He tried to score his own hit, moving past Brandon's guard. Brandon knew he carried a small knife for use in close up fighting and considered this the trick of a coward. He watched Bedlington's free hand and kept his distance while forcing him to continue the fight with his sword. Bedlington failed to score on him, although he tried time and time again.

They continued the fight until both were tiring and sweat rolled down their faces. Brandon decided to end this one way or the other and pressed his attack. They crossed swords and pushed each other until they were at an impasse. The two men broke away. Bedlington was getting his breath in gasps.

Bedlington tried to feint in high carte, but Brandon could tell from his eyes that he planned to thrust low tierce. When he started to thrust, Brandon's sword caught him high on his shoulder, cutting through his clothing and coming out the other side. He pulled his sword out and Bedlington stumbled back, sinking to the floor.

"Dicks, see what the damage is and if this scoundrel will live. First, bring me a tankard of ale," Brandon yelled.

Dicks handed Brandon his ale while Mrs. Dicks hurried to Lord Bedlington's side. Dicks knelt by Bedlington and looked up at Brandon. "He's bleeding all over the floor, my lord. The missus can stop the bleeding. He'll be weak and sore, but he'll live. Don't appear ye touched his vitals." Dicks turned back to Bedlington and handed his wife what she needed for the bandages.

"Too bad. Dicks, find a hack or a sedan chair and have them take him home." Disgust oozed from each word.

Brandon walked over to where Bedlington lay pale and still. He glared at him before he spoke. "I advise you to call a doctor when you return home. I hope I have made one point plain, so even *you* can understand. If you ever darken my door again or attempt to talk to my wife in anything but a passing pleasantry, I will make it my business to let your father-in-law know what you've been doing. From what I hear, he has a temper worse than mine. Your wife, Lady Cordelia, is the apple of his eye. Is that plain enough?"

Bedlington nodded and closed his eyes. A short time later, Dicks returned with a sedan chair and soon had him on his way home.

Brandon stood watching Mrs. Dicks cleaning the floor. He turned to Dicks. "How many times has that man been here while I've been away?" There was no mistaking the anger he still had in his eyes.

"My lord, he's never been in the house, but he came one day while you were away. Jenkins was still here. He said Lady Montagu had just started down the hall to the small sitting room when Jenkins answered the knock. He opened the door and found Lord Bedlington on the doorstep. Lady Montagu recognized his voice and shook her head at Jenkins.

"Lord Bedlington asked to speak to Lady Montagu, but Jenkins told him she had left for the country. He tried to argue and put his foot in the door, but Jenkins closed the door in his face before he entered. Her ladyship told Jenkins never to admit him."

Brandon sensed the strain and anger leave his body. "Thank you. That will be all. I think I'll try to eat my supper again. Please reheat it for me?"

"Very good, my lord."

A short time later, Dicks brought the reheated supper to Brandon. Before he could finish his soup, there was another knock on the door. Yet again, Dicks entered the library.

"My lord, so sorry to disturb you again, but Mr. Pettigrew insists on seeing you."

Brandon cursed under his breath. "Will I never be left in peace? Very well, send him in and take these dishes away."

Mr. Pettigrew came through the door hesitantly and

looking a little flustered. He looked back as he came through the door. "My lord, is that blood in the hallway?"

"Yes, a minor household accident. We had to remove a rat that mistakenly thought it had found a home here." Brandon took a deep breath trying to regain his composure. "How may I help you, Mr. Pettigrew?" Brandon motioned for him to have a seat.

"My lord, I'm sorry to bother you at this late hour. I noticed the light and stopped. I hoped to see Lady Nicole. Something unexpected has come up, and I'm not sure how to handle it."

"My wife is not here. She's in Standon. As you can see, the house is closed. I arrived a short time ago. I'm leaving for Standon in the morning. Is there something I could help you with or a message I could deliver for you?"

"This is most troublesome. I had hoped to speak with Nicole before I journeyed to Standon. I hope you understand that I never, as a rule, discuss my client's finances with anyone, but I find myself in a quandary. If Nicole is in Standon, then I am at a loss as to what to do."

"Has something happened to Lord Waltham?"

"You might say that. Oh, oh, it's fantastic news in one way and awful in another. You remember that Lord Waltham invested crazily in everything that crossed his path before he lost his fortune. Well, he bought a controlling interest in a diamond mine in South Africa. It turned out there were no diamonds, but the lucky buggers have struck gold. Not just any gold vein, but what is believed to be the richest strike in fifty years. I've never seen the like. Lord Waltham could fall on his face in the mud and come up with a plum. His fortunes are made yet again."

"I don't understand. Why is this bad?"

"Since his breakdown, he has not been himself. I don't want to tell him the good news and then have him go off the deep end again. It has been several months since I've seen him, and I wanted to check on his mental health. I intended to ask Nicole before I approached him with the news, how we might handle the income which has started coming into my office."

"Yes, I see what you mean. The last time we were in Standon, Lord Waltham was in excellent spirits and on the road to recovery. This new found wealth will take a burden off Nicole's shoulders and provide him with the means to hire more help. If I might suggest, why not put the money in trust with executors to administer the money, so he does not enter into dire straits again. He could be given a generous allowance, and his bills sent to the trust."

"Yes, that is what I had in mind. I'm so glad you agree. I'll go to Standon on the morrow and talk to him about doing just that.

"Before I leave, I need to tell you something I found out. You and Lady Montagu were not the only ones trying to find Lord Waltham. Before you came to town, Lord Bedlington was inquiring after him. He said he wanted to buy up Lord Waltham's shares in the mine. I told him they were worthless. He intimated that he planned a trip to South Africa, and he wanted to have something to investigate while he was there. He offered to buy the shares at a tenth of their original value. As it stands now, the shares are worth fifty times what Lord Waltham paid for them. At the time, we were not sure if Lord Waltham was alive or dead. I advised him I couldn't do anything until we knew for certain, and then the shares were Nicole's to dispose of as she thought proper."

"Did he know that gold had been found instead of diamonds?"

"That is just what worries me. Two months after he left my office, I received the good news. I don't know why, but this made me uneasy. By some means, I think he knew."

"You need not worry. I don't think Lord Bedlington will bother Nicole or her father any more. Thanks for telling me. That makes a few things plain to me."

"Thank you, Lord Montagu. That takes a load off my mind. I'll bid you a goodnight. Sorry to have disturbed you."

Mr. Pettigrew left, and Brandon ambled up the stairs to his bedchamber mumbling, "So that was Bedlington's game. He knew about the gold all along, and the scoundrel planned to fleece Nicole and Lord Waltham."

The dust covers were removed, a blazing fire set, and his bedchamber warming pleasantly. The fire did nothing to warm Brandon. He longed to have Nicole's arms around him, her body pressed against him, and the warmth of her tender love. Without a will of his own, he could not stop himself from entering through the adjoining door and walking into her bedchamber. Her jasmine perfume still lingered in the air of the closed chamber.

He walked around her bed and sat on the edge. He glanced around the room and noticed the door on her wardrobe had come unlatched. He stood to close it. Upon opening the doors wider, he saw the clothes Madame Fortier made for her. Her old clothes were gone. Puzzled, he went back to his room and tried to sleep. Sleep did not come until almost daylight. He awoke a short time later feeling worse than when he went to bed.

He opened his eyes to Stephens moving around the room. "Get my baggage ready and have the coach stand by. We're going to Standon first."

"Yes, my lord," Stephens said and bowed. He left the room after he laid Brandon's clothes out for the trip.

Once dressed, Brandon made his way down the stairs. He came up short when he noticed Horus at the foot of the stairs. He hurried to where he stood with a smile on his face. Horus turned around with a scowl, and Brandon found himself propelled backward by a staggering right hand. He tripped on the stairs and sat abruptly on a step, rubbing his jaw and staring up at Horus with his mouth open in bewilderment.

"Stand and fight, you bounder," Horus called with his fists up and his legs posed in an aggressive stance.

"Horus, what's gotten into you? I do not want to fight you. What has happened since I've been gone? Has the whole world gone crazy?" Brandon rubbed his jaw. "I didn't know you had it in you. What's this concerning?"

"As if you didn't know. Just so you know that facer was for Nikki."

Brandon stood with his hands palm up in front of him. "Back off, Horus, and tell me what this concerns. I don't know what I've done. I haven't been home a whole day. Believe me when I say I'm in no mood for melodrama."

"You've broken her heart. That's what you've done, you libertine. Now stand and fight like a man."

Brandon found it hard not to laugh. Horus was a head shorter than him and at least fifty pounds lighter. He resembled a banny rooster more than a seasoned tough. "How have I broken her heart? I came back early because I had to see her. For that matter, how did you know I was here?"

"Uncle Charles wrote me a letter concerning Nikki. I came back to town as soon as I received it. Not knowing what to do next, I was out walking, trying to decide, when I saw you arrive in your carriage. I walked around just thinking some more, then I decided I had to come here this morning and have it out with you."

"That doesn't explain why you're angry and why Nicole is heartbroken."

"Maybe you should ask your mistress. Is she here, or didn't she come back with you?" Horus looked around the room and up to the balcony.

"What mistress? You'd better explain yourself."

"Don't act as if you don't know. Everyone knows Lady Bennett was your paramour before Nikki, and it appears you never stopped that liaison."

"I don't know why I should discuss this with you. This is something between Nicole and me. For your information, I cut ties with Lady Bennett before I married your cousin."

"Ha! Another lie."

"Explain yourself, or I'll forget your Nicole's cousin and thrash you to within an inch of your life." Brandon advanced on Horus until he was standing less than a foot from him.

Horus stood his ground before Brandon's menacing stare. "Nikki and I saw you go into Lady Bennett's house after you came to town for the season. You can't deny it. We both saw you and...*her.*" A look of disgust crossed Horus's face.

"After we came to town?" Brandon said shaking his head. A light dawned. "Yes, you doubtless did, but I was not there for the reason you thought. I received a note from Lady Bennett requesting I come. She had some distressing overages. I agreed to pay the bills she had, but I advised her it was the last time."

"Very neatly said. At three balls I know of, Lady Bennett came up to Nikki and insisted on talking to her. She embarrassed and insulted Nikki."

"She what?"

"I know it to be true because I was there and saw the look on Nikki's face. There were tears in her eyes."

"Horus, I swear I didn't know, or I would have put an end to it. Please believe me; I'm more surprised than anyone to realize I love Nicole. It started out as a marriage of convenience, but it has turned into something much more. I came back to tell her and make things right between us."

"Is that how you show your love, by taking your mistress on your trip?"

"No one went on the trip except my four friends. Who told you different?" He advanced on Horus, his face heated up and his temper rose several degrees.

"Lady Bennett came to Nikki and said she was meeting you in Germany. And if that wasn't enough, she knew the conditions of the will. She thanked Nikki—*thanked* her, mind you—for helping you and her with your romantic rendezvous." Horus's finger stabbed the air, punctuating his words.

"Look, Horus, I know this looks shocking, but I think I can explain. Nothing she said is true. I'm at a loss. I can't understand why she deliberately lied. However, I think I know where she got her information. Lord Wharton likes to play cards, and he plays deep. He often goes to Lady Bennett's to play. A few nights before we left, he played at Lady Bennett's and drank too much. Lady Bennett kept bringing him wine and asking questions. He told me he thought he had been indiscreet but couldn't remember what she asked him, or what he said. He thought it had something to do with our trip. That has to be the only way she found out.

"I love Nicole. That's the only reason I came back. I'll go to Standon right away and make this right."

"You can't. Nikki's not there." Horus collapsed on the stair steps next to Brandon, shaking his head.

"Has she gone to Worthington? That's even better." Brandon was still confused by Horus's manner.

Horus put his head down and shook it from side to side. When he looked up, there was the strain of worry in his eyes.

"She's in neither place. That's why Uncle Charles wrote to me. She's in France."

"France! Why has she gone there? It's not safe. The last I heard, the streets of Paris ran red with the blood of aristocrats."

"Because of the damage from a storm, there had to be repairs to the cottage. It took all the money she had and then some. Monsieur and Madame de Custine came along and offered her a position in Paris at a girl's school to teach music. She received a letter from the

French ambassador assuring her it was safe and there were just a few rebel rousers making the news. The letter said the *gendarmes* would soon have everything settled. She agreed to go.

"It wasn't as dangerous as it is now when she left. But after she arrived, things became dire. She wrote to Uncle Charles that she was coming home. That was the last letter he had from her.

"The only thing we know for sure is that the school burned to the ground, and Nikki is a prisoner somewhere in Paris. It sounds as if they suspect her of being a spy. We received this news from the French ambassador. He refused to give us any more information."

Brandon grabbed Horus by the shoulders. "Get your gear and meet me back here in an hour. My yacht is moored off Dover. We're going to France."

"Won't they think we're spies as well? From what I hear, brother is going against brother and father against son. You can't trust anyone."

"I don't doubt if we're caught, death will be fast in coming. If you'd rather not, no one will think any less of you. I know a few people there that can help us. People I can trust with my life without hesitation. Now hurry if you're coming. I want to leave as soon as possible."

"Yes, yes, you can count on me. I'll be back as soon as I can." Horus gripped Brandon's hand and shook it enthusiastically. He waved and ran through the door headed for his chambers.

In the meantime, Brandon composed a letter to Lady Bennett. He explained to her the consequences of speaking to or concerning Nicole again in no uncertain terms. He sealed the letter and had Dicks have a messenger deliver it into her hands personally.

Before he had too much time to consider what he was undertaking, he checked his pistols and took money from his safe. He drew his hand away when it touched the velvet jewelry cases. She left her jewelry and her clothes. Everything he had bought her. This realization saddened him more than anything else so far.

A short time later, a knock on the door caused him to look up. He slammed the safe door and turned around just as Horus entered. Dicks and Stephens packed the coach, and they were on their way. Neither occupant of the coach spoke until they reached Dover. Each had his own thoughts and worries. The lovely scenery passed by them in a blur.

They arrived too late to sail with the evening tide. The fog coming in obscured the coastline. A freezing rain came down in torrents and forced them to book rooms at the Moon and Sixpence Inn.

"We can't stay here long. Every minute counts against Nicole. Surely this weather will let up by morning." Brandon stared out to where the sea should be and shook his head.

There was one setback after another. His head hurt thinking of Nicole and the distress she must be going through. He shook his head and tried to smile when he noticed Horus watching him with concern showing across his face and in his posture.

## Chapter Eleven

The first thing everyone noticed as they entered the Moon and Sixpense coffee room was a huge fireplace at its center with gleaming brass above the hearth. Years of service dulled the oak walls to a mellow hue. Blue Spanish tiles covered the floor, and the ceiling had oak beams and rafters darkened with age adding to the façade of an old, prosperous establishment. Several polished oil lamps stationed around shed their light into the room.

The rotund, balding innkeeper came through the door carrying tankards of ale for his guests. He wore a dark brown waistcoat and light brown corduroy breeches with tan worsted stockings. His low-heeled leather shoes had brass buckles.

"My lord, your rooms will be ready shortly." He grinned at Brandon and rubbed his hands together. "Listen to that rain beating against the windows. It's still coming in from the east. Not fitting to be out tonight. What a time we're having. My inn's full. Not that I mind the custom, mind you, but no one can sail with the storms we've been having."

Brandon glanced around the room at the fishermen laughing and talking at the top of their voices. Servant girls scurried to each of the tables with trays laden with the innkeeper's best home-brewed ale. Smoke from the fishermen's clay pipes settled over the room in a blue cloud. Occasional raindrops traveled down the chimney and sizzled on the glowing logs sending a belch of smoke into the room.

"Do you see any let-up in the storm? It's urgent we sail with the morning tide."

"I don't see how it can keep up at the rate it's been raining. The whole town is gonna wash away. Ol' Jonah over there in the corner playing dominoes said the rain'll let up pretty nigh onto midnight. He's a regular human barometer, I reckon. He says his bones tell him the weather. Strangely enough, he's hardly ever wrong." The innkeeper looked around the room and hurried away.

A servant girl set a fish stew in front of Brandon and Horus. They were just finishing their meal when the door of the coffee room flew open, and a man fell through the door out of breath. "Help...I've run over a small skiff with my fishing boat. I...pulled them out of the water, but they're barely alive...near enough to drowned." He collapsed in a heap on the floor. The entire room jumped into action. They stepped over him, grabbed their rain gear, and ran out the door. The innkeeper helped the fisherman to a chair and gave him a tankard of ale.

The rescuers soon returned with a woman and a small child. They were soaked to the bone. The woman's matted hair had bits of seaweed clinging to it, and sand fell out of the pockets and folds of her dress when they laid her on the tavern bench. She did not open her eyes. It was hard to tell if she was breathing or not. The small child was in much the same condition. Both appeared to be tenuously clinging to life. The woman's eyelids fluttered. She opened her eyes wide, stared around the room, and tried to speak to her rescuers in French. No one understood her. The men looked from one to the other wondering what to do. Brandon stepped forward and translated.

"She says she escaped France in a small row boat. They've been at sea for three days. Her name is Lady Manon De Sarmoise, and the child is her daughter, Alaina.

"Innkeeper, I think it best if you sent for the doctor. Do you have a room for them? They're exhausted and need a place to rest."

"Yes, my lord, but where am I to put them? Every one of my rooms is full. I even have a guest staying in my daughter's room."

Brandon looked at Horus, and he nodded his head in understanding. Brandon turned to the innkeeper. "My room is larger. Move Lord Fleetwood's things into my room, and they can have his room. Does your wife have any dry clothes for these people?"

"I'll take care of it right away." The innkeeper hurried out of the coffee room.

Brandon tried to reassure the lady by telling her a doctor was coming, and a room made ready for her and her daughter. She appeared to be young, perhaps in her early twenties, with blonde hair and blue eyes and sharp features. Her face and her daughter's were gaunt from starvation. Her daughter was very young, maybe in her fourth year. She was small and delicate, with blonde hair and big blue eyes. She lay unmoving on a bench near her mother.

Lady De Sarmoise grabbed Brandon's hand and clung to it as if her life depended on it. Her eyes were closed, but her lips moved as if in prayer. She crossed herself and opened her eyes. Horus poured her a glass of wine and helped her to drink. This helped revive her. She sat up and released her grip on Brandon, stared across the room, gasped for breath, and fell against Brandon. She closed her eyes and lay so still, Brandon feared she had died. Her eyelids flickered in her pale countenance, and he sighed with relief. The wife of the innkeeper came and had the men carry the two travelers up to Lord Fleetwood's room. Brandon heard the landlady tell one of the serving girls to bring broth for them.

The next morning at first light, there was a knock at Brandon's door. The innkeeper came to Brandon with a request. "My lord, I'm reluctant to bother you, but would you be so kind as to visit our French guests? We can't understand their foreign talk, but I think she wants to speak to you."

"Yes, I'll be glad to talk to her. Before I go, I will write a letter to the French Émigré Society in London and advise them to render aid to these people. I am assuming they have no money. I will leave this pouch of coins with you for their care. If more is needed, I'll settle with you when I return."

"You're most considerate, my lord." The innkeeper peered into the pouch. His blue eyes shone, and he smiled at Brandon. "This will do nicely."

Brandon went to Lady De Sarmoise's room and knocked.

"*Entré.*"

He stepped in and crossed to the hearth where she sat in a chair by the fire, bundled in a quilt. "Madame, should you be out of bed? You have had a harrowing experience."

"I'm much better, thank you, but my daughter is not doing as well. The doctor says she will recover with rest and good food. I understand I have you to thank for our room."

"Think nothing of it. Lady De Sarmoise, I'm sorry, but I must ask where your husband is. Was he in the boat with you?"

She shook her head and stared into the fire. "The guillotine claimed his life. He hid us in the chateau. When they searched, they did not find us. My husband dressed as a fisherman and made his way to the coast. He procured passage for us. It cost two thousand crowns to secure our safety. That was every *sou* we had. The government confiscated our money, our properties, everything." She shrugged and gazed at Brandon with the saddest eyes he had ever seen.

"When he came back for us, someone recognized him and turned him in. They brought him before the Revolutionary Tribunal and sentenced him to death. Before he died, he sent word to us about the fishing boat taking us to England. An old family retainer helped get us to the boat.

"We made our way to the ship in the dead of night. They took us on board, and we thought we were saved at last. The boat set sail at first light but had to turn back because of a terrible storm. When we returned to port, the *Garde Nationale* searched our boat. The captain had foreseen this might happen and stowed us in a crate with a false compartment. There was no room to move. We could barely breathe. I thought we would die.

"Thankfully, they didn't find us, and we set sail again, but half way across the channel, the captain and crew became scared. I'm not sure why. They put us in a small boat and set us adrift. We drifted for three days without food or water. I thought death waited for us in the open sea. If not for my daughter, I might have given up and welcomed death. I had to keep trying to reach shore for her sake. With the fog and no visibility, I didn't know where we were, and then the fishing vessel ran over us." She put her hand to her mouth and shook her head.

"I don't know how we survived. Monsieur, what's to become of us?" She looked away from Brandon as silent tears coursed down her cheeks. "We have no money, no family. Everything is lost. I will never see my Armand again, or my dear mother and father. My parents were guillotined before my husband. There were never two kinder or gentler people in the whole world. No one had a word to say against them, but that did not save them. Their only faults were titles of nobility and land."

"Try not to despair, madam. I gave a letter to the innkeeper to be posted to the French Émigré Society in London. I'm sure they will look after you, but in case they are delayed, I have left money with the innkeeper to take care of your needs until someone from the society can help you."

"Monsieur, you are too kind. However, I cannot accept your money. How can I ever repay you?"

"Consider it my duty to a lady in distress, or my penitence for past wrongs, if you will. I've lived a self-centered life, and I'm only now discovering how selfish I have been. My many sins have come to collect. Please accept my help in your hour of need. You can repay me by lending a helping hand to another." He patted her hand and searched her face before he spoke. "I'm sorry to distress you more, but could you tell me how dire it actually is in France?"

"Monsieur, you cannot imagine the horror or the inhumanity. Every aristocrat is suspect. They are running, hiding, or trying to leave France. My husband had done nothing, but they hunted us as if we were common criminals. It is not just the nobility. My husband's old tutor was seventy years old. They thought he was hiding my husband and tried to make him tell where he had him hid. When he did not, or indeed could not tell them, they took him before the tribunal and sentenced him to death. That poor, kind, gentle soul.

"The clergy are asked to renounce their faith and say they have been telling the people fairy tales. When they do not forsake God, they are sentenced to death. Priest and nun are guillotined for their faith, and their magnificent churches are made into detention centers." She choked back a sob and took a deep breath.

"They do not stop at men and women, no, no, monsieur; they guillotine children and the old. It is said they guillotine a hundred people a day. When you go before the tribunal, you are either innocent or sentenced to death. There is no other alternative. There are very few that are innocent." She grabbed Brandon's arm, her fingers digging in, and stared into his eyes.

"The people's thirst for blood has not been quenched. It is not just the guillotine. People are lined up against a wall and shot, or drowned in the sea. I want to pluck my eyes out and stop up my ears so I can forget what I have witnessed. My mother and father are dead. My sister is in a detention house somewhere, but I fear I will never see her again in this life." At last, she relaxed her hold on Brandon and fell back against her chair with her eyes closed, gasping for breath.

Brandon put his hand on her arm. "This news distresses me more than you know. I must go to France now and rescue my wife. She has done nothing wrong, but she is a prisoner there. Pray for me, madame, that I may succeed."

She opened her eyes and shook her head. "I fear you go on a fool's errand. All hope is lost. If you go, you'll lose your life along with your wife. Do you love this woman that much?"

"Madame, I've only just realized how much she means to me. I will give my life for hers without hesitation."

"Then I wish you Godspeed, and may God have mercy on your soul." She leaned against the back of her chair again and sighed.

Brandon bowed over her hand and left. He found Horus waiting for him in the coffee room. Brandon walked over to the table and poured a cup of coffee. "Horus, I believe it is worse than we first thought. We must leave this morning, whether we have visibility or not. Every day we wait puts Nicole in more peril. I believe it's best if you stay here. If we do not return, someone must look after Lord Waltham."

"I can't be fobbed off as easy as that. I understand the danger, and it scares me to death, but if there is half a chance to save Nikki, then it will take both of us. Our bags are packed. Will your men sail in this pea soup?"

"Aye, they've sailed in worse."

Brandon and Horus walked to the dock in search of their crew. A short distance from the dock, his deck hands were making the schooner ready. A long boat took them out to the gaff rigged, two masted schooner named *Gypsy Soul*. She was easy to manipulate and required a small crew. At one time, circumstances forced Brandon to sail her by himself. She had a shallow draft and skimmed over the water with ease. From out of the mist, the imposing hulk of the yacht loomed large in front of them.

"How come you to buy such a craft? It must have cost the Earth."

"Oh, I didn't buy her. I won her in a card game off a Yankee from Connecticut. He came from a family of shipbuilders. He brought her over here to show her off. She's come in handy more times than I can tell you, or should tell you." Brandon winked and chuckled to himself at a private joke.

The tide ebbed, and they were on their way. Once away from shore, the sun burnt off the fog and a breeze filled the sails. Brandon took the helm. Horus stood beside him.

"How come you to take to sailing? I don't know if I could find my way with nothing but open sea and no landmarks."

"When I take the helm and she's skimming across the water as she is now, I don't believe I'm Earth bound. Freedom is mine for the taking. If we didn't have this ordeal ahead of us, I could make myself believe everything was right with the world."

Chapter Twelve

A member of the crew stood at the bow with a plummet attached to a line checking the depth of the water. With hand signals, he guided Brandon into the secluded cove. The small, oval shaped rocky inlet had two craggy arms standing guard at the narrow entrance. Scrubby trees grew out of the rocks near the entrance shielding the yacht from the sea. The hard ridge promontories and trees surrounded the back of the cove shielding the landside. The only problem with this haven was its dependence on the tides. At low tide, it became a mud flat.

"We must walk from here to the village. It's a tad over two miles, if I remember correctly. From there we can hire a horse and be on our way to Paris."

"How do you know this cove and the region?"

Brandon grinned and studied Horus's face. "Well, Horus, old man, you will have to find out some time. At the risk of shocking you, I must tell you I used to be in the smuggling trade."

Horus started toward Brandon and stopped in his tracks. He put his hand on Brandon's arm and stared at him with a puckered brow. "You what?"

"It's true, I'm afraid. My father sent me to France in disgrace to wait out my latest indiscretion. I fought a duel over an opera singer in Black Pete's gaming establishment. The man pulled through by the skin of his teeth. My father put me on a short leash with barely enough money to live on. He thought to teach me a lesson. That's when I found I had a knack for cards.

"One thing led to another, and I fell in with various shady companions. They were smugglers, but you'd never find a better bunch of companions. They taught me the smuggling trade. That's why I needed a yacht. This was one of my destinations."

Horus stood with his mouth agape.

"Horus, are you going to stand there catching flies all day?"

Finally, he closed it. "What did you smuggle?"

"I ran wines, cognac, and chocolate. It was very profitable for a time. The *gendarmes* and British police were figuring out our schedule and drop off points. I could see it was time to call it a day. During that time, my father called me home, but I must say I enjoyed it while it lasted. I guess it was the excitement of the danger and outwitting the authorities, or maybe it was just the rush it gave me." Brandon shrugged and stared off into the distance. At last, he blinked and dragged his mind to the present before turning back to Horus.

"I made an amazing pile of money in a short time and invested it so I could live independent of my father. Even after he called me home, I never told him. I don't know why I didn't tell him. He would not have approved, and that was usually reason enough to tell him, just to get some kind of a reaction out of him. He never asked what I did in France. I don't think he cared. He was more interested in keeping the family name unsullied. Our relationship was such that we were scarcely speaking by this time. As far as I know, he never knew. He restored my allowance, and life went on as it had until his death."

"It's sad you never got on with your father. I miss my father still. He died when I was very young, and so was he."

"Some people aren't meant to be parents. As I look back, I could have tried harder to get to know him. I regret not making my peace with him before he died. I tried once while he was confined to his bed. He pretended to fall asleep while I tried to talk to him. I took that for a dismissal.

"Enough talking. I've let go of what can't be helped or changed. Wait here. I need to get our disguises from the hold. I'll be back shortly." Brandon gave the helm to Jevin, his first mate.

Brandon rummaged in the hold and came up with two laborers' outfits. "Here, put on these clothes. They're the clothes of a French farm hand. We're less likely to attract attention. Be sure to change your shoes for these sabots. Sabots are worn by the lower classes. Shoes are the things people notice first. Don't shave. A few days' growth of beard makes you look disreputable." Brandon found it hard to imagine Horus looking shady.

"Here are our papers. Someone will ask for them. I bought these last night from someone I knew in the town."

"Are these forged?"

"No, my friend bought them off of two émigrés whose description loosely resembles us."

"Lor, you've led a life. I had no idea." He shook his head and sat on the nearest bench to change his clothes.

"You're going to meet several of my partners in

crime. Please don't be shocked. They're a good bunch, and most importantly, people I trust with my life. If we are to be successful, we must have their help. Do you understand? In these circumstances, we can't be choosy."

Horus nodded.

Brandon gave orders to his crew. "Remember, men, if we're caught, they'll undoubtedly execute us as spies. Keep watch on the yacht, but do it from the promontory. If the ship is boarded, you can escape capture that way. Make your way to Dieppe. Ol' Marco will arrange to get you home.

"Jevin, if we're not back in ten days, we're not coming back. The *Gypsy* is yours. Get out as fast as possible. Don't go into the village for food. There's a well-stocked galley on board. Be on guard. It means your life, and ours."

"Aye, aye, sir."

Horus followed Brandon down the rope ladder to the waiting boat; they made it to shore and headed toward the village. They walked through plowed fields, grassy meadows, and skirted around farmhouses before reaching the small village of Bossiercourt. It appeared to be a small, well-kept village. Today was market day. The village buzzed with activity. As they entered, they noticed the little white houses radiating from the central square. The little square, no bigger than a coin, was paved with cobblestones and had a fountain at its center. As it always is, the more affluent had their houses along one side, and the smaller homes of the poor were on the other.

With the bustle of setting up stalls and getting ready for market day, no one noticed Brandon and

Horus as they made their winding way through the gathering crowd. They walked by vegetable stands, pens of grunting hogs, sad looking horses, and fat cattle. There were even a few chickens for sale. The clunk of the peasants' sabots could be heard on the cobblestones as the wives and young girls moved from stall to stall. They came to a small church on the left. Its bells chimed the hour as Brandon and Horus passed. On the right stood a line of shops followed by a neat bleached white inn with a sign painted in white, blue, and gold announcing its name: The Golden Bull Inn. A local artist had painted a ferocious looking bull on the sign in gold.

The ring of the hammer from the blacksmith's anvil echoed through the village and drew them to his yard and livery. There they could rent a couple of nags. Brandon had to pay extra since they had to leave the horses in Paris. The blacksmith would arrange for someone to pick them up.

"We'll never get there on these old swayback nags. They must be a hundred years old," Horus said when they were out of earshot.

"We'll get there, but if we're to give the appearance of farm hands, we have to ride the appropriate horse suited to our station. If we're stopped, we'll just say we have been visiting our parents in Bossiercourt and are headed back to where we work. We borrowed these animals from our employer."

"What if they ask who our employer is?"

"I have a name to give them, and by the time they check it out, we'll be long gone. Stop worrying and let me do the talking, and we'll be all right." Brandon tried to reassure Horus, but he still looked nervous. "Horus, relax. You're as nervous as if we're on our way to the guillotine."

Horus let out a sigh and relaxed his grip on the reins. He tried not to set so straight in the saddle. "This undertaking worries me. It's an almost impossible task. How in the world are we going to get Nikki out of prison?"

"One step at a time. We must reconnoiter and make a plan. Don't worry, we'll get her back." Brandon tried to give hope to Horus, and himself. He did not see how they would do it either.

Two days later, they reached Paris, but the roads leading to and away were barricaded. They stopped the travelers going out and searched everything. They did not pay any attention to two farm hands on two disreputable looking horses arriving in the city. The guards waved them on through the barricade. They left their horses at the livery stable where the blacksmith had given them directions and made their way to the Rue de Belleville on foot. The Rue de Belleville was a notorious section of bars filled with criminals and prostitutes.

Brandon saw that not much had changed since he last visited this section of Paris. The first thing he noticed was that there were no girls in doorways beckoning to the men as they passed on the street. Sometimes they grabbed your arm and tried to drag you into their alcove. They made their way to the Brasserie La Saint Georges by the middle of the afternoon. Brandon peeped into the entrance and looked around the room. At this time of day, it was empty except for the barkeeper sweeping the floor and a patron in the corner slumped over his table with one hand on a wine bottle. His loud snores reached their ears from across the room.

Henri had changed little since Brandon last did business with him. He was a tall, muscular man with a luxurious black mustache, a bulbous nose, and a balding head with a dark brown fringe of hair surrounding it, making him look the image of a monk with a skullcap. He had dark-brown eyes and always wore a sour expression, unless he smiled. Then his face lit up with an inner glow.

They walked in, and Brandon greeted the barkeeper. "*Allo*, Henri!"

Henri looked up with astonishment written across his face. He glanced at the man in the corner and back again at Brandon. He blinked his eyes and stared. Brandon started to speak but stopped when Henri put a finger to his lips for quiet. He motioned for them to follow him downstairs.

Once they were in his wine cellar with the door closed, he sighed with relief. "Brandon, *mon ami*, are you out of your mind? What are you doing here?"

"Nice to see you too, Henri. Is this the way to greet an old friend?"

"*Mon ami*, if you're found here, we will both be sent to the guillotine. It has not been long enough for them to forget that little trick you pulled in Cherbourg. I am not in the old trade anymore. It's too dangerous. I'm just an innkeeper with a wife and two daughters. Please, do not cause trouble."

"Henri, I didn't come here to cause trouble, but I need help. Our cousin." He looked at Horus with caution written across his face. "Our cousin was taken prisoner. She is English and a music teacher at the seminary of Monsieur de Custine. She is being held at a detention center or prison, but we don't know which one. We have to get her out. We need Jules. Can you contact him?"

"I haven't seen Jules in several months. Everyone is lying low, trying to stay inconspicuous. I may not be able to find him. Besides that, what you want cannot be done. Not even by Jules. This is madness. What has this English lady done?"

"Believe me, Henri, she has done nothing. We believe they are holding her as a spy. Jules has many connections. I know he can help. Please help us find him. If we were not desperate, I would not have come here. I don't wish to get you into trouble. I have no other way to find out where our cousin is or how we may get her out of France."

Henri shook his head and walked to the door. He put his hand on the door handle but stopped before he turned it. "You saved my life once, and I do not forget a debt. I will try to find Jules. You must not leave this place. These are dangerous times. There are spies in our midst. The man upstairs sleeping it off can't be trusted to keep quiet. It isn't just the aristocrats who are brought before the tribunal. Any excuse will do. They say they want to rid France of undesirables.

"My wife will bring you refreshments. I'll see what I can do. Sorry, but I must lock the door. I can't take the chance of someone coming across you by mistake. If you need to leave, you know where the secret door is. I hope this doesn't cause the loss of my head. I am much attached to it." Henri made the sign of the cross and left the room. The key turned in the lock with a loud scraping noise.

Henri's wife brought them wine, sausages, and bread. She opened the door wide enough to set the tray inside the door and did not look at them. The door closed, and she turned the key again. This was the first food they had eaten since the day before. They fell into eating, devoured every scrap of food, and drank the wine.

When they finished eating, Horus looked around the room with a puzzled expression. "Henri mentioned a secret door. Do you remember where it is?"

Brandon closed his eyes remembering and nodded before opening them. "Here, help me move this wine cask forward. It doesn't look it, but it is on concealed casters. Ah, here is the door. Henri didn't lie. This door hasn't been used for some time. There's mold and cobwebs growing over the entrance."

Brandon attempted to open the door without disturbing the cobwebs, but there was no way to do that. The dirt floor held the door in place. They dug around it with a piece of lumber they found in the cellar until they had the path cleared. Both men braced their feet and pulled the door free. It opened into a dark, dank passage. They heard the scurrying of small feet and felt the rush of cold, moist air coming from the passage. They walked through the passage and came to the entrance concealed behind an enormous laurel bush and a huge boulder.

"I can't believe how much it's overgrown since I was here last." Brandon pushed against the limb covering the entrance. He moved it, but it broke in the process, making it easier to climb through. He climbed half way out and checked the neighborhood. The broken limb made it an even tighter squeeze coming in that way. Satisfied that they could escape if necessary, they went back in and rested on the pallets brought to them by Henri while they worked on the door.

Two days later after closing time, Brandon heard the key turn slowly in the lock. Henri did not usually come to the cellar this late. Brandon stood with his pistol in hand, moved to the side of the door, and waited. "I have Jule's with me. We're coming in," Henri whispered.

Henri and Jules entered and lit a lantern. When Brandon saw Jules, he relaxed and stepped out of the shadows. An expansive grin covered Jules's face. He reached out his hand to shake Brandon's and then pulled him into a fierce bear hug.

Jules was not a tall man. He had black hair and eyes. Brandon could not remember ever seeing him without a beard. His slight stature was deceptive. Underneath his clothes were muscles of steel. He always dressed as if he were looking for work, but did not care if he found it. He faded into any crowd with little trouble, which came in handy in his chosen profession of smuggling.

Brandon let his breath out slowly. "Jules, *mon ami*, you're a sight. I've thought of you often these many years. Sorry to come to you with our troubles, but we have little time. I need your help to find my cousin and get her out of whatever prison she is in. Do you think you can help us?"

"When Henri found me, he told me what you wanted. When he said Monsieur de Custine's school and an English music teacher, I knew. This will not be easy. She is being held at the College du Plessis. This is where they wait to receive their letters of indictment.

She may be dead by now, my friend."

"Can you try to find out for us? We have to know one way or another."

"How will I know her? From what I have found out, she speaks French like a Parisian. The women and children are required to take the air for two hours in the morning. They walk in an enclosed courtyard that abuts an alleyway. The gate is boarded up, but one can peek through the cracks. The prison guards watch the women carefully, but it might be possible to get a message to her."

"I don't know what to tell you. She's five feet four inches with auburn hair and slate gray eyes. She must look like a hundred others." Brandon ran his fingers through his hair in frustration. He looked up and snapped his fingers. "I know, I know. She wrote a musical composition. The name of it is *Unforgettable.* If you hum the tune, it will attract her attention. Horus, how does it go?"

Horus and Brandon hummed it until Jules had it memorized. "No more, please. I can't get the melody out of my head. I know it's going to haunt me for the rest of my days. I'll go later this morning and see what I can find out."

"How about a drink for old times?" Henri held up a bottle of claret, brought out four glasses, and filled them with his best wine.

"Let us drink to Jules and the confusion of our enemies." Brandon raised his glass high. "Before you go, if she is still there, how can we get her out of that place? To get out of Paris will be hard enough, much less getting her out of prison." Brandon searched Jules's face for the answer.

"I have been thinking of several schemes, but nothing comes to mind that does not have the soldiers on us before you could leave Paris. The roads out of Paris are blockaded, and everyone is searched. I know how to avoid them, but if the soldiers are coming after you, I don't know. I have thought of one thing. It is risky, but no more so than remaining in Plessis."

"Anything! What is it?"

"There is a drug called Devil's Breath. The only place to get it is at Madame Lapointe's Herbal Emporium. It is illegal, but I know she has a small quantity of the drug. If you take too much it will kill you, and if you take too little, it will not have the desired effect."

"What does it do?"

"If you didn't know, you'd think the person was dead. Prostitutes and robbers give it to their victims. When you put someone under the drug's influence, they will rob their own safe if you ask them. Anything you ask them to do, they will do. Once someone takes the drug, the victims have no will of their own. She must do precisely as I say. I will give her suggestions as to how to act. I will give her instructions to read as the drug takes effect.

"Normally, you have to talk to the victim, but maybe reading the instructions will have the same effect. My instructions will have her lower her pulse, advise her she can't feel, and her body must become rigid. The effect lasts for eight hours. The pulse becomes so faint that not even a doctor can find it. If you take too much, the pulse will get weaker and weaker, and death will come for real."

"Explain these risks to Nicole and see if she's

willing. If not, then we must think of another way. Do you have this drug?"

"No, I'll have to go to Madame Lapointe's."

"Get it first. I think Nicole will chance it. When you have her attention, tell her Horus sent you. She'll understand and trust you."

Jules looked at Brandon with a question on his face, but he did not push the matter.

****

A light drizzle chilled Nicole to the bone as she strolled around the garden. No matter the weather, the prisoners were required to take the air for at least two hours each day in the hopes that this prevented the spreading of disease in the over-crowded prison.

This morning she'd received her letter of indictment. She remembered every word the warden said to her. She walked into his office knowing without a doubt why he called her there. "Mademoiselle Waltham, I have here your letter of indictment. You are charged as a spy. Because of a backlog, you will not go before the council until tomorrow morning. I suggest you unburden your soul. Do not keep up this charade of innocence."

"Monsieur, I am innocent. If I am condemned to death, my blood will be on your hands and the tribunal. I still do not understand why are you doing this? Many times I have told you, I'm an English citizen and a music teacher. Why do you think I am a spy? There can be nothing against my character. Please let me speak to the English consulate. Am I not permitted to have counsel with me?"

"You are not permitted counsel. You will be asked questions by the tribunal. If they decide you are a spy, then you will be sent to the guillotine. Monsieur de Custine will appear as a witness against you." He smiled a satisfied smile with a light in his eyes.

Nicole read his look as having no doubt that she would be sentenced to death.

"Mademoiselle, if you have never been to France, why do you speak French so fluently with a Parisian accent?"

"I have explained that several times. I once thought I wanted to visit Paris. Someone told me it was a beautiful city. They said Paris was enlightened and cultured. It appears I have been misinformed." She smiled back at him and held her head high, determined not to let him see her distress.

With a frown, he flapped his hand at the guard to take her away.

On her morning walk through the garden, she stayed close to the walls, trying to get as much shelter as possible. Although it was drizzling rain, she savored her last hours of life in the open air.

Panic had set in at first, but that had changed to an acceptance of her fate. Once acceptance came, there was a surreal release of her cares. She had few regrets, feeling she had lived life, if not well, then as best she could. Her biggest regret was not seeing her father long enough to tell him good-bye. She wrote him a letter, and one of the guards promised to post it for her if she paid him twenty francs. She could do nothing more. Horus could be counted on to look after her father. Her head hurt when she thought of Brandon. Her arms ached to hold him one last time, to feel his warmth and smell his scent. To be carried away by his kiss and glimpse once more his tender smile as he came to her on the waves of passion. Even now in this place, a longing for his touch stirred deep within her.

She walked on in a trance past the boarded gate. A whisper of a tune caused her to stop, turn her head to one side, and listen. It was the melody to *Unforgettable*. Unable to believe her ears, she walked on and, as she passed the gate again, heard the melody once more. Thinking she might be imagining things, she started to walk once more.

Instead of going on, she stopped and listened. "Who is there? How do you know the song you're humming?"

"Mademoiselle Waltham?"

"Yes, please, who is there?"

"Mademoiselle, keep walking. Come around again and stop at the gate. Stumble and pretend to adjust your shoe. I will explain. You must not make the guards suspicious."

Nicole made the promenade again, her nerves on edge. She appeared to stumble but did not have to pretend too much. Her legs were too weak to hold her up. She bent over, undid her shoe, and pretended to shake a stone out of it. "I'm here. How do you know me?"

"Horus sent me," he said.

Nicole found it hard to catch her breath. She leaned against the wall too dizzy to stand. After regaining her composure, she glanced around at the guards. "Horus? How can this be?"

"I don't have time to explain. We will try to get you out of here. I have just pushed a packet through the gap under the gate. Put it in your shoe or somewhere safe. Walk back around and I will explain."

She picked up the packet and placed it in the pocket of her cloak. Nicole walked back around and pretended to stumble several times. She forced her legs to keep moving toward the gate. Her nerves caused her breath to come in measured gasps. With her hand over her heart, she leaned against the gate. "I'm here, monsieur."

"I have just given you a dangerous drug. When you take it whether by mouth or breathing it in, it will cause your heart to beat wildly, and you could hallucinate. I have given you an overdose. Next, you will become rigid and your breathing will slow. Lastly, your pulse will be so slight that your keepers will think you died. They will put you in the death wagon to take you away from the prison, and your friends will take it from there. After you take the drug, read the note I included in the drug packet. After you read it, destroy it.

"This drug is very dangerous, and it could kill you. Do you want to do this?"

"Yes, monsieur. I have no choice. I received my indictment papers this morning. There was a delay, and they did not take me today. Tomorrow morning, I will appear before the Revolutionary Tribunal. It is either your drug or the guillotine. I prefer your way. How long did you say the effects last?"

"Eight hours, more or less. You must time it to where someone finds you in time to put you in the wagon in the morning, while you are still under the effects."

"I understand. Thank you."

"Do not thank me, mademoiselle. Thank me when you are away from France. Godspeed."

"You there, move along!" a guard called out.

"I must go."

The man did not answer her back.

****

Jules waited for nightfall before he made his way back to Henri's where he found Brandon pacing the floor.

"Where have you been? Have you found her? There is no time to lose," Brandon growled.

"Brandon, must I remind you I am the one taking the risks here? I have been doing what you asked. This is the first chance I had to get back to you. There are spies everywhere. I had to be careful. Once or twice, I thought I might be followed. As to your question, yes, she is alive for now."

"You have spoken to Nicole?" Brandon relaxed when Jules nodded.

"Yes, and she says she will take the drug tonight. She is to go before the tribunal tomorrow morning, so she has to do it tonight. There will be two horses in back of the brasserie shortly after midnight. The wagon carrying the dead will come out by the rear gate of Plessis in the early morning hours. It will head for the outskirts of Paris where the wagon driver dumps the remains in a mass gravesite. They put quick lime on the bodies to hurry the decomposition, but sometimes they burn them.

"The wagon goes through a grove of trees. That is your best place to intercept it. After that, you cannot tell which direction to go, or what they have planned for the bodies. There will be no guards. The dead do not run away."

"Sorry, I snapped at you. You've done well. Thank you, my friend. Here, I have something for your trouble." Brandon handed him a purse filled with coins.

"Do not insult me, *mon ami*. I know you would do the same for me, and have in the past. No, this I do for friendship and nothing else. You must bring the mademoiselle back here so she can get rid of the effects of the drug. You must return before daylight. It is too risky if someone sees you. When you return, leave the horses where you found them and someone will take them away. We still have our huts along the way to the cove. You remember where they are located?"

"Yes, I'm not likely to forget. I didn't think from what Henri said that you were in the smuggling business anymore."

"Operations have been suspended temporarily. We're not active now, but the huts have not been torn down. The huts look the same as fishermen's huts so no one suspects their true purpose. At each one, you will find a change of horses. Do not rest any longer than necessary. Leave France without delay, my friend." He looked at his friend and shook his head.

Brandon put out his hand to shake Jule's hand.

Jules grabbed Brandon's hand and pulled him into a powerful embrace. "Go with God, *mon ami*, go with God." Jules wiped a tear from his eyes and left straight away.

The plan did nothing to ease Brandon's mind. It made him more anxious than ever. Horus started to say something but changed his mind when Brandon scowled at him. He continued pacing. Henri's wife brought dinner, but Brandon's nerves made each bite stick in his throat. He stopped his monotonous pacing a few minutes before midnight and prepared to go.

"Horus, we must put on a mask. We can't take a

chance of being recognized. From here on in, we speak only French. When we detain the wagon, you keep your pistol on the wagon driver. I'll get Nicole out of the wagon."

Horus could do nothing more than nod. His eyes were wide with fear. Brandon saw the sweat break out on his forehead. He put his hand on Horus's shoulder and felt him tremble. "Don't worry, old man. We'll get her out. I'm worrying enough for the both of us. I'm not leaving France without her."

Horus swallowed hard and nodded again. He checked his pistol with a shaking hand, put his mask and pistol in the pocket of his greatcoat, and followed Brandon out the escape route to the horses.

The night air had a chill in it. A yellow fog surrounded the streets making it hard to find their way. The fog made the streets wet with its slimy moisture. The sound of their horses' hooves echoed faintly and died instantly in the fog. No one stirred. Brandon and Horus made their way to the rear entrance of the College du Plessis as silently as ghosts upon the landscape. They followed the road away from Plessis and found the best place to ambush the death wagon. The thick cover of the grove of trees and bushes made a perfect hiding place for them. They could not be seen by anyone passing by.

****

Madame Vivien had the means to buy food and shared with her niece and cell mate. Nicole saved a piece of bread and made a hole in it, put the drug in the bread, and waited. She listened to the guards making their rounds after her cellmates were asleep. When she guessed it must be after midnight, she swallowed the bread and read her instructions by a shielded candle. She read them repeatedly until the drug took effect. She felt flushed and numb at first. Her heart pounded rapidly and wanted to fly out of her chest. She tore the note into bits and swallowed the pieces.

She woke Madame Vivien. "Madame, something is wrong. I'm finding it hard to breathe." Nicole sighed and collapsed on her pallet unable to move.

Madame Vivien held the candle up and looked at Nicole. "My dear, you're as white as the driven snow. Here, drink this water."

Nicole could not drink. The paralysis had started. She remembered everything the man at the gate told her and kept running it repeatedly through her mind until she passed out. She came to a short time later and sensed rather than felt Madame Vivien trying to take her pulse.

Madame Vivien beat on the door to no avail. "Monsieur, monsieur, help me. I need a doctor. I think Mademoiselle Waltham has died!"

Even after frantically pounding on the door once again and calling to the guards, no one came for what seemed an eternity. When the guards came, they could not find a pulse and took Nicole away. She could hear everything they said but could not move her arms, open her eyes, or speak. She sensed herself going to a dark place. She tried to fight her way back up but still could not move.

"Strip her and confiscate her trunk. She has no need of it now," one guard said to his friend. He slapped his companion on the back and chuckled.

She had seen them do the same to others, then try to sell to the inmates what they did not want themselves.

A wagon rattled to a stop, and someone threw her in the bed of the wagon. She felt nothing when her body hit the bed of the cart and had no will to resist. There were more noises beside her. She guessed they were putting more bodies in the wagon. Naked and unable to hide her shame, she realized she must lay on top of other nude bodies on the way to the cemetery. Mercifully, she passed out again and had no inclination to claw herself back up out of the dark space.

****

Brandon heard the creak of the wagon before he saw it. He waited until it was within fifty feet before he moved out in the road and pointed his pistol at the wagon driver.

"Halt," he called.

Horus came behind him and aimed his pistol at the wagon driver.

"I have no money, only dead bodies. The guards robbed them before they put them in the wagon. You're too late." The wagon driver kept his hands up, shrugged, and tried to smile.

"We don't want your money. I'll be looking in your wagon. Do not move, or my friend will put another hole in your head."

Brandon dismounted and went around the wagon. He pulled back the cover and found a wagon full of bodies. Some with heads unattached, some with bullet holes, and others with bayonet wounds. He pulled a body aside and found Nicole. They'd stripped her of her clothes and laid her among the dead. In the early-morning light, her white flesh shone like a beacon. She had lost much weight, and he could count her ribs.

Blood dripped on her, pooling on her stomach. His heart stopped beating until he realized it was not her blood. She looked so still and quiet.

*What if she is dead? What can I do?*

Horus walked toward him, but Brandon held up his hand to halt him. He took his greatcoat and wrapped it around Nicole's motionless body. He lifted her off the wagon and carried her into the cover of the forest. With Horus watching Brandon, the wagon driver took this opportunity to put the whip to his horses and race down the road.

"Is she dead? She looks lifeless. Tell me she's not dead," Horus cried out.

"I don't know. She's freezing. They took her clothes. We have to get her back to Henri's. When I mount up, hand her up to me."

Horus stood there staring.

Brandon snapped his fingers in front of his eyes. "Horus, move! We don't have much time. Jules said the effect lasts for eight hours. We have to wait."

Horus shook his head to clear it of negative thoughts and handed Nicole up to Brandon. They started on their way back to Henri's. Darkness, caused more by the fog than the night shrouded the street, and made it impossible to see more than three feet away. On the alert and looking at everything that moved or made a noise, they made sure no one followed them or lay in wait.

They mistook their street in the fog and took a different route going back. Brandon was not a stranger to Paris streets. When he realized their mistake, he steered them back to the right street, and they made their way at a snail's pace to the secret entrance. The entrance was a tight squeeze for a person who could maneuver; Nicole was dead weight and unable to help herself. Horus squeezed through first, and Brandon handed Nicole to him. They struggled to get her through the opening. By the time they made it through, the sun was trying to shine. The fog lifted, and people started to stir.

Brandon carried Nicole to the storage room, placed her on a pallet, and covered her with their blankets trying to get her warm. Her skin was cold as ice. He stopped Henri's wife when she brought food and asked for clothes for Nicole. She looked at Nicole and left. A short time later, she returned with her daughter's dress, underclothes, and shoes. Brandon dressed her in a shift and covered her with the blankets and his greatcoat again. He walked the floor, wrung his hands, and watched her for a sign of life, any sign.

In the middle of the afternoon, Henri brought ale, wine, bread, and cheese. Brandon or Horus did not touch it. They sat and stared at Nicole willing her to wake up and speak. Brandon thought the effects from the drug should have worn off by now.

He turned and started to speak to Horus when a rasping noise made him turn around. Nicole was sitting up wide-eyed with panic. She gasped trying very hard to catch her breath. She opened her mouth and screamed. Brandon put his hand over her mouth to quiet her. He tried not to hurt her as she struggled to catch her breath. She thrashed with her arms and legs in panic, trying to get off the pallet.

Horus called out, "Nikki!"

She stopped and stared around wide eyed until she saw Horus and relaxed. She turned her head and found

Brandon's face. Her eyes appeared to focus; she blinked and looked around the room. Her raised hand touched Brandon's cheek. He removed his hand from her mouth. Tears streamed down her cheeks.

"I thought I would never see either of you again. I resigned myself to the executioner's blade." Nicole's hand reached up and touched her hair. She fingered the sprigs all over her head. "They cut off my hair. They said it was too pretty and some warden's wife needed a wig."

"It'll grow back, my dear. It doesn't matter. All that matters is that we have you." She closed her eyes and slumped against Brandon.

Brandon laid her on the pallet and felt her pulse. "She fainted. Her pulse is rapid, but it is slowing. I think it's best if we let her sleep. If she doesn't stir in a while, we'll get smelling salts from Henri. We have to leave when it gets dark. The soldiers are undoubtedly hunting for us."

"I understand, but I don't know if Nikki can make the journey," Horus said with a worried look.

"I don't know either, but we have no choice."

\*\*\*\*

Nicole's eyelids fluttered, and she opened her eyes. She stared across the room in a daze until her eyes came to rest on Brandon, and the tension left her body. She tried to smile and sit up. Brandon pulled her into a sitting position and propped her up with a pillow.

Horus rang the bell for Henri to make tea and bring something to eat for Nicole.

"Nicole, you had us worried. You actually looked as if you were dead. How are you feeling?" said Brandon.

"I'm as weak as a newborn lamb. I could use something to eat."

"Horus just rang for food. Henri will be here soon to find out what we want. We have to leave when it gets dark. We've stayed too long in Paris as it is. Do you think you can make the journey to the coast?"

"I must. I want to leave here as soon as possible. If I have some food, I'll get my strength back soon." Abruptly, she felt around her blanket and looked under it. "Where are my clothes?" A blush spread across her face.

"I'm sorry, my dear, but the soldiers took your clothes and everything you had. I wrapped you in my great coat when we rescued you. Henri's daughter is more or less your size. She gave you a change of clothes. If you're up to putting them on, just slip behind that wine barrel."

Nicole tried to stand. Her legs were too weak to carry her. She collapsed on the pallet. "Here, let me help you. Horus, keep watch on the door." Brandon carried her behind the wine barrel, dressed her, and let her lay back on her pallet to rest.

Henri brought tea, cheese, chicken, and bread. Nicole ate a little at first, but when her stomach settled, she ate more and felt better. She stood and walked shakily around the room, holding onto the wine racks in the room. Brandon took her through the tunnel to where she could breathe fresh air.

"Brandon, I owe you my life, but you should not have come. It's so dangerous. If something happened to you or Horus, I don't know what I would do. This is my fault. Papa begged me not to come, but my pride said I had to do this on my own."

"I had to come. I had to find you and make things right between us. What else could I do? You're my wife, and I can't imagine my life without you." He put his hands on her shoulders and looked into her eyes. He pulled her to him and put his arms around her. "When we're out of this trouble, I'll explain. Please trust me. Please know that I love you with all my heart." He held her away from him and searched her face for an answer. "Shall we go back now? You're looking tired."

Nicole nodded, and he took her arm and led her back to the storage room. When they returned, Jules was waiting on them. "Brandon, *mon ami*." He grabbed Brandon's hand and shook it warmly. "As you know, the roads out of Paris are barricaded and patrols are on the streets. However, I've mapped out a route for you. You will have to go on foot. This will require you to go through back streets, over apartment roofs, and even through people's lawns, but it will get you out of Paris. I have two horses waiting for you at this point on the map. Two horses are all I could lay my hands on."

"Saying thanks is not enough. I…"

"Please, you make me blush. No more. Just take the lovely mademoiselle and get out of France, so I can take a deep breath again." He slapped Brandon on the back. As fast as he came, he disappeared out the door with a wave of his hand.

\*\*\*\*

When darkness descended over Paris, the three weary travelers left through the secret way out of the brasserie and started on their circuitous route out of Paris. They were making good time and clearing most of their hurdles. At one point, a man who had been watching for them stepped out of the shadows and motioned for them to travel through his apartment. They climbed out of an attic window and ran across various roofs. The houses were so close together that they could jump from one roof to the other.

Brandon held tightly to Nicole's hand and pulled her to the next roof as she jumped. At the end of the row of houses, they went in another window and out the back door of an apartment building. The last leg of the journey was the hardest. It required they go over a wall, through the back garden of a member of the Committee of Public Safety, and out the gate on the far side. Horus gave Brandon a leg up, and he made it to the top of the wall. Next Horus gave Nicole a leg up, and Brandon pulled her to the top of the wall and eased her to the ground on the other side. He reached down the wall again and pulled Horus up. Both men jumped to the ground and, with Nicole, made their way through the garden toward the gate on the other side. They made it to the gate and found it locked.

Brandon tried to unlock it by the light of the moon. All three turned around at the sound of growls coming from behind them. They looked into the angry eyes of two large dogs with bared fangs.

Horus picked up a tree limb from debris by the gate. "Nikki, get behind me. Brandon, hurry. I don't know how long I can hold off these very angry dogs. They keep inching closer."

Brandon continued to work the gate. "I'm almost there. It's hard to see by the light of the moon."

Someone came out of the kitchen door. "Who's there? What's going on?"

Brandon sprung the gate and they rushed through it. He closed the gate behind him just as the dogs lunged. The latch caught and held. The dogs continued to jump at the gate, growl, and bark. The trio ran blindly along the path to the river. They found the small boat left for them by Jules and were across the river before the barks from the dogs died away.

By the time they reached the horses, Nicole's strength had deserted her. Brandon and Horus were holding her up between them. Brandon mounted his horse, and Horus all but threw Nicole up to him. Horus mounted his horse, and they were moving rapidly toward the first hut.

"We've had to keep away from farmhouses and roads and the going has been slow. We should reach the first shelter by sun up. Ah, look up ahead, there it is. Horus, tie the horses out of sight, and make your way to the hut. Be ever watchful."

Without saying a word, the weary travelers entered the hut, fell on to the rough pallets, and slept until the sun made the shelter too hot. Brandon opened the door and found a basket of food waiting for them. He looked both ways, saw no one, and moved the basket inside. When he went to check on the horses, he found fresh mounts waiting. He went back inside the hut. "Horus, Nicole, wake up. Someone has left cheese, bread, and ale. We have fresh mounts, as well."

Refreshed from the night's rest and the food, they mounted up and headed for the second hut.

"Traveling at midday could not be more dangerous, but it can't be helped. Farmers are working in the fields. We must move as silently as possible and try not to draw attention to ourselves," Brandon warned.

They rode several miles out of their way before they could give the horses their head. By the time they reached the second hut, night had fallen. Horus helped Nicole into the hut while Brandon took care of the horses. They found more bread, sausages, cheese, and wine in a basket. Too tired to eat, the exhausted travelers fell onto the pallets and slept soundly into the next morning.

"Wake up. We have one more ride today, and we will be at the last hut. From there it's a stone's throw to my yacht. Someone left us food again. Jules thinks of everything. Try to eat. You must keep your strength up. When we get to my yacht, you can rest. I promise not to wake you until you're completely rested."

Bleary eyed, Nicole looked up at him. "I'm so tired I can't feel my aches anymore. Give me two minutes, and I'll be ready to eat. Don't worry. I'll make it." She gave him her best smile.

He bent, kissed her on the forehead, and ran his fingers through her hair trying to straighten it. Sliding his finger around her jaw, he tilted her head up and searched her face. "That's my girl. I've brought you water to freshen up. Horus is seeing to the horses. I'll go help him while you get ready."

When she looked at him, Nicole saw the tenderness in his eyes. Her heart skipped a beat. She longed to have his arms around her in love once again. In the prison, she believed she might never see his handsome face again let alone feel his tender touch. Tears filled her eyes at the thought of the prison. So many kind people had befriended her, and yet they had gone to the guillotine. She had escaped her fate, received a last minute reprieve. She prayed they would all see England again, and none of this was done in vain.

All too soon, they finished their meager meal and

were on their way to the third and final hut. "We should be there by late afternoon. This last leg of the journey is the most isolated. We won't have to be so careful to not be noticed. We'll be traveling at a breakneck pace. Nicole, do you think you can hang on?"

Nicole nodded, and they were off. When they rested the horses, they shuttled Nicole to a different horse, alternating between Brandon and Horus so the horses could keep up the fast pace.

"Dark clouds are gathering. There's a stiff breeze ruffling the leaves on the trees. I can smell rain in the air. It's getting darker by the minute. Do you think we will reach the last hut before the rain comes?" said Horus.

"It'll be close, but it's not much farther. Keep a steady pace," Brandon yelled over the wind.

At the last rest stop, Horus pointed at the threatening clouds with lightning playing about in them. As they reached the final hut, the afternoon grew dark as night. Big drops of rain fell. They ran for the hut and were safely inside when the storm hit. As soon as it came up, it blew out to sea. Like a tempest in a teacup, it was over as soon as it started.

"Come, let's get to the *Gypsy Soul*. The sooner we're away from the shore the better. She's a fast ship. In the open water, no one can catch her if they give chase."

Half way to the promontory and the trail, Nicole stumbled and fell. Too tired to get up, Brandon picked her up and carried her along. When they reached where the water should be, the clouds cleared and the moon shone on the cove. To his horror, Brandon glimpsed his yacht resting in a sea of mud.

"What the devil?" Horus stopped with his mouth open.

"Blast, I forgot when the tide goes out it leaves a mud flat. We must wait until the tide comes back in before we can sail out."

"That's all well and good, but how do we get on board. I don't think Nicole can tolerate much more. I know I'm so tired. I don't think I can walk another step." Horus sat abruptly on the nearest rock.

"Er...my lord." A voice called behind them. The three travelers turned in unison to look at the man standing behind them.

"Lor, Jevin, you're a sight for sore eyes. How do we get on board?"

"My lord, I found several broad planks in the hut. I can put them on the mud, and we can get across. The planks will get slippery with the more weight you put on them. Tread carefully. We'd almost given you up. The crew was getting nervous with this storm and us stranded in the mud flat. The rest of the crew are on board."

"Put them down. We'll be much safer on board. Hurry, Jevin."

Jevin put the planks on the mud as he went across. Next, Horus went. The planks were becoming slippery and sinking in the oozing mud. "Nicole, I don't think you're able to walk across on your own. I'll put you over my shoulder. We must move fast, or I'll sink with the extra weight."

He looked at Nicole, and she nodded in understanding.

Brandon picked her up and started across. The first plank sank into the mud under their weight. He stepped where he thought the next plank should be and felt it sink deeper in the mud. He kept moving as rapidly as he could while carrying Nicole. Half way there, he slipped and almost landed them both in the mud. He regained his balance and continued. Before he reached the final plank, he sank knee deep into the mud. The plank he stood on continued to sink.

Jevin threw him a rope. In the mud past his knees, he could not move. He tied it around his waist, and Jevin and the rest of the crew pulled him free. He stepped in faith where the last plank had been and sank into the mud up to his knees again. His foot found the plank under the mud, which stopped him sinking farther. Jevin used the rope to pull him to the rope ladder on the yacht. He kept the rope around him, and Jevin and the other crew members helped pull him and Nicole up the ladder and on board the *Gypsy Soul*.

Brandon set Nicole down, and both collapsed onto the deck. He turned to look at the planks through the railing and watched as the last one sank beneath the mud. He leaned his head back and closed his eyes. When he opened them, he saw Nicole and Horus across from him in the same condition. He stood, took Nicole in his arms again, and carried her below deck.

"My dear, I brought your clothes from the town house. Your night rail is here. Get into bed and sleep. After you've rested, I'll have hot water brought in for your toilette. Are you able or do you want me to help?"

"No, I can manage. Oh, Brandon..." She started to cry.

Brandon rushed to her side. "Nikki, please don't cry. We'll make it. This is just a little set back."

She looked up through her tears. "You called me

Nikki."

"It's that blasted cousin of yours. Every word out of his mouth is Nikki this and Nikki that. Now he has me doing it."

"I like it." She leaned back and closed her eyes in sleep.

Brandon smiled at her, removed her shoes, and covered her with a quilt. After placing a pillow under her head, he tiptoed out of the cabin. He walked into an empty cabin and fell into a deep sleep. Several hours later, he woke to Jevin shaking him.

"Sir, we're being hailed from shore. What do we do? The tide's coming in, but there isn't enough to float her yet."

"Who's hailing us?" Brandon stifled a yawn.

"It looks to be the *Garde Nationale*, sir."

"What the dickens?"

Brandon stumbled out of bed and made his way up on deck. He looked across at soldiers with rifles stationed around the promontory and a fancy dressed man he took to be the leader hailing them.

"Ahoy, citizen! Permission to come aboard," the leader spoke in English.

"Blast, blast!" Brandon mumbled under his breath. "Permission granted, but I must warn you my wife is very sick. She may have small pox."

He watched the leader draw back aghast and murmur to one of his soldiers. There appeared to be a lot of discussion and head shaking.

Jevin came up to Brandon. "My lord, the tides coming in, but we're still stuck in the mud. She may come loose any second, but we'll not be able to leave until the tides in. There's no wind."

Brandon nodded in understanding and stared across at the soldiers.

He watched the captain and three soldiers put a small boat in the shallow water. If this went wrong, they had enough firepower to blast them out of the water. Their small boat barely floated with their weight. They used their oars as poles in the muddy water and pushed over to the *Gypsy Soul*.

"Who are you and what are you doing here?" the captain called.

"I'm Lord Montagu. We were on our way to Italy when my wife became ill. She could not stand the rocking of the yacht, so we pulled in here to let her recover. She has become sicker instead of better. We left England to avoid a small pox out break on our estate. I was afraid to send someone into the village to fetch a doctor, lest she has small pox. We were waiting for the tide and plan to return to England."

"I see," he said with a sly look on his face. "What are your wife's symptoms?"

"She started out with fever and vomiting, but now she's complaining of headache and back pain. She is so weak she can't get out of bed. There's no sign of a rash yet." Brandon tried to look distraught.

"We're looking for two men who made off with a corpse from the death wagon. We wish to search your vessel. My sergeant, as you can see from his scars, has had small pox. I'll send him to inspect your ship. If everything is in order, you may be on your way."

"I assure you there's no corpse on board. I have no problem with you coming on board, but I do not think it's wise if she has small pox." Brandon shrugged with the palms of his hands out stretched and turned up.

"Maybe not, but it is necessary. Michoux, take two men and search," he said and flicked his wrist as if he were telling a dog to fetch.

Hesitantly, Michoux and his men drew the boat closer and began the climb up the rope ladder.

****

Horus burst through Nicole's door out of breath. "Nikki, Nikki, wake up. French soldiers are coming on board. What are we to do? There's no place to hide. Brandon told them he thought you had small pox, but their coming aboard anyhow."

"Get me my makeup kit and hurry!"

Horus brought her the makeup kit.

Pale and worn, she needed little makeup to make herself appear sick. Her eyes were red rimmed from lack of sleep and exhaustion. She immediately made dark smudges under her eyes and put her wig on to hide her butchered haircut. Her nightcap on over the wig made it hard to tell it was not her real hair. She made red smudges on the bottoms of her feet and hands with rouge, splashed water on her face, and drenched her nightgown. She lay back moaning with her hand over her eyes.

Horus pulled a chair up to her side and looked on.

Michoux came through the door of the captain's cabin while the other men searched the yacht. Brandon followed behind the soldiers.

Michoux looked at Horus. "Who are you?"

"I'm her brother, Lord Fleetwood. You should not come any closer. We fear she has small pox."

Michoux moved closer to Nicole. "Light a candle. It's too dark in here."

"Sir, the light hurts her eyes. We've tried to make

her as comfortable as possible," Brandon said.

Nicole moaned and glimpsed the soldier through her half-closed eyelids. Before he could light the candle, she sat up in bed and screamed at the top of her voice. Michoux stood back visibly shaken. Horus jumped up from his chair, knocking it over. Brandon rushed to her side.

"Get them off me! Get them off! Spiders, spiders everywhere," she shouted and screamed again.

Brandon pushed her back into the bed. "Hush, hush, my darling, I'll take care of the spiders." He brushed her arms as if knocking spiders off them.

"They're crawling everywhere on the walls, on my bed. Stop them. Make them stop." Nicole looked around wide-eyed. Her eyes strayed to Michoux, and she screamed again.

Michoux did not move. He continued to watch Nicole.

Brandon took a bottle of laudanum out of a drawer and brought it to Nicole's bed. "Here, my dear, I'll give you something to make you feel better, and it will get rid of the spiders so you can rest."

He stood with his back to Michoux and pretended to put laudanum in a water glass beside her bed. She put both trembling hands on the glass and drank it. Nicole let out a sigh and closed her eyes. A few minutes later, she pretended to sleep.

Michoux backed out of the room, sweat breaking out on his forehead. He hurried to where his men were searching. Brandon followed.

****

"Hurry, men. We need to leave this place." He turned to Brandon with a worried look. "I'm sorry, sir, for your trouble."

"Your captain said you've had small pox. Do you think my wife has this affliction?" Brandon laid a hand on his arm.

He shook Brandon's hand off. "There is no doubt. You must leave France as soon as possible. Small pox took my sister. She hallucinated just as your wife is doing. She died two days later."

He motioned to his men. "Let us leave this accursed place at once."

Michoux and his men returned to the waiting boat. Brandon watched him talking to his captain but could not make out what they said. He did not have to hear to know. Panic was written across the men's faces. Michoux was making animated hand gestures and pointing in his direction. His men pushed their oars into the water and dug deep into the mud heading for shore.

"Leave France as soon as possible. I'll post my men to make sure you do not come ashore. If you try to go into the village, you will be shot," the captain called back.

Brandon watched the captain leave after he placed four men around the little cove. The tide coming in made the ship rock. Satisfied they could leave soon, he went below.

Upon entering his cabin, he watched Horus and Nicole give a sigh of relief in unison. "Nicole, what an actress you made. You almost convinced me you had small pox."

"Are they going to leave us alone?"

"Yes, it appears so. They have four men stationed on the ridge overlooking the cove. Jevin says the tide's coming in strong. We should be able to leave before long. We're waiting for the yacht to become unstuck and the wind to come up. I'm going up on deck and will come back as soon as we leave this place."

\*\*\*\*

After Brandon left, Horus turned to Nicole with concern written across his face. "Nikki, are you feeling better? You had us so worried. Of all the harebrained things you've done, this takes the cake. Imagine going to France in the middle of a revolution. You never had any timing. Remember the time I landed you a facer?"

"I'm sorry you were worried, but I thought I was doing the right thing. I never imagined for a second what could happen to me. Even now, my head hurts when I think of what nearly happened. I owe my life to Brandon and you."

"You didn't have to go to France. I could have given you the money."

"Yes, I know but I wanted to make it on my own. It seemed a good idea at the time." She patted Horus's hand.

"I'm still so tired. If you don't mind, I need to get some sleep." She fell against her pillow with her eyes closed.

Nicole awoke to the rocking of the yacht and sensed it moving out to sea. *I'm going home. I'm really going home.* She relaxed and closed her eyes again.

\*\*\*\*

Brandon looked in on her several times but left her sound asleep. She needed it, and he needed to decide what to say to her. They had to be words he had never uttered to another. They had to be the words that would make her want to stay and give her love to him and him alone.

The next time Nicole woke up, she looked around the cabin, and Brandon sat next to her bed with his eyes closed.

"Brandon, are you awake?" she called weakly.

Brandon jerked awake and stood. He rubbed his eyes and looked at Nicole. "Are you all right? Do you need anything?"

"No, I felt the ship moving. Are we out to sea?"

"Yes, we're more than half way across the channel. We'll be coming into Dover shortly." He paced around the cabin.

"Are we safe? We're not in danger now?" Nicole relaxed when he shook his head no. "Come here and sit on my bed. I want to talk to you." She patted the side of her bed.

Brandon came to her bed and sat on the edge. "Please help me to sit up. I don't have my strength back yet."

Brandon fluffed her pillow and helped her up, then held onto her and could not let go. Looking into those slate gray eyes, he felt mesmerized, his mouth went dry, and everything he planned to say left his mind.

"I'm fine now. You can let go. Brandon...I..."

Both of their heads turned as a knock sounded on the door.

"Enter," Brandon snapped.

Horus came into the cabin. "Sorry to disturb you. I say, Nikki, you're looking better. Had us worried there. Uncle Charles will be glad to know we have you."

Nicole stared at him with a questioning look in her eyes that said, *Why are you here, and please leave.*

"Oh, almost forgot why I came. Brandon, we've just sighted Dover. Are we going to dock there, or are you going on to Fiddler-on-the-Sea?"

"If you don't mind, I have a request to make. Could I persuade you to go on to Standon from Dover and ease Lord Waltham's mind? He must be worried sick about Nicole. She needs to see a doctor, rest, and eat decent food. She's nothing but bone. I don't want her father to see her this way. I'm taking her home to Worthington Park. When she's feeling better in a couple of weeks, tell Lord Waltham we'll come to him, or he's welcome to come for a visit to Worthington."

"Be glad to." He came over to Nicole's bed and placed a kiss on her outstretched hand. "Get better soon, Nikki. This will be good-bye for now. After I've seen Uncle Charles, I'll come by Worthington before I return to Oxford." Horus moved to leave, turned at the door, and waved farewell.

Brandon turned back to Nicole and started to speak, but Nicole put up her hand on his arm to stop him.

"Brandon, I have something to say. I can't go on the way we have. I want a real marriage and a family without intrigues or scandals. If I've learned anything from my recent disastrous experience, it's that life is too short. I cannot think back to the prison without getting a knot in my stomach. You saved me, and I can never forget or repay you for that."

"Nikki, you're my wife. I love you. When I believed I might never see you again, my world fell apart. I didn't realize how much I loved you until I thought I'd lost you. I can't imagine nor do I want to imagine my life without you.

"The only people who went with me on my trip were my four friends. I swear it. You can ask them when they return. I know you were told otherwise out of spite or malice." He put his arm around her.

She snuggled closer.

"I told Horus when he came to confront me. I have to make you understand. Lady Bennett means nothing to me. Everything she told you was from spite. Since the day we married, I have not taken another to bed. I have to admit, I cut all ties because of the will at first, and then I remained celibate because of you. I just couldn't... I love you, Nikki. There is no one else. I swear it. I don't want you to give your love to another. If you do not love me now, then I will spend the rest of my life trying to win your love." He ran his finger around her jaw and brought her head up to where he could gaze into her eyes.

"I have not been a good man. I have lived a lifetime in my five and twenty years, but they have not been well spent. There have been many women in my life, and I have not been faithful to any of them. I have done things even I'm not proud of. I'm aware that you deserve a better husband than I am, but no one could love you more. You make me want to be a better man. Do you think you can give your love to such as I? I promise I won't make you regret entrusting your heart into my keeping."

Nicole nodded with tears in her eyes. "Brandon."

"Yes."

"My love, stop talking and kiss me."

****

He could not suppress the smile that crossed his face. He felt the tension leave his body as he bent his head and tenderly kissed the love of his life. She returned his kiss eagerly. Her arm came around his waist, and he slid farther into the bed. When the two finally came apart, Nicole laid her head on his shoulder, and he pulled her closer.

Nicole raised her head to look at Brandon. "I don't care how many women you have had in the past, as long as I'm the last."

"You're the one I love. I don't want another." Brandon kissed the top of her head.

"You know, it's fairly scandalous to be in love with your wife." Nicole laughed and pressed the palm of his hand to her cheek.

"Yes, I know, but I've never been one to avoid a scandal." Brandon chuckled and held Nicole a little tighter. Once again, he kissed the woman too hard to forget.

## A word from the author...

I was born in the shadow of the Blue Ridge Mountains in Western North Carolina. I met my husband, a Canadian, while skiing in Montana. We have lived in many different locations across the United States and Canada. We finally settled in West Virginia with our dog Wesley.

I have always enjoyed history and reading all genres. Until recently I was employed by a major bank in its IT department as a network analyst. I am enjoying having enough time to do research and work on my stories.

http://www.amandabalfour.com

Thank you for purchasing
this publication of The Wild Rose Press, Inc.

If you enjoyed the story, we would appreciate your
letting others know by leaving a review.

For other wonderful stories,
please visit our on-line bookstore at
www.thewildrosepress.com.

For questions or more information
contact us at
info@thewildrosepress.com.

The Wild Rose Press, Inc.
www.thewildrosepress.com

Stay current with The Wild Rose Press, Inc.

Like us on Facebook

https://www.facebook.com/TheWildRosePress

And Follow us on Twitter
https://twitter.com/WildRosePress